THUNDER ROAD

THE WITCHES OF WHEELER PARK: BOOK 2

CHRISTINE POPE

THUNDER ROAD

Copyright © 2020 by Christine Pope

ISBN: 978-1-946435-34-7

Published by Dark Valentine Press

Cover design by Lou Harper

Book formatting by Indie Author Services

1

THE TEARS DRIED ON MY CHEEKS SOMEWHERE outside Winslow, Arizona. By that point, it was a little past one in the morning, and I was just too tired to cry anymore. Instead, I clung to the steering wheel with grim determination, making myself drive past the small high-desert town…and past Holbrook, a half hour or so down the road from Winslow, just because I knew I was still in Wilcox territory and didn't dare stop for fear that Jake had already discovered my absence and had put out the alert on my newfound witch family's grapevine.

Despite my exhaustion, I made it to Gallup, just over the border into New Mexico, at around two-thirty in the morning. I knew I couldn't drive any farther than that; I'd already had a couple of scary moments when I started to nod off and jerked awake just as the car began to drift over toward the shoulder. If the interstate hadn't been so empty at that hour, I could have gotten myself into a lot of trouble. So, I moved over to the right lane, knowing I needed to exit the highway. Although I had no idea who the witch clan was in that particular section of the world, I knew it wasn't the Wilcoxes, and that was good enough for me.

At the eastern end of Gallup, right off I-40, was a newish-looking Fairfield Inn and Suites. By that point, I was so tired that I probably would have checked into a total dive just to get some sleep, but luckily, such sacrifices weren't necessary. The woman at the front desk, who looked like she was most likely Native American, didn't appear that surprised to see a bleary-eyed girl around her own age stumble in at that hour of the night—probably because they got a lot of travelers who stopped there when they realized they couldn't drive any farther. She handed me a plastic card key after I pushed a couple of fifty-dollar bills across the counter toward her.

"My credit card was stolen, and I'm waiting for a replacement," I told her, and luckily, she accepted the excuse and didn't ask any questions I wouldn't be able to answer.

I barely remembered falling into bed. The next morning, I rolled over and gazed, bleary-eyed, at the clock and realized it was already almost ten. Honestly, I hadn't expected to sleep that well, not when I was still agonizing over my decision to leave

Flagstaff—and Jake Wilcox—behind. But it seemed my brain knew I needed the rest, and had left me alone for the remainder of the night.

However, sleeping that late didn't give me much time to get ready for the next stage of my road trip. I took a hurried shower, glad I'd washed my hair the day before and wouldn't have to waste much time on it, then got dressed and put my bag of toiletries and other odds and ends back in the car. There was a Burger King a few blocks away from the hotel, so I got a breakfast sandwich, hash browns, and an extra-large coffee, and continued east.

In my mind, I had fixed on Albuquerque as my destination. I didn't know why for sure, except that was where all the signs on I-40 were pointing me. At the very least, I thought I could lie low there for a day or two while I decided where to go next. Staying in Gallup hadn't seemed safe, not with the Wilcoxes just over the border ten miles or so away. Albuquerque, on the other hand, was buried right in the middle of New Mexico, and didn't seem like the sort of place where I'd have to worry about running into anyone who might know me. Yes, I'd spent part of my childhood in New Mexico, but we'd never lived anywhere near Albuquerque, and the odds of encountering someone from my past seemed pretty slim.

The whole drive, I kept my phone in airplane mode. It wasn't as though I needed to call anyone, and since I'd seen some of the magic Jeremy, Jake's younger brother, could perform with computers and tech, I was worried he might be able to track me through the cell phone's signal. Once I got to Albuquerque, though, I stopped on the western outskirts of town to get gas, and also to use the Yelp app on my phone to guide me to a local hotel, since that was easier than trying to figure out how to make the Fiat's fancy navigation system give me a hotel recommendation. It had been easy to find the Fairfield Inn over in Gallup because it was clearly visible from the highway, but Albuquerque was huge, probably the biggest city I'd ever been in. No way was I going to start driving around there without having a set destination in mind. Using my phone's cellular data was a calculated risk, but one I had to take.

I decided on a place called the Hotel Andaluz because it was right in the center of town, and also because it was offering a midweek special through TripAdvisor. Since I didn't dare risk leaving my phone on the whole way, I manually programmed the address into the Fiat's navigation system—I'd learned how to do that much, if not anything else— and then let it guide me downtown. The whole time, I maintained a death grip on the steering wheel and probably pissed off everyone around me by driving like an eighty-year-old granny. But I wasn't used to big cities and I wasn't used to traffic, and I figured it was better to annoy a bunch of strangers than get in an accident.

Eventually, though, I reached the hotel and had to hand my car off to a valet. I wasn't thrilled about that, but I gathered the mishmash of shopping bags that comprised my luggage and tried to look unconcerned as I headed into the lobby.

Wow. The write-up had said the hotel was historic, and yet I supposed I hadn't been expecting anything quite so elegant, like something out of a Moorish fantasy, with its high ceilings paneled in wood, and the graceful arches and grottoes that made up the enormous lobby. I gave the woman at the front desk the same story about my stolen credit card—along with a fake address—and was guided by one of the bellmen to a pretty room with a canopied bed, small sitting area, and a window that overlooked downtown.

Once I was safely inside and the door locked behind me, I allowed myself a breath of relief and went over to sit down on one of the upholstered chairs in the sitting area. Because it was a warm day verging on hot, the air conditioning was going nearly full blast, and I leaned my head back and shut my eyes briefly.

I was safe. I had made it.

Of course, this was only the first step in my journey. I wished that I'd asked Jake more about the other American witch clans, that he'd given me more information to work with. Maybe then I'd know if there were any other "dead spots" in the U.S., places that witch families had avoided, for whatever reason. Yes, Utah was one of those dead spots, but I didn't dare go back there. Not with Agent Lenz dumped in Kanab, Utah, and most likely going on a rampage as soon as he recovered from being struck by lightning.

If he recovered. Eleanor, the Wilcox clan's healer, had assured me he would be fine after a few days, but I didn't know that for sure. I didn't know how well he'd handled the trip from Flagstaff to Kanab, or whether Jake's cousins Travis and Leland had been all that careful when they dropped him off in a motel there. I supposed it was all too possible that Agent Lenz had suffered a relapse and was quietly expiring in that anonymous motel room because no one who cared about him even knew where he was.

Stop it, I told myself, and bent to pick up the bottled water that had been left in my hotel room as a courtesy. *He's going to be okay. Eleanor wouldn't lie to me.*

At least, she didn't seem like the kind of person who would tell pleasant lies just to make a situation look better. She'd appeared steady and calm and compassionate, all qualities you'd want in a healer.

And then I realized I was obsessing about Randall Lenz because I didn't want to think about

Jake. I didn't want to think about what I'd done to him, what must have passed through his mind when he woke up and realized I truly was gone.

Tears burned in my eyes, and I made myself drink some more water. Losing it wasn't going to help me…or help Jake. Sooner or later, he'd forget about me. Probably sooner, just because…what did we have to tie us together, really? A few kisses, that was all. Sure, those kisses had been mind-blowing, had shown me just a little of what it might be like to be with someone who seemed to be my perfect match in every way, but still. We hadn't professed our undying love for each other or anything close to it. Jake would get over me.

He had to.

I'd just lifted the water bottle to my lips to take another sip when someone knocked at the door of my hotel room. The sound made me jump, started my heart thumping in my chest, even though I knew it had to be the bellman. Maybe I'd dropped something in the elevator, or maybe he'd decided the tip I'd given him wasn't big enough and he'd come back to demand more.

No, it didn't work that way…did it? This was the first time I'd ever stayed in a hotel with valets and bellmen, so I supposed it was entirely possible that I'd unwittingly committed some kind of gaffe.

For a second or two, I contemplated ignoring the knock. After all, whoever was out there couldn't know for sure that I was even inside the room. I could have gone back out again—either to leave the hotel entirely, or to go upstairs to the rooftop bar I'd seen mentioned on the hotel's website. Even in my current depressed state, I'd thought that a rooftop bar sounded pretty cool.

But after the person outside knocked again, I decided I'd better go and see who it was. I put down the water bottle on the table in the sitting area, smoothed my hair as best I could, and headed over to the door.

As soon as I opened it, I got a weird little tingle at the back of my neck, the one that Jake had said meant I was in the presence of a witch or warlock. The man outside was no one I knew, tall and good-looking, probably of Spanish descent, with his near-black hair and eyes, his warm-toned olive skin.

"Hello," he said pleasantly, although there was something about the way his deep brown eyes fixed on me that made a worried little shiver trail down my spine. "I am Gustavo Castillo. May I speak to you for a moment in private?"

"About?" I replied, trying to sound nonchalant, as though strange warlocks showed up on my doorstep every day.

His brows drew together slightly. "I think you know what this is about," he said, then added in an undertone, "You are a witch in another clan's territory, and our *prima* hasn't given you permission to be here."

Well, hell. I'd thought if I just kept moving, if I didn't stay in any one place for very long, then there was a good chance my presence wouldn't be detected. Obviously, that had been a false assumption. How the *prima* of the local clan had been able to divine that a strange witch was moving through her territory, I had no idea, but I supposed the "how" of the situation didn't matter as much as what I intended to do about it.

"I'm sorry——" I began, but the stranger didn't let me get any further than that.

"I am not the one you should be apologizing to," he broke in, although he uttered the rebuke in almost a kindly tone. "You can give your explanations to Genoveva Castillo. She wants to speak with you."

"She's the *prima?*"

Again, I saw the shadow of a frown cross his face before his expression smoothed itself once more. "You didn't know this?"

"No," I replied, realizing even as I spoke the word that it probably sounded like the lamest excuse in the world, even if it was only the truth. But how was I supposed to explain to this handsome warlock, who looked as though he should be off shooting a tequila commercial or something, that up until a few days earlier, I hadn't known anything about the witching world at all?

"There is some mystery here, it seems," he said. "But you can tell Genoveva about it when you speak with her."

"She's here?" Even as the words left my lips, I realized it was probably stupid to think that the head of the local witch clan was cooling her heels in the lobby of the Hotel Andaluz. Wishful thinking on my part, I supposed, because the thought of going anywhere with this stranger wasn't exactly appealing.

A ghost of a smile touched his finely molded lips. "No. Her home is in Santa Fe. I will take you there."

Worry thrilled through me, and almost subconsciously, I sent a glance over my shoulder, back toward the windows in my hotel room. They still showed a serenely sunny blue sky, with absolutely no clouds overhead.

If a stranger had confronted me like this just two days before, I was pretty sure storm clouds would have already been circling overhead. But, thanks to the insights Joanna, the Wilcox clan's weather-worker, had given me only a few days earlier, I now knew how to keep my roiling emotions from interacting with the air currents high above. Yes, I could call the winds to me, or bring the lightning the way I had to protect myself from

Randall Lenz, but if I did so, it would be because that was my conscious decision and not because of my emotions raging out of control.

I owed the Wilcox clan that, if nothing else.

"But—but I just got to Albuquerque," I stammered, realizing that was probably a silly argument. Like the guy cared when I'd arrived, or that I'd paid for my hotel room in advance.

"I will get you a refund," Gustavo said. "Please…fetch your things."

I was running out of excuses, but I tried anyway. "What about my car?"

"I will drive your car," he said smoothly. "I had an Uber drop me off here against this eventuality."

Damn it. "So, I'm supposed to go off to Santa Fe with a complete stranger, just like that?"

"Not 'just like that.'" He pulled a sleek black iPhone from the pocket of his jeans, touched the screen, and then waited for a few seconds. "Genoveva?" A pause. "Yes, I'm with her now. She is reluctant to come, which is understandable, I suppose." He took the phone away from his ear and handed it to me.

I really didn't want to take it, but I realized I didn't have much choice. "H-hello?"

"This is Genoveva Castillo," came a woman's voice, brisk and low-pitched, the voice of a woman who was used to being in charge…and getting her own way. "It is my right as *prima* of this clan to speak with any strange witches or warlocks who enter Castillo territory without my permission. Who are you, and what are you doing here?"

"I'm—I'm Addie Grant," I said. All right, technically I was a Wilcox, and I even had a fake Arizona driver's license giving my last name as such, but it seemed strange to call myself Addie Wilcox when I still felt like Addie Grant.

"I don't know that clan. Where are you from?"

"Everywhere," I replied. That might have sounded like a non-answer to Genoveva Castillo, but it was only the truth. My mother and I had never stayed anywhere long enough for it to feel like home to me. Maybe Flagstaff could have become home…if Randall Lenz had left me alone to find out for myself.

A long pause. "Are you being impertinent, Ms. Grant?"

There was a word I hadn't expected to hear in casual conversation. "Um…I don't think so. It's just kind of a long story."

"All the more reason for you to tell it to me in person. I will see you in an hour."

The call ended there, and I handed the phone back to Gustavo. He watched me carefully, as if waiting to hear my response to Genoveva's demands before he decided what to say.

And honestly, what could I do? Call down the lightning to defend myself? Being so overtly hostile would only have the wrath of the entire Castillo clan descend on my head, and I had enough problems as it was. No, the best thing to do would be to see this Genoveva, explain why I'd been traveling through Castillo territory without permission, and then—with any luck—either go on my way or be allowed to have a small breathing space there in New Mexico before being forced to confront my destiny.

I managed a wan smile at Gustavo, who lifted an eyebrow but otherwise didn't react.

"Let me get my stuff," I said wearily.

2

JAKE WILCOX SAT UP IN BED, MIND ALREADY thrumming with possibilities for the coming day. Sure, there was still some lingering unease lurking in the back of his brain, thanks to the way Agent Lenz had turned up out of nowhere the night before, but Addie had managed to defend herself just fine, and Jake's ever-resourceful clan members had handily taken care of the fallout. Since Lenz's memory of the past few days had been completely scrubbed, there didn't seem to be much to worry about. Randall Lenz might have managed to track Addie to Flagstaff once, but Jake doubted he'd be able to manage such a feat again.

Even if Lenz somehow found his way back to northern Arizona, the Wilcoxes would be waiting for him...only this time, the price for his interference might be a little more severe than a few missing memories and a painful recovery after being struck by lightning.

Humming under his breath, Jake climbed out of bed and got in the shower, figuring he might as well start getting ready for the day ahead. He hadn't heard any sounds from the guest room across the hall that Addie was using as her crash space, but he guessed she was probably exhausted after everything that had happened the day before and was sleeping in. Who could blame her?

Twenty minutes later, Jake was out of the shower and dressed, leaving his wet hair to air dry after he'd run a comb through it. When he went out into the hallway, he saw his dog Taffy lying on the floor in front of the guest room door, as though keeping watch over the woman inside.

"Good dog," Jake said, then knelt so he could reach down and scratch the dog's ears. Taffy immediately got up and pressed herself against him, asking for a thorough back scratch. Suppressing a grin, he went along with the dog's demands, although after a moment, he gave her a pat on the head and straightened up. "I can't keep petting you forever," he said, to which Taffy quirked a lopsided ear and gave him some serious side-eye, as if to tell him that yes, of course, he could, because petting dogs was what humans were for. "Anyway," he went on, "it seems as if Addie's sleeping in pretty late, don't you think? Should I knock, or just go downstairs and make some coffee?"

In response to this question, Taffy pawed at the door and gave a hesitant little bark. Not too loud, but still, the sound made Jake stare down at the dog, unease growing within him. Normally, Taffy didn't bark very much. And that hadn't sounded like an excited bark, or a warning bark, but more as though she was worried about something.

Doubt stirred in Jake's mind, even as he told himself that he was probably making a big deal out of nothing. Still, while he would have preferred to avoid waking up Addie if she was sleeping peacefully, neither did he want to stand out in the hallway and do nothing if something was seriously wrong. What if summoning the lightning the night before had taken more of a physical toll on her than she'd wanted to admit? What if she'd injured herself in some way, had suffered some kind of painful after-effects that had only manifested themselves as the night wore on?

Those disturbing questions served to settle the matter. He lifted a hand and knocked on the door, saying softly, "Addie? Is everything okay in there?"

No response. Jake looked down at Taffy, who cocked her head to one side and whined slightly. A low sound emerged from her throat, too soft to be called an actual growl, and yet something about it made a shiver of cold work its way down his spine.

What if Lenz had somehow remembered what had been done to him and had made his way back to Flagstaff under cover of darkness? What if he'd stolen Addie right out of her bed?

No, that was ridiculous. The man had been struck by lightning and was still unconscious the last time Jake had seen him. He highly doubted Agent Lenz would be in any kind of shape to go crawling up the side of a house…but what if he had?

That frightening image seemed to decide things. Mentally rehearsing apologies for barging in on her like this, Jake put his hand on the doorknob. It turned easily, and the door swung inward.

The curtains were still shut. In the dimly lit room, he could just make out the huddled shape of Addie's body under the quilt that covered the bed. She didn't stir at all as he entered, and once again worry lanced through him.

"Addie?"

Still nothing. With Taffy padding along a pace or two behind him, Jake went over to the bed and lowered his hand to the approximate spot where he thought her shoulder would be located, thinking he would touch her lightly, give her a very small shake to wake her up.

Except when his fingers closed on what was

supposed to be her shoulder, it felt curiously soft under his fingertips, not like a shoulder at all. In fact....

Suspicion growing, he grasped hold of the quilt and pulled it back, revealing not the startled and possibly annoyed Addie he'd hoped for, but a couple of pillows shoved under the covers, clearly put there to mimic the shape of a sleeping body.

God damn it.

She was gone. But where?

More importantly, *why?*

A hurried glance around the room and in the closet proved that all her things were gone—her new purse, the few clothes she'd purchased over the past couple of days. And when he went to the guest bathroom to check inside, there was absolutely nothing left to show she'd ever been there...no toothbrush, no toothpaste stored in the vanity drawer. The cup on the counter still had some water in it from when she'd brushed her teeth the night before, but otherwise, the bathroom looked as though no one had even used it.

Somehow, he doubted Agent Lenz would have been quite so thorough if he'd actually managed to gain access to the house and take Addie away. No, it seemed fairly obvious to Jake that she'd packed her things and stolen out in the middle of the night... and that realization was like a blow to the gut.

He left the bathroom and ran down the stairs,

Taffy following, toenails clicking on the polished wood. Of course, the dog wasn't so much interested in the missing woman as getting a chance to pee on the front lawn while Jake stood there on the flagstone path, staring at the empty driveway in consternation.

Addie's brand-new Fiat was gone.

Right then, Jake cursed himself for being so eager to buy her that damn car. At the time, he'd thought it a good thing to get her some wheels, allow her to have some independence while she familiarized herself with Flagstaff and grew into her new role as a member of the Wilcox clan and the daughter of a former *primus*. Now, though…now he could only think that she might not have had such an easy time getting away if he hadn't made her so mobile.

Think. He needed to think.

Where could she have possibly gone? She didn't have any family—or rather, the only family she had in the world was right there in Flagstaff. Yes, she must have had maternal grandparents somewhere, but since Addie had never mentioned them, Jake had a feeling they hadn't approved of their daughter's unexpected pregnancy and had thrown her out of their lives. Positively Victorian, as far as he was concerned, but he knew there were still people in the world who thought that having children out of wedlock brought disgrace on a family.

Unfortunately, even though Addie might not have had any real refuge waiting for her, what she did have was years of experience in moving from place to place, of continually starting over. True, it must have been her mother who'd handled the logistics of those moves, at least until Addie was old enough to contribute, but even so, she still knew more than most people what it was like to start all over again in a new town, and therefore wouldn't have been as afraid of the prospect as someone who'd spent their entire life in one place.

Which meant she could have gone anywhere.

He dragged his hand through his hair and wished he could throw back his head and shout his frustration at the clear blue sky. However, that sort of display would only make his neighbors —all nonmagical folk, except his cousin Alan's family down the block—wonder what the hell was the matter with him, and it certainly wouldn't bring Addie back.

Why? *Why?*

Except…he could guess exactly why she'd bolted. He might have only known her for a few days, but he'd noticed the troubled expression that had passed over her face as Connor and Angela explained their plans for disposing of Agent Lenz. She'd dutifully gone along with all of it…while at the same time inwardly fretting that their scheme wouldn't be effective in the long run, that he'd still be able to figure out what had happened to him and would return to take her away despite all their precautions. Since Jake and his brother had already pretty much come out and said that the Wilcox clan would remove such a threat if it actually reared its head, Addie had known Lenz's return could bring a hell of a lot of trouble with it.

So, she'd run. She'd run because she didn't want to see anyone else get hurt. And Jake couldn't even say she was overreacting, not when that same agent had shot her mother dead right in front of her.

Damn him. Jake would never have said he was a vengeful person, but in that moment, he found himself wishing Addie had killed the bastard with the lightning bolt she'd summoned, rather than merely knocking him out.

As soon as the thought passed through his mind, though, Jake immediately rejected it. As far as he was concerned, Agent Lenz was a miserable excuse for a human being, and if there was any justice in the universe, he'd get what was coming to him sooner rather than later, but the last thing Jake wanted was for Addie to bear the burden of the guilt for his murder. She didn't deserve that.

He turned back toward the house, and Taffy trotted toward him, gaze expectant. This was usually the time of day when he'd take her for her morning walk, but he'd never felt less like spending the precious time that activity would require. Still, none of this was the dog's fault, and of course, he wouldn't neglect her in such a way.

But he would make her wait for a minute or two. First, he needed to call Connor.

His head felt as though someone had taken a mallet to it. Holding back a groan with some difficulty, Randall Lenz rolled over on his back and stared up at the unfamiliar ceiling overhead. That he didn't recognize the ceiling in question wasn't too strange, since he spent a lot of time on the road, searching for new subjects for his agency to investigate and add to the Daedalus Project if it turned out they were the real deal. However, the disorientation he currently seemed to be experiencing showed no sign of going away any time soon. Usually, once he blinked and took stock of his surroundings, he remembered right away where he was.

That didn't seem to be happening at the moment.

He scowled and made himself sit up, even though his head hurt even worse in an upright position. And it wasn't only his head—his entire body felt like he'd gone on a bender and had spent the overnight hours participating in the local version of *Fight Club*.

Not that he knew what constituted "local,"

precisely, because he was damned if he could even remember where the hell he was.

Frown deepening, he glanced around the room and saw that he appeared to be in a motel or hotel room of some sort—slightly shabby, carefully anonymous furniture, the ubiquitous notice tacked to the back of the door advising guests about check-in and check-out times and providing information about emergency exits. Probably, the wisest thing to do would be to get up and walk over to the door so he could read the sign for himself, since they almost always provided the name and address of the hotel in question. At the moment, though, he didn't know whether he was even capable of that much exertion. Everything just *hurt*.

All right. Time to go back to the beginning and figure out where the hell he was. Unfortunately, he couldn't seem to recall what the beginning was supposed to be.

He pressed his thumb and middle finger against his forehead, rubbing slightly. In the past, that simple trick had often helped with his headaches, but it didn't seem to be doing much at the moment. If anything, he felt slightly worse.

But there was an unopened bottle of water sitting on the nightstand, and he made himself reach for it, crack open the lid, and take a long swallow. Yes, that was a bit better. Not a lot, but if nothing else, the sensation of the tepid liquid slipping down his throat helped him feel a little more grounded, helped him to return to himself.

What had happened to him?

He was dressed, although his shoes sat on the floor by the nightstand and his suit jacket had been draped across the foot of the bed, with his tie lying on top of it. Clearly, he'd been in good enough shape to remember to take off his jacket, shoes, and tie, although he didn't recall removing any of those clothing items. Hell, he didn't remember even coming to this room in the first place.

Although it hurt more than he wanted to think about, he forced himself to lean over to the foot of the bed and rifle through his jacket pockets. Worry mounted in him as he went through all of them… twice…and realized his cell phone appeared to be just as MIA as his memory of how he'd gotten there.

His gaze roamed the room, but he didn't see the phone anywhere, not on the nightstand, not on the little round table over by the window. He supposed he could have left it in the bathroom, but searching for the damn thing would require him to get up off the bed to find it, and he wasn't sure whether he was physically capable of that sort of exertion at the moment.

No sign of his laptop, either. Lenz reached into his trouser pocket and was somewhat relieved to find his wallet there…a relief that was short-lived once he realized that his official Homeland Security I.D. also seemed to have disappeared. All he had on him was his Virginia driver's license and his own personal Visa card, not the official one he used when traveling. Oh, and a couple of hundred dollars in cash, all twenty-dollar bills, as if he'd withdrawn the daily maximum from an ATM. He couldn't remember carrying that much money with him, or making that kind of a withdrawal, but since he didn't seem able to recall much of anything useful at the moment, he supposed that wasn't so strange.

Obviously, the mystery wasn't going to clear itself up any time soon. Gritting his teeth, he swung his legs over the edge of the bed and then sat there for a moment as he allowed himself to recover from the painful exertion. Crazy how he could be so incapacitated when he didn't even know what had happened to put him in this state in the first place.

Had he been in a car accident? Possibly, but even though he hurt all over, it was a sort of generalized ache, nothing obvious like the sort of sternum injuries that were common when an airbag exploded. He didn't have any obvious cuts, scrapes, or other lacerations, no broken bones, and he wasn't covered in the fine white dust that was the telltale fallout of an airbag letting go.

His bladder told him that it seemed to have

escaped serious injury, and needed to be relieved. Well, he supposed he would have to stand up sooner or later.

When he did so, the room spun around him, and he grabbed a corner of the nightstand and held on, willing himself to remain upright. A lancing pain shot through his head, almost blinding in its intensity.

Blinding....

The word—or possibly the mental image—seemed to jar something in him, although right then, he couldn't say exactly what it was. Something about a bright flash of light.

Maybe it had been a car accident after all. Maybe what he was remembering were the headlights of the car that had crashed into him. But if that had been the case, why was he here in this hotel room instead of in a hospital somewhere? With as banged-up as he was feeling, he highly doubted any EMT would have let him walk away from the scene of that kind of accident.

Somehow, he managed to take a step, and then another. It hurt, but he forced himself to keep going. The bathroom wasn't that far away—ten feet, maybe twelve. He could do this.

Eventually, he got to the doorway and held on to the jamb for a moment to steady himself. Once he thought he was strong enough to totter the last three or four steps to the toilet, he moved forward again. Undoing his pants told him how unsteady his hands were, but he kept going, took care of business, and then zipped his trousers closed again. No blood in his urine, so at least that was a good sign.

That task handled, he turned toward the mirror. Big mistake. A hollow-eyed, pale-cheeked reflection stared back at him, hair mussed, dark stubble covering his chin and cheeks. If he'd encountered that mirror self while walking down the street, he probably would have given the man in question a wide berth, figuring he had to be an addict or mentally ill.

Well, he needed to do something about that. With a shaking hand, he reached for the tap and turned on some cold water, then splashed it on his face and ran it through his hair, doing his best to finger-comb it into submission. The shock of the water brought a little blood to his cheeks, although there were dark circles under his eyes that made him look as though he'd gone a week without sleep, rather than being unconscious for…well, however long he'd been passed out in that hotel room.

Those rough ablutions sapped his energy enough that he knew he didn't have the strength to do much more than stumble back to the bed and fall down on it. At some point, he'd have to force himself to walk over to the motel office and try to find out how he'd gotten there in the first place, but for the moment, Lenz knew the most important thing to do was to get his strength back.

No…actually, the most important thing to do was try to remember what the hell had happened to him.

He knew he'd gone to Kanab, Utah, in search of Adara Grant, a young woman who appeared to have some sort of strange influence over the weather. That was his job at the division of Homeland Security where he worked—to track down people who possessed unusual abilities and bring them back for study and possible weaponization under the umbrella of the Daedalus Project. And no, the truth of the project's mission statement had never been outlined in quite so bold a manner, but Randall Lenz and everyone he worked with knew exactly why the government wanted to get its hands on those people.

Again he saw a flash, only this time he realized it was the muzzle flare from his service pistol. It hadn't been his intention to kill Lyssa Grant, Adara's mother; he'd drawn his pistol to intimidate her and Adara, nothing more. But something had hit his head and the gun had gone off, and then…

…and then he'd awakened in this hotel room. That didn't feel right, though, as though his brain had skipped over something vitally important, even if he couldn't recall what it was supposed to be. He remembered feeling a burst of triumph as the skies over Adara Grant's house had opened up, her own fear and rage obviously calling the storm to her. That storm had told him she truly did possess the power to control the weather.

But nothing after that. No, wait…there had been a man. A stranger had shown up on Adara's front porch, had asked for her by name as if he, too, knew there was something special about her. A dark-haired man, middle or late twenties.

A name came to him.

Jake.

Jake what?

Lenz wrestled with the name but couldn't seem to come up with anything more than that single syllable.

Still, it was another clue, another piece of the incomplete puzzle that his memory had apparently become. Sooner or later, he'd figure out who Jake was.

And where he'd come from. Lenz didn't know much right then, but he somehow knew if he found Jake, he'd find Adara, and then he could do his best to salvage something worthwhile from this entire miserable situation. If he failed, Daedalus would be taken from him, and he'd never be able to recover professionally from such a blow. Worse, he couldn't expect any of his successors to give the project the delicate care it deserved. A myriad of nightmare scenarios danced through his head, and he gritted his teeth and did his best to push them to the back of his mind where they couldn't distract him.

For the moment, he needed to heal.

However long it took.

3

"She *what?*" Connor demanded.

"She left in the middle of the night," Jake said, feeling a low-level headache continue to throb somewhere behind his temples, despite the two cups of coffee he'd drunk and the bagel he'd forced down, more because he knew he needed to eat something than because he had any actual desire to consume the damn thing. "I was asleep, so I don't know what time exactly."

"Shit. Did she leave a note?"

"No."

In a way, that was the worst part about all this. Addie's leaving truly sucked, was something he still didn't quite want to acknowledge had actually happened, but if she'd at least left him a letter telling him why she'd fled, then maybe he wouldn't be feeling quite so abandoned. And yes, he'd already guessed that her departure had been motivated by a worry that Randall Lenz would awaken and come back to finish the job that had been cut short by her lightning attack, and yet…and yet, it still wouldn't have hurt quite as much if he had some actual facts to work with instead of only educated guesses.

"Any idea where she went?"

"Jeremy's working on it."

His brother had warned him that tracking her via traffic cams was going to be difficult, since they weren't super high-resolution at the best of times, and any images recorded during the overnight hours would be grainy and dark, and without a lot of detail. But better crappy images than no images at all. If nothing else, they had the lower traffic density of the overnight hours working in their favor, since there wouldn't have been nearly as many people out and about after midnight. Jake figured Addie couldn't have sneaked out much earlier than that, since they'd gone to bed a little before eleven and she would have wanted to wait a while until she knew he was safely asleep.

"In the meantime," Jake went on, since Connor hadn't replied right away, probably because he wasn't even sure what to say, "I figure I might as well head east and start making inquiries. Maybe she stopped for gas or stayed at a hotel somewhere."

"Why east?"

"I don't know." Actually, Jake had already realized he was grasping at straws, since it was entirely possible that Addie had headed west, hoping to lose herself in Southern California's enormous suburban sprawl. But he couldn't travel nearly as far in pursuit of her before he butted up against Santiago territory —that particular clan controlled the southern half of California, from Santa Barbara down to the Mexican border—and he supposed he was hoping she'd gone east because at least that way there was a higher likelihood of someone in the Wilcox clan having seen her.

Unless she'd gone straight into Castillo territory without stopping, in which case, he was screwed. True, the Castillos and the Wilcoxes had been more or less friendly for generations, thanks to Jeremiah Wilcox's sister Emma providing healing to a Castillo clan member as the Wilcoxes traveled west to Flagstaff in the 1870s, but relations had been strained for the past couple of years. Not because the Wilcoxes had done anything on purpose to draw the ire of the Castillos, but because their former *prima,* Isabel, had died several years earlier helping Connor and Angela defeat Joaquin Escobar, the dark warlock who'd seized control of the Santiago family and had threatened to do the same thing to the Arizona clans. Isabel's death certainly wasn't the fault of anyone except Escobar himself. However, her daughter Genoveva still was less than happy with the Wilcoxes and the McAllisters. After all, if they hadn't reached out to the Castillos for assistance, her mother would most likely still be alive.

At any rate, waltzing into Castillo territory and asking for help looking for a runaway witch probably wasn't the most politic thing to do, considering the current state of affairs between the two clans. Even so, Jake knew he'd walk right into the lion's den if necessary to get any information that might lead him to where Addie had gone.

He just sort of hoped matters wouldn't require him to do anything quite so drastic. Although he'd never had any direct dealings with Genoveva Castillo, he'd heard that she could be one cold-hearted witch.

Since Jake could tell that Connor was waiting for him to go on, he added, "Logistically, it makes more sense. She can't leave the country because she doesn't have a passport, so that rules out going south into Mexico, and she wouldn't head north because she knows we dumped Randall Lenz in Kanab, and she'd have to go through there if she was traveling to Utah or Idaho, unless she went the long way around by heading west to pick up I-15."

"Right," Connor said, sounding distracted. "Getting rid of him went well, by the way. Travis and Leland just told the motel manager that their friend had had a few too many, and that they needed to leave him there because they were due back at work and couldn't wait for him to sober up. They paid for two nights, just to be safe. Eleanor assured me he'd be mostly functional by that point."

Too bad. Jake knew he wouldn't shed too many tears if Lenz died in his sleep, but his death would invite the sort of inquiry none of them needed. And anyway, Jake had already told himself that he didn't want the man's death on Addie's conscience, even if he had brought the lightning strike on himself by refusing to back down. "And back at his agency, telling tales."

"Minus his phone and laptop."

"True."

They'd decided to keep those items, along with his I.D., partly because they didn't see the need to make things easier for Lenz whenever he did wake up, and partly because Jeremy had wanted to get his hands on them and see what sort of data he could pry out of the devices, the laptop in particular. So far, he wasn't having much luck, just because they were encrypted to a level that made the traffic cams and satellites he'd hacked seem like breaking into some high school kid's Chromebook, but Jake was confident that his brother would succeed at some point. His magic hadn't let them down so far.

"Still," Jake said. "They're going to be able to start piecing things together, even with his memory wiped and his phone and laptop missing. He had to be working with support people back at his agency, people who would have been tracking his movements."

"Well, we'll deal with that when the time comes," Connor replied. He didn't sound worried, but then, Connor always had been good at acting casual even when something was bothering him. "It's pretty obvious that Lenz and whoever he's working for are all about doing everything in stealth. If they show up in Flagstaff and start throwing their weight around, people are going to notice. And when people start noticing stuff, that's when it ends up on the evening news."

"I hope you're right."

"It's going to be okay, Jake. You go look for Addie—and in the meantime, I'm going to reach out to both Genoveva Castillo in New Mexico and Marisol Valdez in Southern California, just in case she went into either of their territories."

That sounded like a good idea...and also made Jake very glad that Connor was the head of the Wilcox clan and not him. While their relationship with Marisol was a bit better because Connor and Angela had actually been responsible for freeing her from the mind control Joaquin Escobar had exerted over her, she was still dealing with the effects of being under the dark warlock's control... and having his child. From what Jake had been able to tell, Marisol had done her best to keep a low profile the past couple of years, and he doubted she'd be overjoyed to hear from the Wilcox clan's *primus*, if only because speaking to Connor would probably dredge up memories she'd rather keep buried.

"The Ludlows?" Jake asked then. A touchy subject, because the Ludlow clan in northern California had actually thrown in their lot with Joaquin Escobar, then had to quickly backtrack when he was killed. There hadn't been any real contact with them after his death; like Marisol Valdez, they'd been keeping their heads down and their clan affairs to themselves.

A sigh came through the cell phone speaker. "With any luck, I won't have to talk to them at all. Let's wait and see if we can get some other leads on Addie before I walk into that particular hornet's nest."

"Sure," Jake said easily. They all had plenty on their plates to get started, and they'd deal with the Ludlows when—or if—the time came. "I'm going to stop by Trident HQ and check with Jeremy on that laptop, and then I'll get on the road."

"And I'll put out the word to the Winslow and Holbrook relatives to see if anyone noticed something out of the ordinary last night."

Probably a long shot, just because Jake realized that Addie's new car had been delivered to her with a full tank of gas, and they hadn't used much on their little trip out to Williams, which meant she wouldn't have had any real reason to stop before she hit the New Mexico border.

Weird to think that their outing to the town that billed itself as the "gateway to the Grand Canyon" had happened just the day before. It felt like a hundred years had passed in the intervening time.

"Thanks," Jake said, mostly because he didn't see the need to point out that such measures were probably futile. Connor was only trying to help. "I'll try to keep you posted."

"Same here." A brief hesitation before his cousin added, "I'm really sorry about this, Jake. I could tell there was something starting between you and Addie."

"You could?" Jake asked, startled. He'd been playing it cool when he first brought Addie to meet Connor and Angela in Jerome, since back then, he'd barely begun to admit his attraction to her even to himself. There certainly hadn't been any public displays of affection between him and the girl he'd found in Kanab. And when Connor and Angela had rushed over to the cottage after Addie attacked Agent Lenz with her lightning, the scene had been tense enough that Jake wasn't even thinking about anything except doing his best to comfort her.

Connor didn't laugh, but there was an undercurrent of amusement in his voice as he replied, "After experiencing the consort bond with Angela, it's kind of easy for me to see when a witch and a warlock have that same chemistry between them."

"But Addie's not a *prima*," Jake protested.

"No," Connor replied, his tone turning serious. "But she's the daughter of a *primus,* isn't she? That means we're kind of dealing with uncharted territory here. Anyway, I guess what I'm trying to say is that if you were both feeling the same kind of strong connection, then leaving had to be just as hard on her as it was on you. And I can't help thinking...."

"Thinking what?"

"Thinking that, even though it might not look that way right now, she wants you to find her."

Putting on his shoes had been exhausting enough that Randall Lenz had to sit down on the chair by the window to catch his breath afterward. Even so, he looked on his current state of affairs as a small victory. At least he was no longer lying in bed, and he was sitting upright and wore a pair of shoes and a jacket. In another ten or fifteen minutes, he might feel well enough to actually walk out the door and go to the motel's office. Lacking his cell phone, it seemed to be the only place he could get any real answers.

He'd brought the half-drunk bottle of water with him to the table and chair, and he swallowed some more, preparing himself for the ordeal ahead. Then he pulled the shabby striped curtains aside so he could look through the window and get some idea as to the lay of the land.

The motel where he'd been dumped consisted of a single story. It formed a squarish U-shape, and looked out onto what appeared to be a fairly busy street. The parking lot currently contained only four vehicles, none of them particularly noteworthy—a dusty beige Camry, two older-model SUVs, and a pickup truck with oxidized red paint. From where he sat, he couldn't really make out any of the license plates, but the soaring red sandstone cliffs off in the distance seemed vaguely familiar. As he stared at them, it suddenly clicked.

Kanab, Utah. Somehow, he was back in Kanab. For a single disorienting moment, he wondered if he'd imagined the confrontation at Adara Grant's house, had suffered some kind of strange episode that returned him where he'd started, but he was able to shake that nightmarish possibility almost as soon as it popped into his head. This wasn't the same hotel where he'd been staying when he first came to town, and so he knew some time had to have elapsed.

But how had he gotten here? None of the vehicles he'd spied in the parking lot were the black Ford Taurus he'd been driving as his agency car. He had absolutely no idea what had happened to it; clearly, its fate was lost in the same haze that had swallowed all his memories from the past few days.

At least, he hoped he'd only lost a few days. Technically, as soon as he was late checking in with HQ, they should have sent someone out to retrieve him, but they would have honed in on his cell phone and used that to track him. Since his phone was MIA, they would have no idea where to find him even if they somehow recovered the phone.

He needed to call in, let Dawson know his current location. He didn't know why he hadn't thought of that when he first woke up, except his brain felt as scrambled as a plateful of eggs.

Except…he couldn't remember the number for HQ. Which was ridiculous, because he had it memorized. Then again, his memory was currently as full of holes as Swiss cheese, so he supposed it wasn't so strange that he'd lost such a vital piece of information.

No matter. He wouldn't try to force it; his experience was that such things tended to resurface when you least expected them to. For the moment, he needed to focus on his upcoming expedition across the parking lot, daunting as that particular prospect seemed to him. When he'd looked out the window, he'd spotted the neon "Office" sign over to the left and up at the front of the building, so at least he had a destination in mind.

All he had to do was get there.

Another swallow of water to fortify him, and then he stood up. That actually felt a little better; the room hadn't spun all the way around him the way he'd been expecting it to. He still felt like deep-fried shit, but at least he didn't feel as if he was about to pass out.

In fact, he wondered if he might actually be hungry. He considered that possibility for a second or two, and decided he probably could eat something. Actually, he was ravenous, stomach aching with need. There was no food in the room, so he'd have to go out to find something to eat.

First things first, though.

The key to the room—an old-fashioned metal key on a plastic fob, not the credit card type that had supplanted metal keys at most hotels—was lying on the table. Lenz didn't remember leaving it there, but then again, he really didn't remember much of anything, so he couldn't be surprised by that particular gap in his recollections. Nonetheless, he picked it up and put it in his jacket pocket, then let himself out.

The air was much warmer than he'd been expecting. Downright hot, actually. Rather than feel uncomfortable in his black suit, though, he welcomed the sensation of the sun beating down on his head. If nothing else, it helped to bring some warmth to his cold hands and feet, extremities which shouldn't have been that chilled, based on the temperature of his hotel room.

Drawing strength from the heat, he began to slowly walk across the parking lot. As he went, he fancied he could almost feel himself soaking up the sun's rays, letting them move through his body and recharge his fried nerve endings. It still took a great deal of effort to put one foot in front of the other, but he was steadier than he'd expected, which could only be a good thing, and he reached his destination more quickly than he'd expected.

A kid who looked as though he was barely out of high school sat behind the desk in the motel office. He blinked as Lenz approached and paused in front of the desk.

"Can I help you, sir?" the kid asked.

Staring down at him, Lenz guessed that the young man seated at the desk couldn't have possibly been working the night before. No one in their right mind would have left someone that age in charge during the overnight hours; he was probably on duty now because it was the middle of a weekday and the place wasn't all that busy.

Still, he had to ask the question.

"Were you working here last night?"

"No, sir," the kid said.

Belatedly, Lenz realized the kid was wearing a name badge, and that the name on it was Byron.

Who the hell named their kid Byron in this day and age?

That was no concern of his, though. "Do you know who *was* working?"

"My father," Byron replied. "My family owns the motel, and we all take turns running the office. I'm on summer break now, and—"

"Can I talk to your father?" Lenz cut in, plowing through the kid's words with the ease of long experience. It wasn't the first time he'd had to cut past the chatter and get to the meat of a witness's story.

Not that this kid was a witness. He hadn't been around the night before, wasn't the person who might have seen whoever had dumped Lenz at the hotel under cover of darkness.

Byron squinted up at him. He was a sandy-colored specimen, eyes pale brown, hair an indeterminate color between blond and brown, skin tanned enough for him not to be pasty but definitely not the color of someone who spent a lot of time outdoors. "He's not here."

"I understand that," Lenz replied. He was somewhat proud of himself for maintaining a level tone, especially after having to make that arduous trek across the parking lot. "What I meant was, can you call him? I need to ask him a couple of questions."

"You a cop?" the kid asked, now looking vaguely worried.

"Not exactly."

A blink. "Oh. Well, what I meant is that he's not *here,* here. Here in Kanab, I mean. He and my mom went to St. George for the day."

Of course, they did. Lenz tried not to grind his teeth. Then again, even a primitive place like this one probably had resources he shouldn't overlook.

"Do you have a security camera here in the office?" he asked.

"Sure." Byron pointed up at an old-fashioned CCD unit bolted to the ceiling behind the desk.

Perfect. At that angle, it should have picked up anyone who'd come and gone in the office the night before.

"I'd like to look at your footage from last night."

The kid blinked again. "Um…I don't think I'm allowed to let you see that."

"Of course you are," Lenz replied, his tone silky, persuasive. "You asked if I'm a cop, and I said 'not exactly.' That's because I'm with Homeland Security, and you may have information vital to our national defense stored in the footage that camera recorded last night."

This pronouncement was met with widened eyes. "Homeland Security?"

"Yes, son."

"Do you have a badge?"

"No. I'm undercover."

Apparently, the kid didn't see anything wrong

with that line of reasoning, because a knowing light entered his eyes and he nodded. "Oh, right. I should have thought of that. Just give me a minute, sir—I need to pull it up."

"No worries," Lenz told him, doing his best to sound unconcerned…even though he knew he had far too many hopes pinned to whatever might be on that security footage.

A moment later, Byron said, "Here you go, sir," and actually got up from his chair so Lenz could take a seat there.

The controls were simple enough—he just had to use the mouse to click on a set of arrows superimposed on the footage to scroll back and forth—and so he fast-forwarded through several hours' worth of extremely dull images, none of which showed anything more exciting than a man in a backwards baseball cap coming in around 11:30 to have some sort of argument with the heavyset individual watching the front desk—Byron's father, Lenz assumed. And the rest of the evening seemed similarly uneventful.

Was it possible that whoever had dumped him here had taken him straight to the room and not come into the office at all? That scenario didn't make much sense, though; if that were the case, he doubted they would have left a key behind.

"Do you want to check the night before?" the

kid asked. "Your room was actually rented two days ago."

Lenz blinked at him. "It was?"

"I think so." He reached in the desk and pulled out an old-fashioned ledger, scanned its contents, and then nodded. "Yeah, Room 16, Sunday, June seventh."

Had he really been passed out in that motel room for nearly forty-eight hours? It didn't seem possible, but then, considering how he couldn't remember a damn thing about what had happened to him, he supposed it might be the simple truth.

"Okay," he said, trying to sound casual. "Then show me the footage from Sunday night into Monday morning."

He stepped out of the way so Byron could navigate from the Monday night video feed to Sunday night's images. If anything, that evening seemed even less eventful than Monday had been, since the only people who entered the office after nightfall were a couple who appeared to be in their fifties, trim and wearing hiking clothes. They had a brief exchange with the man Lenz assumed was the owner, and departed.

However, at a little past 1:30 in the morning, two young men entered the office, both of them appearing somewhat furtive. A casual observer probably wouldn't have noticed anything strange about their demeanor, but Lenz had been trained to look for certain tics in people, and he could tell from the way they never quite made eye contact with the man behind the desk and kept glancing out the windows that looked on the parking lot that they were clearly uncomfortable being there.

They didn't look like criminals, though. No, they both looked like a couple of clean-cut college kids, maybe a little older. Twenty-five at the most, dark-haired, wearing casual but good clothes—no rips or stains, nothing worn out. No visible tattoos or earrings. Hair cut fairly short. In fact, they appeared to be the kind of upstanding, attractive guys that a father would be glad to have his daughter dating.

Even so, Lenz knew right away that they had to be the ones who had dumped him at the hotel. How he knew such a thing, he couldn't exactly explain, except that he often had such hunches, and they almost invariably proved to be accurate.

"Those two men," he said, pausing the footage so a fairly clear shot of the two of them remained frozen on the screen. "Have you seen either of them before?"

Byron squinted at the still image and shook his head. "No, sir. They're not local."

"Do you have camera surveillance of the parking lot?"

"No. We used to, but people kept breaking or stealing the cameras, so my dad just gave up. He figured if something happened to someone's car, their insurance could take care of it."

A pragmatic solution to the problem. Still, Lenz wanted to curse. If there had been footage of the parking lot, then he could have gotten a look at what they were driving, maybe even caught a glimpse of their license plate. As it was, he had an image of a couple of twenty-somethings and not much else.

However, he'd long ago learned to work with what he had. "Can you print out a copy of that image?"

"Yes, sir," Byron replied. "Actually, all you have to do is hit Control + P."

He should have known that. Frowning at himself, he entered the command and then waited as an old-fashioned inkjet off in the corner began humming away as it warmed up. A moment later, it spat out a copy of the image in question. Grainy, yes, and black and white because the camera apparently didn't shoot anything else, but even so, the two men in the photo were recognizable enough.

"Thanks," he said, and folded the piece of paper and put it in his pocket. "Is there anywhere in walking distance to eat?"

"Yes, sir," the kid replied, and pointed toward the front of the motel. "Just another block down to your left and across the street. Grady's."

"Just" another block seemed like a very great

distance, but he'd manage. After all, he'd gotten across the parking lot…and picked up a valuable piece of intel. There was still a great deal to do, but for the first time since he'd awakened in that strange motel room, he felt a flicker of hope.

It might not be happening as quickly as he'd like, but sooner or later, he'd get to the bottom of this mystery.

4

I SUPPOSED IN THE BACK OF MY MIND, I'D BEEN expecting the Castillo *prima's* home to look something like Angela and Connor's gracefully restored Victorian house in Jerome. However, as Gustavo pulled my Fiat into the driveway of Genoveva Castillo's house, I realized I'd been woefully naïve in thinking that all *primas* did things the same way as Angela McAllister-Wilcox.

For one thing, the Santa Fe *prima's* place was huge. From what I could tell, it took up half the block, an enormous compound surrounded by a high adobe wall and shaded by old, old trees. As I got out of the car, the breeze which caressed my face was almost cool, telling me that summer's heat didn't assault this part of the world the same way it did Kanab or a lot of the other places I'd lived in the Southwest.

"This way," Gustavo said, and I followed him through a gate and then along a path that meandered toward a huge hacienda-style house, with green lawns and neatly trimmed flowerbeds on all sides. The rich perfume of roses drifted on the air, underlaid by the sharper scent of freshly mown grass.

Beyond all that, however, I got a sense of age, a realization that the place had probably stood there for hundreds of years and planned to be around for at least a few hundred more. It was sort of strange, that feeling of tradition, of history, because it wasn't something I'd really been expecting to encounter, maybe because I honestly didn't know all that much about Santa Fe. My mother and I had lived in New Mexico off and on, up until the time I was ten, but we'd made our home in places like Tucumcari and Truth or Consequences, and I'd never gotten the same feeling from either of those towns.

We walked up a low set of steps to the front porch. Even though Genoveva Castillo surely must have been expecting us, Gustavo still paused at the large double doors and politely rang the doorbell rather than simply waltzing in.

A moment later, the door opened, and a handsome man, probably around thirty or so, looked out at us. I could see the family resemblance between him and Gustavo in the night-dark hair and equally dark eyes, the somewhat long, patrician nose, but this man's expression seemed much friendlier. In fact, he smiled broadly when he saw me and extended a hand.

"Adara?" he asked, and I nodded, figuring it wasn't worth the effort to tell him that I preferred to be called Addie.

"Yes, I'm Adara Grant."

"Wonderful. Genoveva is expecting you. I'm her husband Eduardo. This way, please."

He moved out of the way so Gustavo and I could enter the house. However, Gustavo hung back as Eduardo gestured for me to follow him and didn't tag along as the two of us left the foyer—a grand space with dark, polished wood floors and walls of thick adobe, the heaviness of the decor relieved a bit by a large blue glass vase filled with red and white and yellow roses—and moved into what had to be the living room. The furniture there was heavy and dark as well, the room somewhat dim, thanks to the thick velvet curtains at the windows.

A woman got up from one of the sofas as we approached. On the phone, she had sounded crisp and mature and utterly self-assured, but as I approached, I realized she probably couldn't be much more than four or five years older than I was, so twenty-nine at the most. Still, I felt cowed by her, by how sleekly elegant she was, dark hair pulled back into a heavy knot low at the base of her neck, effortlessly chic in a slim dark skirt and gray silk blouse, a heavy coral cross—Native American work, I thought—hanging from a thick silver chain at her neck, sleek black pumps with heels I would never have attempted on her slender feet.

"How nice to meet you, Adara," she said. "Please, sit down."

She spread a manicured hand toward the sofa nearer the window, and I found my feet propelling me forward, almost as if she'd cast some sort of spell on me. Since she was a *prima,* I supposed she might have been capable of such a thing, but I thought rather that I obeyed because of the sheer force of her personality.

Something in her expression softened as she glanced over at her husband, and I couldn't miss the warmth and admiration in his eyes as he looked back at her. Intimidating as she appeared, it seemed the two of them truly cared about each other.

The *prima* bond Jake had spoken of? I supposed so, although I wasn't sure I wanted to think about that, about how I'd responded almost as strongly to him, even though I certainly was no *prima.*

Despite its heavy appearance, the velvet-upholstered sofa I sat down on was surprisingly comfortable. With the window at my back, I felt some of the warmth of the sun on my shoulders, strangely reassuring.

"Iced tea?" Genoveva asked as she took a seat. "Or lemonade?"

"Iced tea is fine," I replied.

She smiled up at her husband, and he left the room, presumably to go to the kitchen so he could get our refreshments. Was it the consort's job to fetch and carry for his *prima* wife? I didn't know, but maybe I was reading way too much into his actions, and he was simply being hospitable so his wife could get down to business.

Which was exactly what she did. Her smile faded, and her jaw set slightly as she stared across the massive coffee table of carved mahogany that separated us.

"So, Adara," she said. "What is it that brings you to Castillo territory? I am anxious to hear this 'long story' of yours."

Maybe she was, but I sure as hell wasn't eager to tell it. Partly because I didn't think it was any of her business, but also because I didn't want to explain anything of what had happened between Jake and me. I'd just gotten a tenuous grip on my emotions and didn't much relish the thought of possibly losing control in front of the steely Castillo *prima*.

Unfortunately, I could tell from the way her gaze was fastened on me that I didn't have much of a choice. And, to be fair, I was breaking the rules. Of course, a few days earlier, I hadn't even known such rules existed, but still, I had a feeling that sort of excuse wouldn't fly with Genoveva Castillo.

"I suppose I'm a Wilcox," I said slowly. "Except I didn't know that until a couple of days ago."

Her brows drew together. "You were not raised in the Wilcox clan?"

"No. My mother had a—a fling with Jackson Wilcox. I'm his daughter."

That revelation startled her, I could tell. Surprise flared in her dark eyes, exotic with their heavy lids and perfectly arched brows. "But I was led to understand that the curse—"

"I know," I cut in, realizing belatedly that interrupting a *prima*—especially the Castillo *prima*—might not be the best idea in the world. But since stopping myself there would have been even more awkward, I forced myself to go on. "No one can really figure it out. But it's the truth. Jake Wilcox discovered me a few days ago and brought me to live with the Wilcoxes after my mother...after my mother died."

There. I'd said the words and hadn't dissolved into tears. Actually, my tone had sounded almost too matter-of-fact, but I supposed that was better than bursting into noisy sobs in front of Genoveva Castillo.

Even though I hadn't provided any details about the how or when of my mother's death, Genoveva seemed to have picked up on some of the subtext, because her tone was gentler when she spoke again.

"I'm sorry for your loss...but glad that one of

your cousins located you and brought you to be with your father's family." A pause as she studied me for a few seconds before adding, "But clearly, that wasn't the end of it. Did they mistreat you in some way?"

"No," I replied quickly, wanting to make sure I disabused her of that notion. "No, everyone was very kind. But the problem was…."

"Yes?"

I gathered myself. While Genoveva definitely didn't seem like the sort of person I'd want to go shopping with or hang out with at a club—unlike my cousin Laurel—she appeared at least somewhat sympathetic. I knew next to nothing about her clan, but I knew they definitely deserved to hear that Randall Lenz was out there somewhere, hunting down people with extraordinary abilities.

In other words, witches and warlocks.

"There's a man," I said, the words coming out quickly, knowing I needed to say them as fast as possible before I lost my nerve. "He works for the government, Homeland Security. He—he found me somehow, because of my talent."

Genoveva looked as though she was about to ask a question, but was interrupted by the return of Eduardo, who carried a silver tray laden with a pitcher of iced tea and three heavy blown-glass tumblers. Apparently, he would be allowed to sit in on this convo, unlike Gustavo, who I assumed was still cooling his heels in the foyer...unless he'd decided to go hang out on the porch and enjoy the mild summer day.

After Eduardo had poured tea into the glasses and handed one to Genoveva and another to me before taking the last one for himself, the *prima* spoke. "This man 'found' you? How? What is your talent?"

"Weather-working," I replied. "Only—only I couldn't control it. And so he was tracking me through unexplained weather phenomena."

Comprehension flickered in her dark eyes. "You had no control because you weren't raised in a witch clan."

"Exactly. And—and I got some bad news, and there was a bad thunderstorm, and this man— Randall Lenz—showed up on my doorstep. He tried to get me to go with him, but then Jake appeared and—" I faltered, wondering if I had to recount the whole terrible story. Probably, but there was no reason to go into excruciating detail. "There was a—a confrontation. Lenz shot my mother, and Jake and I ran."

"I am so sorry," Eduardo said, and I knew just by looking at him that his concern and sympathy were real, not emotions he'd assumed because they were appropriate to the occasion.

"Yes, that is terrible," Genoveva added. "So... you ran, and got away?"

"For a time," I replied. There was also no reason to explain how quickly Jake and I had come to care for each other. My worry about what Agent Lenz could do to the Wilcox clan as a whole should be sufficient motivation to explain why I'd decided I had to leave. "But then Randall Lenz showed up in Flagstaff, and even though we took care of him, I realized that I couldn't stay with the Wilcoxes. I'd be putting them in danger, because I could tell Lenz wasn't the sort of guy who gave up easily. I decided I needed to get out of there before anyone else showed up, asking questions."

Genoveva and Eduardo glanced at one another. I didn't think *primas* were psychic, necessarily, and yet I got the feeling they exchanged some sort of silent communication. When I met Connor and Angela, I'd noticed them doing much the same thing. It must have had something to do with their consort bond.

"You said you 'took care of' this Randall Lenz," Genoveva said then. "What happened to him?"

"Connor and Angela stripped his memories, and they confiscated his laptop and cell phone," I replied, realizing I'd just described what could only be a series of criminal offenses. However, I got the feeling that witch clans were a law unto themselves, even if they had to pay lip services to the law of the land as well. "And then a couple of Wilcox cousins dumped him back in Kanab, Utah—where I was living and where he originally found me. But even though Angela and Connor and—and Jake—seem to think that's the end of it, I don't believe that. I think Lenz is going to keep looking for me, especially if he remembers enough to...." I faltered there, not sure whether I should reveal how I'd managed to neutralize him...almost kill him...by sending a lightning strike his way.

But the damage was done, because Genoveva seized on my words immediately. "Remembers enough to what?"

I reached for the glass of iced tea Eduardo had poured for me and took a sip. It was cool and strong, not sweetened at all, which was a shock at first. After a second swallow, I thought I might prefer it that way, bracing and almost astringent, even though my mother had always dumped enough sugar in our iced tea that it might as well have been soda. "Remembers enough to realize that my gift—talent, whatever—is even stronger than he thought. That it's...easily weaponized."

Eduardo, who'd sat down next to his wife, sent me a worried look. "How do you mean?"

"When he found me in Flagstaff, I—" There wasn't any easy way to say it, so I just blurted out the words. "I called the lightning to strike him down. I didn't kill him," I added hastily. "He's okay. The Wilcox healer patched him up. But still...if the government already wanted me because of my talent, then I have to believe they're going to want me that much more when they realize what I can do with it."

The *prima* sat very still, staring at me like someone who thought they'd picked up a harmless garter snake, only to realize it was actually a black mamba. "You can do that? Bring down the lightning through sheer force of will?"

"Well, sure," I said. It was impossible to ignore how startled she looked...and I had a feeling Genoveva Castillo wasn't the sort of person to startle easily. "Isn't that what weather-workers do?"

"Not exactly," she replied. She'd recovered some of her composure, but she still seemed a bit off balance. "Weather-workers can summon the clouds to come and go, to coax them to rain...or snow...or hold off if fair weather is preferred. Never too much, because it's not good to upset the natural balance of things. But I've never heard of a weather-worker who could make the very lightning itself her servant."

And if Genoveva Castillo, a *prima* from a very old and established clan, had never heard of such a talent, that meant it probably hadn't existed before I came along. At the very least, even if weather-workers maybe had once been capable of such feats, they hadn't performed that particular trick for a very long time.

Was it Jackson Wilcox's blood and talent

running through my veins that made me so different from the weather-workers who'd come before me? Or was I just a freak, some kind of weird mutation? Neither Connor nor Angela had looked that startled by what I'd done, but they'd been thinking on their feet, trying to figure out what to do with Randall Lenz, rather than stopping to analyze the nuts and bolts of what I'd done.

If I'd been back among family, I might have asked whether I'd demonstrated some kind of previously unknown weather-working ability. I sure as hell wasn't going to ask such a thing of Genoveva Castillo. She was still looking at me as though she wasn't quite sure what sort of witch she'd just invited into her living room.

"But," she went on, when it became obvious that I didn't have any idea how to reply to her comment, "yes, I think you're probably right in assuming that this Agent Lenz would find you quite valuable. Now I can see why you felt it necessary to run."

I didn't quite let out a sigh of relief, but I couldn't help but be glad that she was able to see my side of things. However, I was less than heartened by her next words.

"And if you were a danger to the Wilcoxes, then you are a danger to us as well." A pause, as if she expected me to protest, but since I only sat there on the couch, hands knotted together, she apparently decided she might as well continue. "I have sympathy for your situation, Adara, but I have to think of my family, my clan."

"That's fine," I said. Although I honestly hadn't expected her to offer me any sanctuary, now that I knew doing so was an impossibility, I experienced a flare of annoyance. I did my best to tamp it down as I added, "I wasn't lying when I told Gustavo I was only passing through. I never planned to stay here more than a day or two at the most."

Genoveva nodded, but I thought I detected a certain abstraction in her expression, as if her thoughts were already ranging ahead to my eventual fate. "Where do you plan to go?"

"I don't know," I said. "I figured I'd keep running until I ended up someplace so obscure that Randall Lenz would never have a chance of finding me there. The Wilcox weather-worker taught me how to control my talent, so it's not as though I'm going to be summoning random cloudbursts or tornadoes and sending up red flags."

"A good plan," she replied. "But you should do your best to avoid any witch clans, and hide among the civilian population."

"Well, I'd love to do that," I retorted. "Problem is, I have no idea where most of the witch clans even are."

Genoveva finally reached for her glass of iced tea and sipped from it before replacing the tumbler on its carved wood coaster. "We're in nearly every state, but that still leaves plenty of places where you could go. My advice, however, is to head to Wyoming."

"Why Wyoming?" I asked. My mother and I had lived near Casper for about six months, and it seemed to me that Wyoming with its wide-open spaces was exactly the sort of place where Agent Lenz would be able to spot me from a mile away, even if I managed to keep my magical gifts from revealing my location.

"There are no witch clans there, for one thing," she replied. "I'm not sure why. But as witch-kind settlers came to this land, they pushed on through Wyoming and kept heading for points west, or south. And also, there is a sizable Native American reservation in the state. I can't think of a better place for you to hide yourself than among the Native American population, since they generally tend to be wary of the government."

That all sounded very logical, except…. "I'm not Native American," I pointed out.

"No," Genoveva said, looking singularly unworried by that fact. "And neither are quite a few of the people who live and work near the reservation. But if you're looking for an obscure place to hide yourself, the sort of location where this Agent Lenz is unlikely to look, I can't really think of a better plan…unless you intend to leave the country altogether."

That option wasn't really open to me, since I didn't have a passport. And yes, I knew I could probably get a fake one somewhere, but I had no idea how or where. Besides, I doubted Genoveva Castillo would want me hanging around Santa Fe for the length of time that sort of project might require.

And even though I didn't want to admit such a thing to myself, I didn't want to leave the country where I'd been born. I might have moved around a lot and never been able to call a single town or state home, but in a way, that made the entire United States my home. Desperate as I was feeling, I still wasn't quite ready to make myself an exile.

"Wyoming sounds good," I said at last.

"Then it's settled."

Eduardo looked at his wife in some alarm, obviously worried by the finality in her tone. "Surely you're not going to send her off to Wyoming right this minute?"

Frankly, the thought of getting in my car and driving a thousand miles or so—or however far it was to Wyoming…my knowledge of geographical distances wasn't the best—made a wave of dismay go through me. However, if Genoveva wanted to send me packing, then I'd go. I wasn't going to presume on her hospitality.

She said calmly, "No, of course not, Eduardo." Her gaze flickered back in my direction as she added, "Tonight, you can be my guest. I'll get you a room at one of the hotels not too far from here, make sure you're adequately supplied for your journey." One brow lifted slightly. "Do you need money?"

I thought of the wad of bills still shoved in my wallet. Even after my shopping expedition two days earlier and paying for gas and the hotel room in Gallup, I still had almost two grand on me. That was more than enough to get me where I was going, with a bit of a cushion until I could find a job. Which shouldn't be a problem; if all my moves with my mother had taught me anything, it was that it was usually pretty easy to find a job waiting tables wherever I landed.

Besides, I hated the thought of taking charity from Genoveva Castillo.

"No, I'm fine," I said, trying my best not to think of all the money Connor had transferred to me, now sitting unused in a couple of Chase accounts. That money might as well be on the moon, though. I didn't dare touch either of those accounts for fear of sending up a flag that either Randall Lenz—or Jeremy Wilcox, Jake's computer whiz brother—could see from space. "But thank you."

Genoveva's slender shoulders lifted in a shrug under the fine silk of her blouse. "If you're sure."

I nodded.

Eduardo rose from his chair, looking resigned. "I'll call the La Fonda."

And that, it seemed, was that. Within the half hour, I was ensconced in a lovely hotel right by the Plaza downtown, in a large suite that was even nicer than the room I'd rented at the Andaluz. I didn't know how Genoveva knew that I'd been lugging all my stuff around in a series of Kohl's and Dillard's and Macy's shopping bags, but a suitcase and matching overnight bag were waiting for me in that hotel room, so at least I'd be able to continue my travels in style. The room service I ordered for dinner was comped, and so was my parking in the garage overnight. The Castillo *prima* might not have wanted me hanging around her territory, but it was obvious she would do what she could to make my journey a little easier.

I supposed I had to be grateful to her for that.

Even so, I cried myself to sleep that night.

5

As Jake had expected, he found Jeremy in the PC room at the renovated house that was Trident Enterprises' headquarters. To his relief, he didn't see Laurel anywhere. It wasn't that he intended to hide Addie's disappearance from his cousin, but she'd probably want to ask too many questions, and most likely would figure out quickly enough that his interest in their first "orphan" witch wasn't exactly professional.

Not that Jake and Jeremy were really in the habit of sharing confidences—their conversations rarely got very personal—but at least Jake knew his brother already had an inkling about his feelings for Addie, and so there was no reason to say much of anything else. And because Jeremy was always so focused on his computers, he wouldn't have the inclination to go talking to other people in the clan about subjects that Jake would prefer were left private.

"Any luck with that?" he asked, noticing that his brother had Randall Lenz's laptop on the desk in front of him, although at the moment, he didn't seem to be doing anything with it beyond staring at the screen in annoyance.

"Not yet."

Jake had halfway expected as much, but he still couldn't help experiencing a flicker of worry. "What happens if you can't hack into it?"

"Nothing, because I'll get into it eventually." Jeremy shoved a hand through his hair, making half of it stick up on end, and swiveled in his chair to glare at his older brother. "Did you have a reason for coming by, or did you just decide it would be better to bug me about this laptop in person?"

If someone else had used that tone on him, Jake might have bristled. However, he knew his brother's short temper was inversely proportional to the difficulty of whatever computer project he was working on at the moment, and so he knew better than to take offense. Whatever Lenz and his team had used to lock down that thing, obviously it was some high-level stuff.

"Just wanted to check in," he said easily. "I'm going to drive east for a while, see if anyone out that way might have spotted Addie."

"Why east?"

"Why not?"

His brother seemed to consider that statement, then shrugged. "You could do all that on the phone," he pointed out.

Something Jake had already considered, but he knew if he went back to his house and sat in the living room and made phone calls all afternoon, he'd go crazy. He needed to be doing something physical, something that got him outside and made him feel as if he was accomplishing some kind of goal. "I could call the Wilcoxes out there, true," he replied. "But I couldn't talk to the people in the gas stations and the hotels."

"You're going to talk to every gas station attendant and front desk clerk between here and the New Mexico border?"

"If I have to."

Jeremy lifted an ironic eyebrow but didn't say anything. Instead, he turned back to the laptop, whose screen was dark blue except for an ominous "enter username and password" block floating in the exact center. Obviously, he hadn't gotten very far with that particular project. Sounding resigned, he said, "I suppose you want me to watch your dog."

"Could you?"

"Sure," Jeremy replied. He rolled his office chair over to another computer and began typing in a series of commands. What they were for, Jake had no idea. Probably, his brother was attempting to find a way into Lenz's computer that didn't involve figuring out his password or username. Without looking up, he asked, "Are you coming back tonight, or should I bring Taffy over to my place?"

Good question. Jake had thought he'd drive as far as he could and then circle back to Flagstaff, but if he made it as far as the border, then he'd have at least a five-hour round trip ahead of him…and that didn't even count all the stops he was planning to make. He definitely wouldn't make it back before dark.

"Better take her to your place, just to be safe," he said. "I'll run back to the house and pack up her stuff so all you have to do is grab it off the kitchen counter."

"Okay," Jeremy said, already sounding distracted. His eyes had the familiar glazed look they always got when he was fixated on a problem, his attention far away in some otherworld of coding that Jake couldn't begin to comprehend.

He had to hope that Jeremy wouldn't forget completely about going to fetch the dog, but he figured he could send a text to remind him. Besides, his brother would have to come up for air at some point. While he tended to lose himself in his projects, he still had an uncanny ability to snap out of his coding haze when it came time for a meal.

And if all else failed, Jake knew he could call Laurel to have her swing by and get Taffy.

"Thanks," he said, since he knew his brother would be useless for any further conversation.

Without saying goodbye, he let himself out and got back in his truck, then drove over to the house and set out all of his dog's things—her spare bowls and her treats and a bag of food. During all this, she sat on the kitchen floor and watched him warily, as if she knew full well that he was about to abandon her.

"Sorry, kiddo," he told her, doing his best to ignore the guilt that surged through him at his dog's reproachful stare. "But I don't know how long I'm going to be gone, and I don't want to leave you alone if it turns out I'm away all night. You're going to Jeremy's."

At Jeremy's name, Taffy's tail wagged a little. He'd been on her favorite people list ever since he fed her an entire hamburger from McDonald's. Without the bun, of course, but still. Anyway, ever since that momentous event, she'd looked forward to the time when she might get another burger of her own, and so Jake couldn't feel too guilty about having his brother dog-sit.

In fact, he'd send a text suggesting that maybe Jeremy should get Taffy a burger tonight…just in case.

A quick run upstairs to throw together a bag of his own, again, just in case. A change of clothes, his toothbrush and razor, a small bag of toiletries, and within five minutes, he was back out the door, promising Taffy as he went that Jeremy would be over later that afternoon. She wagged her tail but still looked a bit dubious, as if she—like Jake himself—wasn't quite sure whether her owner's brother would remember to tear himself away from his computer to fulfill his obligations.

But since he had contingencies in place, Jake tried not to let himself be too worried. He climbed back into the Gladiator and headed south on Milton so he could pick up the eastbound I-40, making a brief stop to fill up his tank before he got to the highway. From there, though, it was just him and the open road.

No point in stopping anywhere before Winslow. He highly doubted Addie would have paused in her flight so close to Flagstaff itself. In fact, Winslow was probably too close as well, but he would give it a try all the same. A couple of Wilcox cousins owned a diner downtown on Route 66, and although the beautiful La Posada Hotel was owned by people from out of state, one of the managers was a Wilcox as well and might have seen something.

A long shot, sure, because La Posada wasn't right off the freeway, and not the sort of place you'd generally drop into after midnight, but Jake knew better than to dismiss the possibility out of hand. Maybe Addie would have chosen to stay in such a place precisely because it wasn't the obvious choice for someone on the run.

Also, Amtrak's Southwest Chief stopped at La Posada, although Jake guessed that she wouldn't have abandoned her vehicle in order to take an alternative form of transportation. She'd be a lot more flexible driving a car. Then again, she'd also known that he and any other Wilcoxes looking for her would be keeping an eye out for a brand-new green Fiat 500X, so maybe the train would be a safer bet.

And so on. His thoughts danced around themselves as he drove east, even as he did his best to ignore the single glaring one that should have dominated all of them.

She'd left him. No note, no discussion, no nothing. Jake supposed he should have been angry, but he was more hurt than anything else. Had the moments they'd shared really meant nothing to her? Or was she simply so scared, so worried that she might bring disaster to the Wilcox clan, she just wasn't thinking straight?

He wanted to believe it was the latter possibility. Although she hadn't talked much about her past, he thought he could read between the lines and decipher just as much from what hadn't been said as what had. With the way she and her mother had moved around so much, he had a feeling Addie hadn't formed a lot of attachments.

Maybe a casual boyfriend here and there—she'd told him theirs wasn't her first kiss, and he'd believed her—but probably nothing that had felt as though it would last. How could it, when she knew she might have to pull up stakes and leave at any time?

And when she'd finally allowed her heart to open up a little and accept the possibility of an attraction and most likely much more, the universe had clapped back at her by delivering Randall Lenz on her doorstep. No wonder she'd bolted like a frightened horse.

When he found her—and Jake mentally repeated that "when" to himself, not even allowing the word "if" to enter his mind—he'd have to do his damnedest to reassure her that she wasn't alone any longer, that not only did she have him at her back, but the entire Wilcox clan as well. There was no need for her to be scared, because they'd find some way to figure this out.

Of course, the first thing he had to do was track her down.

He reached Winslow and pulled off the interstate at the first exit. Near the off-ramp was a 76 gas station and convenience store, and so he maneuvered his truck onto the lot and parked in one of the spaces near the entrance to the store. The man working behind the counter appeared to be Native American, old and weathered, iron-gray hair pulled back into a ponytail. His impassive expression didn't change as Jake approached the counter.

"Hey," Jake said. "Were you working here last night?" Probably not, since it was now past one in the afternoon and anyone who'd worked the overnight shift would be long gone, but he figured he needed to start somewhere.

However, the man surprised him by saying, "Yep," although he stopped there and didn't appear eager to volunteer any more information.

Still, that one syllable was more than Jake had been expecting. "Do you remember seeing a girl come in here, long brown hair, driving a green Fiat with paper plates?"

The man stared back at him, expression still stony. "You a cop?"

"No," Jake replied. "I'm a friend of hers."

"Hmph."

That single syllable could have had a host of meanings, none of them positive, but he knew he needed to keep going. "Look, she's a friend, and she's in trouble. You don't have to give me any details, but can you at least tell me if you saw her?"

"Nope."

"No, you didn't see her, or no, you're not going to tell me?"

The attendant's dark eyes narrowed for a fraction of a second, but otherwise, his features might as well have been carved from stone. "Didn't see her."

"You're sure?"

"Yeah."

For a moment, Jake hesitated, wondering whether he should attempt to pry more information out of the guy, like the exact hours he'd worked the night before. However, he could tell that any further overtures would probably get summarily shut down, and so he decided to quit while he was ahead.

"Thanks," he said, mentally adding, *For nothing*. Then he headed back out to the Gladiator, scowling the whole time.

And although the attendants at the other gas stations he visited were a lot friendlier than the first guy, no one had seen anyone who looked like Addie Grant, or had spotted a car that matched the Fiat's description. Which wasn't so strange, since Jake had already told himself she probably hadn't been anywhere close to running out of gas when she passed through Winslow.

His cousin wasn't working at La Posada that day, so he came up empty there. Muttering an inner curse, he got in his truck and guided it back to I-40, this time with Holbrook as his destination.

He really didn't want to go to Holbrook.

Sarah's family lived in Holbrook.

It was an irrational aversion, he knew. Holbrook was still Wilcox territory, and there was no reason for anyone to question his presence in that particular small town...except that he'd never been back after Sarah's funeral. She was buried in the cemetery there, along with past generations of the Holbrook branch of the Wilcox clan, and he'd never been able to bring himself to visit the place. Maybe some people found solace in seeing the graves of lost loved ones, but Jake knew he wasn't one of them. Standing there and looking at the headstone, reading the dates that so starkly spelled out the reality of a life cut short, would have only driven home to him the enormity of his loss. He didn't think he had the strength to do such a thing.

And he also couldn't help thinking that if he had the singular bad luck to run into Sarah's parents during this particular errand—or her younger sister or older brother—they might not be overly sympathetic to learn his only reason for being in town was to track down the woman who'd currently stolen his heart. True, three years had passed since Sarah's death, but maybe her family wouldn't consider that a long enough expanse of time to recover from losing the love of his life.

Especially since….

No, he didn't want to entertain that thought. But once he'd allowed it into his mind, he realized he couldn't ignore the traitorous notion, as much as he might want to.

He'd always thought of Sarah as his soul mate, his one true match. When he lost her, he thought he'd lost everything.

The last few days had taught him differently. He'd responded to Addie in a way he hadn't thought possible. She meshed so well with him that he'd begun to ponder a truth which would have been unthinkable even a week earlier.

Maybe Addie, not Sarah, was truly his soul mate. Not a pale second best, not the proverbial "second chance," but the person his heart had always yearned for. He'd already told her that he'd begun to realize it was possible to have more than one soul mate, and yet the possibilities running through his mind now told him something else. His love for Sarah had been deep and true, and he knew if she'd lived and they'd built a life together, they would have been happy, but…

…but she'd never set his soul on fire the way Addie did.

That realization woke a deep shame in him, even though he knew it was impossible for him to have guessed that there might be something more to love than what he'd shared with Sarah. He shouldn't be comparing the two women, not when they were so utterly different. Sarah had been quiet and steady, the sort of person you could depend on to lend a helping hand without question, which was why she'd wanted to get her master's in education and teach junior high. Addie was fiery and spirited, forthright, elemental. There was very little the two women had in common, which was why he knew they'd appealed to different parts of him.

And now...now, his heart recognized what his brain still didn't quite want to accept.

All the more reason why he really didn't want to go to Holbrook. It wasn't a big town, only had a population of around five thousand people or so, but still, the chances of running into anyone he knew were pretty damn small. The Wilcoxes who lived there were ranchers, or worked for the big APS power plant over in Joseph City. They didn't work at the gas stations or the motels. But....

But nothing, he told himself. *You're going to get your ass in there and ask the necessary questions, or you might as well have stayed back in Flagstaff and watched Jeremy hack Lenz's computer. Stop being a coward.*

Addie didn't deserve a coward. She deserved someone who would do the work and make the hard choices, no matter what.

That inner admonishment seemed to settle things. He pulled off the highway and made the rounds, but, as he'd feared, no one had seen anything. After Holbrook there wasn't much, only a few wide spots in the road like Houck and Lupton, along with a couple of large travel centers that catered to truckers. It was looking more and more likely that Addie had pressed on toward New Mexico without stopping.

Then you won't stop, he told himself. *You'll keep going, just like she did.*

Which could be a problem. Clan etiquette dictated that he should reach out to Genoveva Castillo for permission to enter her territory. However, he wasn't sure he wanted to tip his hand in such a way, especially if Addie had managed to get intercepted by the Castillos. He didn't want her to get wind of his pursuit and slip away before he had a chance to speak with her.

That seemed to settle things. In his experience, he'd found it was generally easier to ask for forgiveness than permission....

The diner the kid at the motel had recommended was only a block away, but it still felt like a mile to Randall Lenz. Eventually, though, he managed to shuffle in and take a seat at the counter. The place felt oddly familiar, from the red, white, and chrome decor—an obvious nod to the restaurants of the 1950s that were the inspiration for the restaurant—to the brassy-haired woman who came over and asked if he'd like a cup of coffee.

"Back so soon?" she asked as she poured him some, then took a closer look at his face. "Looks like you've had a rough couple of days, if you don't mind me saying so."

He made himself focus on her name badge. Tammy. The name didn't mean anything to him, but again, something about her exaggeratedly golden-blonde hair and heavily penciled brows seemed familiar as well. "No, I don't mind," he said. "Has it really been a couple of days?"

Those brows drew together for a second or two as she appeared to consider his question. "Think so. You were last in…Saturday morning. And now it's Tuesday."

Well, there was the confirmation he needed. He really had been passed out in that motel room for the better part of two days. "I had a hell of a long weekend, Tammy," Lenz replied, and she gave him a sympathetic smile.

"Well, some coffee should perk you up." Her blue eyes twinkled as she added, "Perk you up…get it?"

He managed to smile back, although the effort hurt his cheek muscles and he wondered if the expression had looked more like a grimace. "I get it. Say, could I have an omelette and some hash browns?"

"Denver, like last time?"

"Yes, please."

She scribbled the order down on her notepad, then tore off the top sheet and wedged it into the little carousel doohickey that hung above the raised shelf which separated the serving counter from the kitchen. No computerized ordering system here, that much was obvious. Lenz glanced around, trying to see if anything in the diner jogged his memory. But while everything in his surroundings still seemed vaguely familiar, nothing stood out to him particularly. He couldn't remember eating a Denver omelette here, even if that was what Tammy said he'd ordered the last time he was in.

The coffee was good, though, strong and hot. He took a few sips and allowed himself to sit quietly on the stool and simply observe what was happening around him. Maybe a booth would have been more comfortable, but his balance seemed to be improving, and it would be easier to chat with Tammy sitting here than off at a booth across the way. Even though it was almost eleven o'clock and past the morning rush, the diner was still pretty crowded. Mostly tourists, from what he could tell; he spotted several families with kids, and a few older couples who most likely were driving the RVs he'd glimpsed in the parking lot.

All in all, it looked like a perfectly normal Tuesday morning. Nothing particularly jumped out at him, but he still made himself sit there and drink his coffee, watching as people came and went. When Tammy came by with his omelette a few minutes later, he asked, "You get a lot of tourists here?"

"Oh, yeah," she replied. Her gaze moved past

him, as if she wanted to make sure she wasn't neglecting anyone as she stood there and talked, but two of the tables she'd been waiting on were now empty, their occupants leaving to get on with their day. "People want comfort food when they're on the road. And we're on the way to Bryce Canyon and Zion, so we get more than most places." Something in her blue eyes seemed to sharpen as she regarded him for a few seconds. "You're not a tourist, though, are you?"

"Not exactly," he said. Ignoring the food she'd just set down in front of him, he reached in his pocket and drew out the muddy-looking printout of the two strangers who'd dumped him at the hotel down the street. "Do you recognize either of these two men?"

She stared at the paper for a few seconds before shaking her head. "No, I don't think so. I mean, we get a lot of people coming through here, but those two would kind of stand out."

Probably because they were both young and dark and good-looking, but Lenz wasn't going to comment on that. Their looks weren't what concerned him. "You're sure?"

"As sure as I can be. Like I said, we get a lot of tourists in here, so I don't pretend to have memorized everyone's faces, but I know they're not local."

Just what Byron at the motel had said as well,

but Tammy's input seemed to confirm that the two men were definitely not from Kanab.

"You sure you're okay, mister?" Tammy asked then, her expression one of concern.

No, Lenz thought, but of course, he wasn't going to give her such a self-pitying answer. "I'm fine," he said as he folded the piece of paper and stuffed it back in his pocket. "Just need some fuel in me." And he picked up his fork, figuring he'd better go ahead and eat the food she'd brought him before it got cold.

"Okay," she said, still looking slightly worried. "You just call if you need anything."

"I will."

He dug into his omelette, glad of the cash in his wallet, glad that at least he didn't have to worry about paying for his meal—or leaving Tammy a big tip. While she hadn't been able to provide much useful information, at least she'd shown some worry over his condition. It was kind of amazing what a little bit of old-fashioned human concern could do to improve a person's outlook.

Not that his view of the world was all the way improved. The mere fact that he'd been MIA for two days meant that no one at the agency truly had any idea where he was, or they would certainly have come and extracted him by now. Even though he'd already told himself that forcing the issue wouldn't help, he couldn't help digging through his brain, trying to see if he could somehow unearth a single helpful piece of data. The names of the people he worked with. A phone number.

Anything.

But those answers seemed determined to evade him. He ate all of his omelette and the hash browns that accompanied it, and drank his cup of coffee and a second one when Tammy came by to give him a refill. The food quieted the ache in his stomach, and he felt almost human again, thanks to a full belly and the caffeine from two cups of coffee coursing through his system, but that still didn't seem to be enough.

"'Bye, Roy!" Tammy called out then, addressing a thickset man in his late forties or early fifties who wore an Arizona Cardinals T-shirt and matching baseball cap. "Have a safe drive to Flagstaff!"

Flagstaff. In his mind, Lenz saw a series of tall mountain peaks, dark ponderosa pine forests...a street lined with perfectly restored Victorian and Craftsman houses. A flash of Adara Grant's face, smiling as she tilted it up toward the man Randall Lenz knew only as Jake.

He'd gone to Flagstaff. He still couldn't remember what had happened when he was there, except a dim recollection of blinding pain, but it was as if hearing the city's name was enough to unlock other memories—the drive to Las Vegas... the way he'd dropped two twenty-dollar bills into the jar that had sat on the counter here in the diner, collecting money for Lyssa Grant's funeral.

His assistant, Kelly Dawson, pale brown hair pulled into its habitual ponytail.

More importantly, the number for Dawson's extension.

He signaled to Tammy, and she came over, carafe of coffee in one hand.

"More coffee, mister?"

"No," he said, glad of how steady his voice sounded. "I need to use your phone."

6

THE DRIVE FROM SANTA FE TO THE WIND RIVER Reservation in central Wyoming was supposed to take a little more than eleven hours. I knew there was no way I could manage such a trip in a single day—well, if pressed, maybe I could, but I didn't want to take the risk of falling asleep behind the wheel like I almost had on my way into New Mexico. But Genoveva had that handled, too, telling me I could stop in a town called Walden that was still in Colorado but around the midway point of the drive, and then conclude my journey the following day.

"That's in Harper territory," she told me over the phone, after I'd had dinner and called her using the landline in my hotel room. "But I'll call in the morning and let them know you're coming through, and it should be fine. Just stick to the route I gave you."

Because she'd actually faxed to the hotel—who had a fax machine anymore?—a map and a set of detailed driving directions, along with the explanation that there were long stretches along the route that didn't have good cell service, and so it was better for me to have a hard copy of where I was going. That was a relief, just because I knew it would be safer to keep my phone in airplane mode, and even though the car had a state-of-the-art nav system, I was still learning how to use it. Thanks to Genoveva's thoughtfulness, I had a much better chance of getting where I needed to go.

"I will," I assured her, then asked, "And the Harpers won't mind me coming through?"

"Not with the proper warning," she replied. "They tend to keep to themselves anyway—and they're mostly concentrated in Denver, Boulder, and Fort Collins. Places like that. There probably aren't a lot of them along the route you'll be taking."

Well, that was something. It would be great if I could make it all the way to Wind River without any witches or warlocks taking note of my progress, except for maybe some Castillos while I was still in New Mexico. I thanked Genoveva for everything, and was maybe a little too effusive in my expressions of gratitude, because she didn't seem to want to hear it.

"It's nothing," she said, her tone almost curt. "Honestly, Eduardo has been chiding me all evening for not letting you stay here in Santa Fe. But of course, you understand why that's impossible."

"I understand," I replied. And I did. The last thing I wanted was to bring disaster down on the Castillos. I was already dealing with enough guilt, thanks to the way I'd drawn Randall Lenz into Wilcox territory.

So, there was no one to say goodbye as I unceremoniously hauled my new luggage out to the car, loaded it up, and then drove slowly out of the parking garage at the hotel. I'd eaten breakfast in my room, and was fortified by an enormous breakfast burrito and some spicy homestyle potatoes to go with it. Strangely, the spice in my morning meal made me think of the spice in the Indian takeout I'd shared with Jake at his house.

The taste of that spice on my lips as he kissed me.

Tears burned in my eyes, but I set my jaw and told myself I needed to focus on the road. I didn't have time to turn into a weepy mess, not with six-plus hours of driving on unfamiliar roads—and in an unfamiliar car, albeit one I was getting to know pretty quickly—ahead of me.

I'd bought bottled water in the gift shop and got a large coffee to go from the espresso stand in the lobby, so I figured I should be fine for a few hours.

Most likely, I'd need to stop to go to the bathroom before I needed gas or anything else to drink. I decided that Alamosa in southwest Colorado was a likely place for a pit stop, although I figured I'd play it by ear and decide as I went.

This was a part of the country I'd never explored before. Yes, I'd lived in both Colorado and New Mexico, but all those places had been way east of Highway 285 where it wound its way north through dry, high-desert terrain, brown and plain except for the scrubby dark forms of juniper trees and the occasional bit of farmland. When I finally crossed the border and entered Colorado, I began to see more fields, some of them oddly circular in appearance, as the landscape grew a little greener.

But I couldn't spend a lot of time staring at my surroundings, since I had to keep my eyes on the road and make sure I stuck to my route. In a way, I was glad of that necessity, because by focusing on the highway ahead of me—and making sure I didn't get squished by any of the over-aggressive truckers who were taking the same road—I didn't have as much time as I feared I might to obsess over Jake Wilcox.

Oh, I couldn't get him completely out of my head. That would have been asking the impossible. Even so, the farther I got from Santa Fe—and therefore, that much farther from Flagstaff—a strange calm began to settle over me. Maybe I'd gotten to the "acceptance" stage of grief. I didn't know, but I was glad that apparently I didn't have to worry about making the entire drive with tears running down my face.

It still hurt, though. I wanted to ask the universe why someone who'd only been in my life for a few days could make such a lasting impression on my soul, on my heart and mind and body, but since the universe had never been all that kind to me, I decided that asking it to explain itself was probably a waste of time. Yes, I was in love with Jake Wilcox. Yes, it had broken my heart to leave him behind. And yet….

Broken hearts could mend. I couldn't see my way clear to that day, not yet, but I figured it had to happen at some point. For the time being, best to focus on the here and now.

I stopped for gas in Alamosa, bought myself some more bottled water and a package of trail mix at the convenience store, and then got on the road again. The entire stop had taken me less than five minutes, and I felt rather pleased with myself for being so efficient. At the rate I was going, I'd make it to Walden by five o'clock. For a second or two, I wondered if it was silly to stop there, whether I'd be smarter to push on toward Wyoming. But then I realized that even with minimal stops and speeding ever so slightly, I still wouldn't make it to Wind River before eleven at the very earliest, and that didn't seem like a very good idea. Yes, I had a room waiting for me in the town of Riverton, thanks to Genoveva's efficient travel planning, but coming into a strange place after dark could be nerve-wracking. Better to wait.

The rest of the drive to Walden passed without incident, and I arrived at my destination to find that the "hotel" was actually a set of rooms above one of the local restaurants. However, everything was neat and clean, the space obviously recently renovated, so I had to send a mental "thank you" to Genoveva for finding the place for me.

The restaurant wasn't very busy when I came downstairs after getting settled in, but it was still early, barely five-thirty. Despite the hour, I wanted to eat, since I hadn't had anything for lunch except some trail mix, and at least the place appeared to be open for customers.

I looked around for a hostess, didn't see one, and went ahead and sat down at one of the smaller tables. Maybe the counter would have been better, just because that way, I wouldn't be taking a table away from a couple or a small group, but sitting at the counter opened up the possibility of having to be social, and I just didn't have the energy right then. No, I only wanted to get some food inside me and go upstairs, watch TV, and get some sleep.

A woman who reminded me a little too much of my mother—middle forties, pretty, with blonde hair and bright blue eyes—came over to introduce herself as Andrea and ask me if I wanted anything to drink. Even though it probably wasn't the smartest thing to do, I requested a glass of wine. Now that I'd safely reached my destination, I was starting to feel jangly again, as if my brain had just figured out that it didn't have to spend as much energy focusing on the road and so thought it was perfectly fine to start torturing me with thoughts of Jake.

"And a steak," I added, figuring I might as well eat hearty.

"Baked potato with everything on it?"

"Sure." I didn't know if it was a witchy thing, or whether both my mother and Jackson Wilcox had bequeathed fabulous metabolisms to me, but I never had to worry too much about what I ate. Maybe when I hit my fifties, everything would start to catch up with me, but for the time being, I felt safe consuming sour cream and bacon bits and a medium-rare steak.

Andrea smiled at me and said she'd be back with my drink in a moment, and I settled against the back of my chair and let out a breath. Not of relief, exactly, but more just knowing that I'd made it this far without incident. My mother and I had traveled all over the place, so I certainly was no stranger to long road trips, but this was the first time I'd ever driven so far completely on my own. In an odd way, it made me feel more like a real adult, someone who was capable of making her own decisions and managing her own life.

Not that any of this had really been my choice. No, I'd much rather still be in Flagstaff, sitting on the couch in Jake's cozy living room, maybe perusing takeout menus and deciding what we wanted to get for dinner that night.

Damn it. There were those stupid tears again, stinging my eyes. I picked up the paper napkin at my place setting and touched it to my face to erase the tears, then shoved it hastily down onto my lap when Andrea approached, glass of wine in one hand.

Even though I'd only overflowed a little and hadn't broken down into sobs or anything, she seemed to notice something was wrong because she said, "Everything okay, sweetheart?"

The casual endearment only made me want to cry that much harder. I'd seen my mother do the same thing with customers at the various restaurants where she'd worked, always ready to reach out and offer a bit of comfort, or just a sympathetic ear for those lonely souls who desperately needed someone to talk to. More than once, I'd found myself envying the way she could strike up a quick rapport with people, as if she had a magic of her own that allowed her to know exactly the right thing to say. I was never like that—or at least, I was never given the chance to be that way, just because as soon as my weather-working gift awoke and started causing me such grief, I'd had to be on guard at all times, always worried about what might set me off.

As Andrea set my glass of wine down in front of me, I managed to smile up at her. "Oh, sure," I said, trying to sound breezy and confident. "I've just been driving all day, and I guess I'm tired."

"Going far?"

My first instinct was to lie about my destination. But I didn't see how anyone could track me to Walden, and I desperately needed to talk to someone. "To the Wind River Reservation. I—I have a job waiting for me there."

A complete lie...or maybe not. After all, I did plan to look for a job once I got to Wyoming, even if I didn't yet know what or where it would be. And as much as I hated to admit it to myself, my hope of finishing my degree had pretty much disappeared. Maybe there was a community college near Riverton, but that wouldn't help me, since I'd been about to begin my senior year at the university and a two-year college wouldn't do me a bit of good.

Well, my mother had survived without a college degree, and I supposed I would, too. Life was all about readjusting expectations, after all.

Andrea nodded, not looking too surprised by my stated destination. "Oh, a job at the casino?"

"Yes," I replied, even though that was the first I'd heard of it. Although I'd brought my new

MacBook Air with me, I hadn't quite dared to pull it out of its case and use the wi-fi at the La Fonda to do some research on the place I meant to make my new home. Maybe it would have been perfectly safe, but I'd feared that Jake's uber-hacker brother might somehow have managed to locate me if I went on the internet. Stupid, probably, and yet I just couldn't make myself take the risk.

Anyway, a casino sounded like a good place to land a job, if one was available. People gambling and drinking tended to be big tippers. Or at least, that's what I'd heard, although I'd never worked at a place like that. My mother had—briefly—when we lived near Durango. But when flooding caused by torrential rains that I'd called had damaged several of the quaint downtown area's streets, we'd left in a hurry. It was too bad, because we were doing well there. Then again, that was where I'd been dating Tom McKenzie, who'd wanted things between us to get more serious. I didn't know whether I wanted to contemplate what might have happened if I'd stayed.

"Did you come far?" Andrea asked.

"Pretty far," I said. "From Albuquerque."

Another lie, but just a little one. As much as it felt better to hear a friendly voice, I wasn't stupid enough to tell Andrea I'd come from Flagstaff...or Kanab. That was being just a little too specific.

"Well, then, a hearty meal is just what you

need," she said. "Let me go check on your steak."

"Thanks," I told her, and she headed off toward the kitchen, leaving me alone to drink my wine.

I reached for it and took a large swallow, enjoying the friendly warmth in my stomach as it sank downward. Yes, that was better. A glass of wine to take the edge off—or maybe two, since all I had to do after I finished my meal was head upstairs and go to sleep, and it wouldn't matter if I got a little tipsy. I certainly wouldn't be driving or anything.

As I sipped again—a much more modest swallow this time—the door to the restaurant opened, and a couple of loud male voices echoed through the restaurant. Instinctively, I stared down at my glass, pretending to be engrossed by the dark garnet-colored liquid within. The last thing I wanted was for anyone to notice me sitting over at my little table off in one corner.

Unfortunately, the universe didn't appear to be listening to my needs, because a moment later, two guys around my age, maybe a little older, came walking up to the table. The one who appeared to be in the lead leered down at me and pushed his baseball cap a little farther back on his head.

"Well, what do we have here?" he inquired rhetorically, light blue eyes roving toward the modest cleavage my T-shirt revealed, while his friend, who was a few inches shorter and much darker, rocked back on his heels and grinned.

"She's not from around here, that's for sure," he said.

Since I knew from past experience that ignoring them wouldn't do me any good, I looked up from my glass of wine and said politely, "Can I help you with something?"

"Can you help me?" the first guy said, pale eyes crinkling at the corners. "Oh, honey, I think there are a lot of things you could help me with. Isn't that right, Cal?" he added, and jabbed his companion in the ribs with an elbow.

The other guy winced slightly, but his grin didn't fade. "Damn straight."

Where the hell was Andrea? I wasn't too worried about things getting out of hand, not with my newfound ability to keep my weather-working talents from spinning out of control, but even so, I only wanted to have a quiet drink, not be harassed by a couple of local yokels.

"Look, my food will be out in just a minute—"

"Great," said the first guy. "Then we'll join you."

He pulled out one of the empty chairs at my table and sat down, and his friend followed suit. About all I could do was hope Andrea would arrive soon and send them packing. I had a feeling this wasn't the first time they'd overstepped their bounds with a woman.

Thunder growled overhead, and I jumped. Cal, the shorter and darker of the two guys, sent me a condescending smile. "Scared of a little thunder, sweetie?"

"No," I said coolly as I lifted my glass of wine to my lips. "I just wasn't expecting it. The skies looked clear when I came into town."

"Things blow up quick around here," his friend put in, leaning over the table as if to get a closer look at my lips as I sipped from my wine.

It tasted sour in my mouth, but I swallowed it anyway. Those two had absolutely no idea how quickly things could "blow up" around me....

"Cal, Arnie—what the heck do you two think you're doing?"

Andrea, thank God, coming over to my table with a plate of steak in one hand and a basket of dinner rolls in the other. Her mouth was tight with annoyance, her blue eyes snapping fire. Clearly, she didn't have a very high opinion of the two interlopers.

"Why, just welcoming a pretty newcomer to our town," Arnie drawled as he leaned back in his chair.

"From the looks of her, she isn't too happy to be 'welcomed,'" Andrea retorted. "Did she invite you to sit down?"

"Well, no—"

Thunder cracked again, and she jumped slightly, the plate with my food dropping with unintended force onto the table's worn wooden surface. "That was close!"

Yes, it was. I reached out with my gift toward the storm that had decided to descend on the town, and realized I hadn't called it. We might not have gotten to the official start of monsoon season yet, but apparently no one had told the weather currents in that part of the world. It was a volatile storm, though, crackling with the energy of late afternoon and powered by an odd eddy of warm air that had drifted through the valley where Walden was located.

"All the more reason we should keep this young lady company," Arnie said, an unpleasant smile pulling at his mouth. Even on his best day, he probably wasn't a good-looking guy, with those pale brows and a nose that appeared to have been broken more than once, but right then, I thought he was just about the ugliest man I'd ever seen. "You know, so she won't be scared by the storm."

Oh, boy, are you barking up the wrong tree. "Storms don't scare me," I told him.

"See?" Andrea said. "She's not scared. Now, let her eat her meal in peace. Go on, or I'll tell your dad you were in here harassing the girls again."

Again. It seemed my hunch that this was typical behavior for Arnie and Cal had turned out to be correct.

"Like he cares," Arnie scoffed. "You're just angry because he tried to cozy up to you last Friday."

Andrea planted her hands on her hips. She

wasn't wearing a wedding ring, so either she wasn't married, or she preferred to leave it off while she worked. "And, just like my guest here, I wasn't interested. Now, go on, you two. Don't make me call the sheriff."

A scowl furrowed Arnie's nearly nonexistent brows. "You wouldn't do that."

"Try me."

Cal pushed his chair back from the table. The grin he'd been wearing had faded, and he now looked almost worried. "Maybe we should go—"

"I'm not going anywhere," Arnie cut in. During the entire exchange, his gaze had never left me, and a little shiver of worry descended my spine. Andrea was doing her best, but I knew there was no way she could physically force the bastard to leave the restaurant, not when he was at least five inches taller and probably seventy to eighty pounds heavier than she was.

"It's okay," I said, and stood up. "I can take my food up to my room, and you can put it on my tab."

Obviously, Arnie wasn't impressed by my solution, because he reached over and snagged my plate, pulling it over toward him. "No, you can sit right here and eat with us."

Anger flared in me, and thunder crackled. Maybe I hadn't called the storm, but it was still responding to me, was still receptive to my magic. I knew I needed to tamp it down, to do what I could to send it away…

…but I really didn't want to. No, what I wanted to do was show this punk ass who he was dealing with.

"I don't think so," I said calmly. Once again, lightning glared, followed by thunder so quickly that I knew the storm was almost directly overhead.

Andrea's face was white now, her expression strained. "It's okay," she told me. "I can have them make you another steak and have it sent up to your room."

"No need for that," I said, voice still cool and flat.

"Maybe you'd better—" Cal put in. Judging by the worry on his face, almost an echo of Andrea's expression, he clearly thought the game had gone far enough.

"Shut the fuck up, Cal," Arnie growled.

That seemed to settle things. Now that I was standing, I could see the entire length of the restaurant, could look through the window that faced out on Main Street and see a large white pickup truck parked in front of the place. I knew it hadn't been there when I pulled up, which meant it most likely belonged to Arnie or Cal. Probably Arnie; I had a feeling he wasn't the type of guy to let his friend chauffeur him around. No, he'd want to feel in charge at all times.

Well, his truck was about to feel a hell of a charge.

It took hardly any thought at all, just the slightest of mental nudges directed toward the storm cloud that sat directly above the restaurant. Another flash of brilliant light, followed by the tinkling of glass. I blinked, and opened my eyes to see that the white pickup in question had been hit directly, its windshield and the glass from all its windows shattered and lying in pieces across the hood—and, probably, the sidewalk next to it, although I couldn't tell for sure from where I stood.

"My truck!" Arnie groaned, all thought of baiting me apparently abandoned now that he had something far more important to focus on.

"Oh, my," Andrea said, eyes widening in feigned concern as she looked out the window at the wreckage. "Some people might call that an act of God."

He shot her a glare of pure venom but didn't bother to retort, only hurried out the door, Cal tagging along a pace or so behind. The second they went out the front door, they were drenched, since the rain had only intensified following the destructive bolt that hit the truck.

"Definitely a useful coincidence," I said, then sat back down and pulled my plate in front of me. "Do those two act like this all the time?"

She glanced out the window again. The two men were circling the truck, apparently taking stock of the damage. Arnie now had a cell phone pressed to his ear and was speaking to someone—a tow truck driver, I assumed, or maybe Triple-A. Did they have Triple-A in Colorado? I couldn't remember, since my mother had never been able to afford it.

"More than I'd like to admit," Andrea replied. "On his own, Cal isn't so bad, but he and Arnie get bored and egg each other on. I'm sorry I took so long in the kitchen—they probably wouldn't have even sat down at your table if I'd been out here."

No way would I let her feel guilty for their bad behavior. "It's not your fault," I told her. "But at least it looks as though the universe gave them the clap-back they desperately needed."

An unwilling smile tugged at her lips. "Yes, it does look that way." She paused, and tilted her head as she looked down at me. "Another glass of wine?"

Why not? I should probably celebrate this clear evidence that I had my powers firmly under control, even in a stressful situation. I wanted to think that Joanna Wilcox would be proud, even if she hadn't been there to see my handiwork. Somehow, I guessed she also wouldn't have had much patience for Arnie and Cal's bullshit.

I looked up at Andrea and nodded in answer to her question.

"Absolutely," I said.

7

Just outside the defunct Fort Defiance compound, about forty minutes from the New Mexico border, Jake's cell phone rang. He'd left it propped up in one of the cupholders, so he lifted it out and took a quick look at the screen.

Jeremy's number.

"What's up?" Jake asked.

"I got in."

"What?"

"The laptop. Lenz's laptop. I'm in."

"That's great!" Jake told him, which of course, it was. Not that he'd had any doubts about his brother eventually finessing his way into the agent's computer; he just hadn't expected that particular feat to happen so quickly. Jeremy was insanely talented, true, but even he'd admitted that the security on Lenz's laptop was pretty hardcore. "Thanks for the update."

"I didn't call to give you an 'update,'" Jeremy replied, sounding irritated. "I called because I need you to come back to Flagstaff. Now."

What the hell? "Jeremy, I'm almost to the border. It's going to take me the better part of two hours to get back there."

"I don't care. It was stupid of you to think you could just waltz into Castillo territory without permission. Anyway, what I found is more important than this wild goose chase of yours."

Privately, Jake couldn't think of anything that was more important than tracking down Addie, but since his brother obviously didn't share that particular sentiment, he didn't bother to protest Jeremy's choice of words. "What'd you find?"

"I'd rather not tell you that over the phone."

"What, you think someone's listening?"

"Maybe." A pause, and then Jeremy added, "I didn't spend all this time getting into the laptop to have you broadcast everything we're saying on an open line. Just get your ass home. Addie's already got probably an eight-hour lead on you, if not more, so it's not as if you had a chance in hell of catching up with her anyway."

Those words were true enough that Jake didn't bother to dispute them. In the back of his mind, he'd been hoping that, even though there was no way he could overtake her in a direct pursuit, she might have stopped somewhere to hunker down and plan her next step, and he'd be able to catch up to her that way. If he stopped now...if he turned around as Jeremy was requesting...then even that faint hope would be gone.

"It's really that important?" Jake asked.

"Yeah, it's really that important. Come home."

The call ended there, and Jake muttered a curse under his breath. True, with a couple of hundred miles separating them, there wasn't much Jeremy could do to prevent him from continuing into New Mexico, but, on the other hand, he'd sounded pretty damn urgent. Just what the hell had he discovered on Randall Lenz's laptop?

Only one way to find out, and Jake gritted his teeth, wishing he had the magical ability to split himself in two so he could send one version back to Flagstaff and the other into New Mexico. However, he'd never heard of any witch or warlock possessing that particular talent, and he knew he sure as hell didn't have it. Too bad, because it seemed eminently more useful than the ability to move solid objects around with his mind.

An exit was coming up. If he didn't get off the highway here, he'd have to travel another three or four miles before another opportunity presented itself.

Fuck it.

He pulled off at the exit in question, crossed under I-40, and got on the access road that took him back to the westbound side. The whole time, he was cursing his brother, cursing himself…and definitely cursing Randall Lenz, who was the real guilty party in this particular scenario. If he'd just admitted defeat and gone back to Alexandria—or wherever the agency he worked for was located— then none of this bullshit would even have been necessary.

Speeding now, going up to ninety or even ninety-five in spots, eyes continually checking the rearview mirror because magical talents weren't a guarantee that he could escape the watchful eye of any Arizona state troopers or local sheriffs patrolling this stretch of the interstate. The whole way, Jake kept wondering if he'd just monumentally screwed up, whether he'd abandoned his last chance of finding Addie by acceding to his brother's wishes. All right, he didn't even know whether she was in New Mexico at all, but at least by heading in that direction, he'd felt as though he was accomplishing something.

Returning to Flagstaff seemed like defeat.

He'd already decided on this course of action, though, and so there wasn't much he could do except see it through to the end. By the time he exited the highway and pointed his truck toward Wheeler Park and Trident Enterprises HQ, he was in a thoroughly foul mood. He entered the renovated house, stalked past the Macs in the main room, and found his brother and his cousin Laurel in the PC center, both of them hunched over Randall Lenz's confiscated laptop.

"All right," Jake growled, not bothering with a greeting. "What's so goddamn important that I had to come all the way back here to see it?"

Laurel startled a bit at his approach, but Jeremy merely shrugged. "Addie's not the only one. Look."

He swiveled the computer so Jake could see the screen more clearly. On it were multiple windows, each of them appearing to be a dossier of some sort, complete with photos and lists of vital statistics, accompanied by paragraphs of text that were too dense for him to make out from where he stood several feet away. "What am I looking at?" he asked.

"They're witches and warlocks, Jake," Laurel said, her tone almost hushed, as if she was too horrified by what she'd seen to speak any more loudly than that. "All of them. People that Lenz's agency has captured."

In the back of his mind, Jake had entertained such a possibility, but it was one thing to think of such a concept in the abstract and quite another to be confronted by the reality of so many individuals somehow caught in Randall Lenz's web. Their faces stared up at him from the laptop's screen, eyes almost accusing, as if they wanted to know how he could have let such a thing happen to them.

Because he hadn't known. None of them had known. How could they? These people were like Addie, unaffiliated with any witch clan, completely unaware that they were anything more than genetic freaks with strange and unwanted powers.

Or at least, he assumed those powers were unwanted. Addie sure as hell hadn't wanted hers.

He managed to find his voice. "How many?"

"Fourteen altogether," Jeremy replied. "Addie would've made fifteen."

"Any Wilcoxes?"

An eloquent lift of his brother's shoulders. "I have no idea. One or two look like they could be… maybe…but it's impossible to know for sure, just from looking at some photos. We'll have to inter-view each of them, find out where they're from, what their stories are."

"Plus, there's just the teeny little detail of them all being held in a government facility in Virginia," Laurel put in, her expression worried and more than a little scared. Jake couldn't really blame her; they'd expected to encounter challenges when setting up Trident and carrying out its stated mission, but none of them had thought they'd run afoul of the federal government on their very first try.

Since all the photos in the file looked like they'd been lifted from driver's licenses or some other form of state-issued I.D. and were probably at least a year old, if not more, Jake had no idea how their captivity might have affected Lenz's prisoners. He cleared his throat. "How long have they been held there?"

Jeremy toggled back and forth between a few files, although he didn't seem to be looking that closely at the screen, as though he'd already memorized those particular bits of information. "Depends on the person. The most recent 'acquisition'—although I know that's a horrible way to phrase it—was brought in about five months ago. This guy"—he maximized one window to fill the entire screen, showing a thin-faced man in his early thirties—"has been there for almost three years."

"'Three years'?" Jake repeated, aghast. "Three years without being charged with anything? What happened to due process?"

To his surprise, it was Laurel who answered him. "It's not a prison, Jake. It's a research facility. Basically, these people have just...disappeared. When Jeremy started cross-checking their identities, every single one of them is officially dead."

Just like Addie herself. The fire Randall Lenz had set in her house in Kanab had served the purpose of covering up her mother's murder, but it also had the important secondary function of making the world believe Addie had perished along with her mother.

And if everyone thought you were dead, then no one was going to be asking questions about why you'd disappeared.

He didn't know why he should be so surprised. After all, the world had taught him some fairly harsh lessons over the past three years. Still, he supposed he must have been pretty naïve to think the government had the best interests of its citizens at heart. His own family history had taught him how ruthless men could be when in pursuit of a goal they thought would benefit them.

Jeremy and Laurel were both watching him, clearly expecting him to give some guidance on what to do next. Problem was, he had no idea. They'd definitely stepped into a hornet's nest with this one. The moral thing to do would be to figure out some way to rescue the poor souls that Randall Lenz had been keeping as his personal guinea pigs, but how in the hell were they supposed to manage that particular feat? They might be a bunch of witches and warlocks with their own unique talents and gifts, but they weren't exactly an army.

Well, he'd let Connor and Angela know about what Jeremy had found, and see if they had any ideas. They were the leaders of the two local clans, and ultimately, it would be their decision as to whether a rescue mission was the right way to go. Some might have said it was a moral imperative to rescue fellow witches and warlocks from such horrible captivity, but even greater than the kinship all witch-kind shared was the need to keep the truth of their existence hidden from the world. If attempting to rescue Agent Lenz's captives resulted in exposure for the rest of the witch world, it didn't take a rocket scientist to figure out what Connor and Angela's answer would probably be.

"We'll circle back to that later," he said, trying to ignore the disappointment in his cousin Laurel's clear amber eyes, the slight frown that pulled at Jeremy's brows. "None of this digging around is going to give away our position, is it?"

His brother's lip curled. "What do you think I am, an amateur?" A lift of his shoulders as he added, "I also had to neutralize the geotracking on Lenz's phone so it wouldn't broadcast its current position, but that was easy enough, a lot easier than dealing with the encryption on the laptop. Anyway, of course they don't know I'm in their system, poking around."

"Wait—you're *in* their system?" Jake asked. Alarm flared within him, and he did his best to ignore the panicky feeling that grew somewhere in the pit of his stomach. "This wasn't all on the laptop's hard drive?"

"Lenz didn't have much on his hard drive. Some notes…Addie's case file. But once I was on his laptop, I was able to use it to drill into the agency's servers." Jeremy didn't even look particularly pleased with himself for accomplishing such a feat, as though penetrating the data banks of a secret government organization was all in a day's work for him. "By the way, our friends function under the umbrella of the Science and Technology Directorate in the Department of Homeland Security, and go by the name of Special Enforcement Division. Nice and vague, isn't it?"

Jake nodded. A name like that could cover just about anything…which he was sure was exactly what its creators had intended.

"The project itself is called Daedalus, and has a staff of forty people. Lenz runs Daedalus and reports directly to the Under-Secretary of Homeland Security." Jeremy minimized the window that had contained the image of the man who'd been held for three years, and brought up another, this one a document containing what looked like various vehicle bills of sale and their accompanying documentation, including driver's license photos.

And there was Jake's own face, staring back at him.

"Son of a bitch," he breathed.

"Pretty much, yeah," Jeremy said. "That was how Lenz knew who you were—I hacked your files to give you a fake address in California, but once Addie opened her bank accounts here in Flagstaff, he obviously put two and two together and figured out this was where he should have gone in the first place."

Jake ran a hand through his hair. Probably, he shouldn't have been too surprised that Lenz had all this information on him, but he still hated the thought of being tracked so easily. "Great, so they know exactly who I am and where to find me. Now what?"

"Piece of cake." Jeremy entered a few commands, and the file disappeared.

That didn't seem terribly impressive. "So, you closed the window. Big deal."

Not even a blink, although one corner of Jeremy's mouth lifted slightly. "No, I introduced an untraceable worm that'll go through their entire system and erase everything associated with Addie's file, including all those vehicle records and the notes that Lenz's assistant, Kelly Dawson, has been keeping on the entire incident. Unfortunately, I don't have Connor and Angela's brain-scrubbing abilities, so I can't make her forget the whole thing existed."

"Then they'll just find Jake all over again, won't they?" Laurel asked, anxiety clear in her tone.

Jeremy cracked his knuckles, and Jake tried not to wince. He hated it when his brother did that.

"O ye of little faith," Jeremy said. "For now, 'Jake Wilcox' has been purged from the motor vehicle division database, and anyone searching for the deed to your house will find that it's now in the name of a false identity I created for you."

"You took my house away from me?" Jake asked, not sure whether he should be impressed or appalled. "And what if I get pulled over?"

Jeremy didn't look at all concerned by the sharp edge in his brother's voice. "No, I didn't take your house away from you. You still have the deed, don't you?"

"Well…yeah."

"Then you can prove it's yours, push come to shove. And, like I said, I set up a fake identity for you in the MVD database—you just need to get Jasper to make you an I.D. to match it."

From the sound of things, Jeremy had all the bases covered. Jake knew his cousin Jasper could make an impeccable forgery, one that, backed by what looked like a valid entry in the state of Arizona's files, wouldn't send up any red flags.

"Besides," his brother went on, apparently undeterred by Jake's lack of response, "all this is temporary. Once we know we have Randall Lenz and his goon squad off the scent permanently, then I'll put everything back to normal."

Which of course Jeremy would, with the same sort of ease most people usually reserved for making a shopping list. "So, who am I now?"

"Tyler Andrew Greene," Jeremy replied. "Twenty-eight, hometown Gilbert, Arizona."

"Why Gilbert?"

"Why not?"

Since that was basically inarguable logic, Jake shrugged. "Okay. I'll go see Jasper after this and get set up."

"Good," Jeremy said. "Because you'll want some valid I.D. when you hit the road again."

For a second, Jake just stared at him, wondering what his brother was playing at now. Sometimes, Jeremy's thought processes could be downright impenetrable. "'Hit the road'?" he repeated.

"Oh. I found this."

He set down Randall Lenz's laptop and got up from his chair, Jake and Laurel following him, and moved into the main room where the Mac Pros were located. The one Jeremy paused in front of currently had a screensaver of panoramic northern Arizona landscapes filling the screen, but he touched the mouse and it woke up, showing an image that was clearly Addie, standing next to a coffee bar in the lobby of what appeared to be a fancy hotel, handsome and very Southwest in style.

"Where was this?" Jake demanded.

"The La Fonda Hotel in Santa Fe," Jeremy replied. "This morning. I didn't *see* it this morning," he added quickly, probably because Jake had just sent an epic scowl in his direction, and even Laurel was frowning a little. "I found it this afternoon while you were driving back. But I figured I'd wait to tell you until you got here, since you were on your way to Flagstaff anyway."

This explanation didn't do much to mollify him. "So, she was in Santa Fe. And if I'd kept driving—"

"You still would have missed her," Jeremy cut in. "Because this is what I saw next. And don't worry— this is all downloaded to a local drive. I already purged anything that showed her driving around Santa Fe or the highways near there. She's not track-able at this point."

He touched the mouse, and the still-frame image in the screen switched over to what looked like a security camera capture from inside a parking garage. Jake watched Addie hand over a ticket to the attendant and then pull out, disappearing into a glare of sunlight outside. The time stamp on the image was 10:40 a.m.

Instead of commenting on the image, Jake only said, "Were you able to track where she went?"

"Up to a point. She was headed north on Highway 285. But a couple of cameras outside Ojo Caliente were down, so I didn't see her come through. She could have turned off before then and headed toward Taos."

"Any sign of her on that route?"

Jeremy shook his head. "Nope. Best guess is that she continued north on 285, but I haven't been able to find her so far. There's lots of places where she could have turned off, including I-70 if she wanted to go east into Denver."

Denver would have been a good place to lose herself...except the Harper family had controlled that part of the country for the past hundred and fifty years. Would they be all right with a strange witch turning up in their midst? Probably not, unless Genoveva Castillo had smoothed the way for Addie. The Castillo *prima* must have offered some assistance, because Jake doubted that Addie would have spent the previous night holed up in an expensive downtown hotel without Genoveva's help. If that was the case, then he supposed she might have called ahead and asked if they would take in the fugitive Wilcox witch.

That scenario didn't make a lot of sense, though. Addie's whole reason for fleeing in the first place had been to draw any unwanted attention away from her newfound family. She certainly wasn't callous enough to move in with a new witch clan and, by doing so, open them up to interference by Randall Lenz and his team.

No, she had to have been headed somewhere else.

"What's north along the route she's taking?" Jake asked.

It was Laurel who answered him. "Not a lot, really," she replied. "If you keep heading north, you get into Wyoming. First big town is Casper."

Where Addie had lived, if only for a short period. She'd made the comment in passing, as if Casper hadn't made much of an impression on her, but would she still have been tempted to go someplace familiar?

That didn't make much sense, either. She wouldn't take the risk of returning to a town where she had any kind of history. And anyway, that was wrong. He realized then that she'd said she lived in Cheyenne, not Casper. Jake didn't even know how far apart the two cities were; he'd never paid that much attention to geography in school, since being a warlock meant you generally had to stay put in your clan's territory.

Jeremy was frowning, rubbing his chin as he stared at the screen, even though there obviously wasn't anything revelatory about that final image of Addie's car pulling out of the hotel parking garage. "Wyoming," he said, his tone musing. "No witch clans in Wyoming."

"There aren't?" Laurel asked, expression a bit startled. "Why not?"

"Don't know," he replied. He leaned back in his office chair, hands clasped behind his head. "I just remember that because a while back I got on sort of a kick and went through Marie's databases and memorized all the different witch clans across the United States. There was a big gaping hole in Wyoming, and another in Utah."

That was news to Jake as well. Just as with geography, he'd never bothered much with learning about the clans outside Arizona, California, Nevada, and New Mexico, mostly because he knew that his odds of traveling where he would run across any of them were slim to none. Absently ruffling the hair at the back of his head, he asked, "You think Genoveva told Addie to head that way?"

"It makes sense," Jeremy said. "If there aren't any witch clans in that part of the world, then there isn't anyone Randall Lenz would be interested in. It would make a good place to hide."

Probably. Lots of empty country out there, not a lot of big cities or neighbors who'd want to pry into your business. Still, he needed to know for sure.

"Thanks," he said. "I think I need to go talk to Connor."

"Why?" Laurel asked, although Jeremy gave a faint nod, as if he'd guessed why his brother would want to visit their *primus.*

"Because," Jake said as he fished the key fob for his truck out of his pocket, "I think Genoveva Castillo would blow a gasket if I called her directly."

~

Thank God Connor and Angela were already safely ensconced in their Flagstaff home for the summer; Jake was pretty sure he didn't have the necessary stores of patience to drive all the way down to Jerome at the moment, especially not after that abortive trip east earlier in the day. But their house was only fifteen minutes away, and although he had to spend a little time explaining to the twins why he didn't have Taffy with him this time—"but I want to see your dog again!" Emily begged in plaintive tones, big green eyes earnest and pleading—not too much time elapsed before he and Connor were sitting in the living room, with a sympathetic Angela coaxing Ian and Emily and Miranda outside to play in the wide, pine-shadowed backyard so the two men could talk in peace.

"We had a sighting in Santa Fe this morning, so I'm pretty sure Genoveva Castillo must be helping Addie," Jake said after he and Connor had sat down in the living room, a place that looked relatively untouched by the kids, although numerous photos of them adorned the mantel and several accent tables placed around the room. "I was hoping you could call her and see if she knows where Addie is heading."

Connor, who'd brought a couple of glasses of iced tea with him, paused with the tumbler halfway to his lips. The glance he sent Jake was half incredulous, half almost pitying. "If Genoveva really is helping her, do you think she's going to admit to that, let alone reveal where Addie's going? She's going to tell us to butt out, Jake."

"Butt out of our own clan's business?" he responded calmly, since he'd already done his best to anticipate the sort of protests Connor might make and come up with reasoned counter-arguments. "One of our own going AWOL affects all of us."

"Some more than others," Connor observed, then set down his glass of iced tea. "I'm not saying I'm not sympathetic, but I really think this is out of our hands."

Although he'd been glad many times over the past several years that Connor and not his late brother Damon was in charge of the Wilcox clan, right then Jake found himself wishing that the current *primus* wasn't quite so *laissez-faire*. Lord knows that Damon Wilcox wouldn't have sat idly by and allowed one of his clan's witches to take off for parts unknown…especially if the witch in question happened to be his half-sister.

"She belongs with us," Jake said, doing his best to sound earnest but not desperate. "We can protect her. What if Randall Lenz finds her before we do?"

Connor's shoulders tensed, but his tone was level enough as he replied, "You made it sound on the phone as if he wouldn't be able to find her. You said Jeremy had purged all the videos that showed her leaving Santa Fe."

True, he had explained all that to Connor when he'd called and requested this interview, but Jake still wasn't sure whether Addie was safe. "He purged what he could," he told the *primus*. "But if they're looking for her hard enough, she's going to turn up eventually. Do you want that to happen when she's a thousand miles away from anyone who could help her? There aren't any witch clans in Wyoming. She'll be entirely on her own."

A long silence. Connor picked up his iced tea and tapped his fingers against the side of the tumbler, appearing to consider Jake's words. His gaze moved to the windows; outside, the sound of the kids playing with Angela in the yard was just barely audible, cheerful noises that—rather than reassure Jake that life went on no matter what—made him realize how thin was the thread happiness hung from, that everything could change in an instant. He didn't want one of those instants to happen to Addie when he was too far away to do anything to help her.

He'd already gone through that once and didn't want to experience that sensation of helplessness ever again.

"Okay," Connor said, with a breath that wasn't quite heavy enough to be a sigh. "I'll call her, but I can't promise that she'll help you. Genoveva does things her own way."

"That's okay," Jake replied, relief coursing through him. "At least we'll have tried."

The *primus* didn't look entirely convinced that the attempt would be worth the effort, but he didn't say anything, only dug his phone out of his jeans pocket and scanned through the contacts list. He touched his finger to the screen and held the phone up to his ear. A pause as it rang, and then he said, "Genoveva? It's Connor Wilcox. I—" He stopped there, as if interrupted before he could get any further. "No, but—look, I've got my cousin Jake here with me. Mind if I put you on speaker? Thanks."

Connor pulled the phone away from his ear and set it down on the coffee table. A woman's voice emerged from the tiny speaker, sounding somewhat irritated. "Can you hear me?"

"Yes," Jake said. "Thanks so much for speaking with me, Mrs. Castillo."

"Genoveva," she corrected him. "I'm not going to have someone almost my own age calling me 'Missus.' I assume you're calling because you've discovered that your fugitive came through Santa Fe."

"Yes," he replied, almost tacking on *ma'am* and realizing that wouldn't have gone over very well. The Castillo *prima's* voice was so crisp and businesslike, he had to remind himself that they were nearly contemporaries. "I was really hoping you could tell us where Addie was going."

A pause. Then Genoveva said, tone almost amused, "Do you think she would be very happy if I told you that?"

"Probably not," he responded. There was no point in lying; he figured the best way to handle this was to be brutally honest and hope she'd respect him for that much, if nothing else. "But I don't think she understands what she's risking by trying to go it alone."

"I would say she understands more than you give her credit for. After all, she survived just fine on her own for more than twenty years."

"She wasn't alone—she had her mother watching out for her."

Another of those brief silences. Then Genoveva said, "True, but her mother was not a witch. She did not offer the same protections that one of us might."

There wasn't any way to really argue with that comment, because the Castillo *prima* was right. Over on the couch, Connor raised an eyebrow, as if also acknowledging that she'd scored a point.

However, Jake wasn't about to give up that easily. "Maybe so, but before a few days ago, Addie didn't have a rogue government agency chasing after her, either. The stakes are a lot higher now."

"She seemed to get away just fine," Genoveva said. "She told me how she called down the lightning to strike the agent who was threatening her. I have no doubt she will be able to do it again if necessary. Her talent sounds quite formidable."

True, but Jake chose not to voice his agreement on that particular point. "And they're going to know that about her, and be prepared. She's not going to catch them off guard again."

Once more, the *prima* didn't respond right away. When she spoke, her tone was calm, measured…but also unyielding. "I'm sorry, Jake. I really am. But Addie and I spoke in confidence, and I would be betraying her trust to tell you where she's gone. I can say that she'll be safe there. She'll be in a place with its own protections, even if they aren't the same protections that the Wilcox clan could offer her."

Damn it. Jake looked over at Connor, but the *primus* only gave a very small shrug and looked heavenward, as if to say, *What do you expect me to do?*

Not much, apparently. That wasn't being fair to Connor, though. He was a very strong warlock, and the leader of the Wilcox clan, but it wasn't as though he could coerce Genoveva Castillo into doing anything she didn't want to do. He'd opened the lines of communication. In the end, it was up to Jake to convince her that revealing Addie's intended destination was the right thing to do.

"Haven't you ever been in love, Genoveva?" he asked desperately.

A chuckle drifted out of the iPhone's speaker. "I'm the *prima* of my clan," she responded, still sounding amused. "Of course, I know what it means to be in love…probably more than you do.

And I understand your worry for Addie and your need to be with her. But you will have to find her in your own way. It's not my place to give you that information."

"Okay," he said, his voice tight with pent-up frustration. As much as he wanted to unleash that frustration on Genoveva, he knew better than to do anything that would cause an inter-clan incident. "Thanks for listening."

"It's no problem," she replied. "And Jake—"

"Yes?" The syllable came out clipped and angry, but right then, he didn't much care. As long as he said the correct things, it didn't matter as much *how* he said them, did it?

"If you're meant to be with Addie," Genoveva said, "you'll find her…one way or another."

8

ALTHOUGH I DOUBTED I'D HAVE ANOTHER RUN-in with Arnie and Cal—a tow truck had come along to haul Arnie's damaged Ford F-250 away, since the lightning bolt hadn't just shattered the windows but had also burned out the vehicle's computerized "brain"—I still got up early and dressed hurriedly, wanting to get out of Walden as quickly as possible. There was a diner serving breakfast down the street, but I didn't dare run the risk of meeting anyone who might have been friends with either of the two men. Probably, neither of them had made any connection between their harassment of me and the lightning strike that had blown out Arnie's truck, and yet it felt safer to slink away without anyone noticing. I still had some trail mix left over from the day before, and I figured I'd stop to grab something more substantial to eat farther up the road, once I was safely away.

As it turned out, I had to drive more than an hour before I got anywhere that even began to resemble a town, but they had a McDonald's, and I went inside to use the bathroom and then get a breakfast sandwich and an iced coffee to go. No one paid me the slightest attention, which seemed encouraging. So far, I hadn't seen even a hint of pursuit, telling me it appeared that I'd managed to give both Jake and Agent Lenz the slip.

Probably, I should have been a bit more cheered by that outcome than I actually was. Oh, of course I was damn glad that I'd left Randall Lenz far behind in my rearview mirror, but at the same time, I began to wonder how hard Jake was working to track me down.

Which I knew was foolish. I didn't want him to find me. I wanted him to be safe. At the same time, though...

...I wanted *him*. It was a lot easier to act confident and independent when I was around other people, like the waitress Andrea at the restaurant the night before. She'd apologized profusely to me about Arnie and Cal, and I'd told her it was fine, that it wasn't the first time I'd had to dodge a couple of over-eager jerks who wouldn't take no for an answer. My reassurances seemed to put her at ease, and she'd left me alone to eat my steak and drink my second glass of wine after that.

And yes, I'd looked cool as a cucumber, but inwardly, I'd still been trembling. Maybe that was delayed shock from the encounter, or just the realization that once again I'd used my gift as a weapon, but either way, I sure as hell wasn't as calm as I'd pretended to be.

Now, though, as the empty miles between Walden and Riverton, the town where the Wind River Casino was located, slowly shrank and the day wore on through the morning and into the afternoon, I couldn't keep myself from dwelling on Jake—the flash in his dark eyes as he smiled, the warm tones of his resonant voice, even the scent of his hair, which could have been his shampoo or just a sun-drenched combination of fresh air and pine forest. All of those things made him uniquely who he was, the man who'd crept into my heart and claimed it for his own.

I didn't know whether he'd ever leave it. Not really. I tried to remind myself of all the reasons why I needed to stay far away from him and the Wilcox clan, and they sounded sensible enough. But sense was cold comfort when contrasted with the way his arms had felt around me, strong and sure. In his embrace, I'd been utterly myself and yet completely part of him as well, our two selves blending so beautifully that it didn't even matter where one of us ended and the other began. I might not have known much about the world, but I knew that kind of oneness was damn hard to find. Once in a lifetime, maybe…if you were really, really lucky. Twice?

As they supposedly liked to say in New York, fuggedaboutit.

You don't have to think about falling in love again, I scolded myself as I came through a wide spot in the road called Lander and turned east onto Highway 789 for the last leg of my journey. *All you have to think about is getting to your hotel and crashing for the night. And after that….*

Well, after I'd gotten a good night's sleep—and, with any luck, didn't have a repeat of my traumatic experience with those two jackasses in Walden—I'd head over to the Wind River Casino and see if they were hiring. I wasn't actually staying there; Genoveva had arranged for a room at the Fairfield Inn and Suites, presumably the highest-rated place in town. Yet another echo of my stay in Gallup, but really, it hadn't been the hotel's fault that I was such an emotional wreck when I'd stayed there.

I figured that was the best way to manage my current circumstances. Don't look more than a couple of steps ahead. Always have a contingency, but don't try to manage everything. Go with the flow.

That had been my mother's mantra. She'd always said we created the greatest trouble for ourselves when we tried to force things, that doing so created resistance to the way the world was supposed to work. I figured she'd gotten that particular piece of advice out of some self-help book or another—she was always reading those things during her downtime, rather than the mysteries and romance novels I favored—but in this particular case, I thought the reasoning seemed sound enough.

Besides, what real choice did I have?

I realized I'd thought of my mother in that particular moment with love, with a bit of inner amusement, but very little sadness. Oh, of course, I missed her, wished fiercely that I had her sitting in the passenger seat, sharing this road trip with me, and still…the hollow, burning ache that had torn at me immediately after her death seemed to have eased. It wasn't fair that she was gone, and I fiercely hoped that someday, somehow, Randall Lenz might be brought to justice for what he'd done, but at the same time, I understood that I could mourn her and wish things had been different, and at the same time understand it was okay—more than okay…*necessary*—for me to go on with my life.

My route took me directly past the Wind River Casino on my way into town, and I craned my head to take a longer look than was probably safe, just to see as much of it as I could before I passed it by. The place was bigger than I'd expected, looming up out of the flat prairie like a monolith, four stories high and with a large neon sign at the entrance beck-oning travelers to come in and try its gaming tables and slot machines, its restaurants and bar.

Tomorrow, I promised it, even though of course, I wouldn't be going there to game, but to apply for a job. That glimpse had reassured me a bit, however. The place looked big and prosperous; there had been a lot of cars in the parking lot, even on a Wednesday afternoon. Now all I had to do was hope they were in need of a waitress or even a host-ess. Yes, I'd graduated from hostessing years earlier and knew I'd earn a lot more as a waitress, but I told myself I'd take what I could get.

Too bad I'd never gotten my bartender certifica-tion. I'd thought about it, but my mother had told me I'd be better off earning a four-year degree and getting an office job somewhere.

"Bartender hours stink," she'd told me, which was only the truth. It was hard to have a life when you had to work mostly nights and weekends.

Not that I was having much of a life at the moment.

I pushed the self-pitying thought away as best I could, and headed into Riverton proper, which was bigger than I'd expected, and quite green and lush even in this dry period before the summer rains, thanks to the river that wound its way through the town, giving its water and energy to the trees I saw on every side. At my previous pit stop, I'd programmed the Fairfield Inn's address into my nav system, and so it wasn't too difficult to make my way there and come to a grateful stop in the half-full parking lot.

Since I'd arrived a little before five and not earlier in the day, my room was ready and waiting for me. I took my bags upstairs—again grateful that Genoveva had had the foresight to provide me with some decent luggage instead of the shopping bags I'd been using—and found a room almost identical to the one I'd rented in Gallup.

In a way, the corporate blandness was reassuring. It reminded me of how big this country was, how it was so easy to lose oneself in its vast expanses and yet still have your new surroundings be somewhat familiar.

The room was mine for three nights, so I unpacked everything, hanging my shirts and blouses in the closet, stowing my underwear and jeans in the dresser. That particular task didn't take me very long, and so I figured the best thing to do was go out and roam around town a bit, get the lay of the land. By that point, I was fairly hungry, since I'd been eating trail mix—padded with some white cheddar popcorn I'd bought at a convenience store in Avon—all day.

Because I didn't dare use the Yelp app Jeremy had installed on my phone…which still in airplane mode…I wandered downstairs and asked at the front desk where the best place was to get something to eat, and maybe a drink.

"Definitely Bar 10," the girl at the desk told me. She was pretty and dark, probably Native American. "Just head back into the center of town—it's about two miles from here, on Broadway just below Main Street."

I thanked her and went out to my car. Since I'd already noted that the Fairfield Inn wasn't really within walking distance of most of the local attractions, I knew I'd have to drive.

No more than two drinks, I told myself. Which wouldn't be that hard. Drinking alone wasn't much fun.

The bar itself wasn't as easy to find as the woman at the hotel had made it sound, but after a couple of false starts, I located the entrance and went inside. By that point, it was getting closer to six, and it seemed as though happy hour was in full swing. All of the tables were taken, but I managed to grab an empty seat at the end of the bar. The bartender, a friendly-faced woman with bright red hair pulled up in a messy twist at the back of her head, raised a hand to acknowledge my arrival and called out, "Be over in a sec, hon!"

"Thanks!" I responded. There was a menu lying near the spot where I'd sat down, so I picked it up and gave it a quick inspection. Lots more variety than I'd expected, and almost everything sounded good. And the wine list looked like something I would have seen in one of the restaurants Jake had taken me to in Flagstaff, not some hole in the wall in Riverton, Wyoming.

Well, that had to be a good sign, didn't it? Maybe it wouldn't be as hard to live here as I feared it might. Of course, I still had to get past moping over Jake, but, like my grief for my mother, perhaps that pain would also lessen as time wore on.

"What can I get you, hon?" the bartender asked.

"A glass of pinot noir, please."

"I.D.?"

I dutifully dug my license out of my wallet and handed it over. The bartender inspected it briefly and gave it back, and I let out an inner sigh of relief. Even though I knew that my fake license had already passed muster several times, I still couldn't quite prevent myself from tensing up every time someone wanted to take a look at it.

No drama this go-'round, though, and I put the Arizona license back in my wallet as the bartender went over to pour me my glass of wine. She came back right away and said, "Just passing through?"

"I hope not," I replied with a smile. "I'm hoping to find a job at the casino."

"Ah," she said, now looking a bit guarded. "Well, it's a good place to work—if you can get a position there. They mostly like to hire Native Americans, though."

Oh. I supposed I should have thought of that. It made sense that the local tribe would want to provide job opportunities for its own members, but I figured it couldn't hurt to try.

"Well," I said, my tone probably too falsely bright, "my great-great-grandmother was Navajo." All right, I knew there were a few more "greats" involved in that particular relationship, but it still was nothing more than the truth.

The bartender looked cheered by that revelation. Her hazel eyes twinkled, and she appeared to give me a quick once-over, as if looking for that bit of Native American heritage in my appearance. "Is that a real Navajo great-grandmother, or the sort of Indian ancestor half the people in this country like to claim they have?"

"A real one," I replied, not at all offended by the question.

"Then you might have a shot," she said as she set my glass of wine in front of me. "I'm Carolyn, by the way. Where'd you come from?"

"Tucumcari," I told her. Again, not really a lie. I'd lived there for a few months years earlier, but she didn't have to know how far back in the past my time in Tucumcari actually was.

She frowned slightly, as if trying to puzzle out exactly where that was. "Colorado?"

"New Mexico."

"Ah. I guess that explains why you'd have a Navajo great-grandmother."

Not really, because the Navajo were mostly in Arizona, and the part of New Mexico they claimed as their own was far to the west of Tucumcari. But I didn't see the need to give Carolyn a geography lesson, so I just smiled and nodded, and picked up my drink.

"I'll check back in a minute, give you some time to decide on your food," she said, and headed down to the end of the bar, where a group of guys who looked as though they'd been working on a road crew all day were ordering another round of beers.

It was loud and kind of rowdy and, oddly, exactly what I needed right then. No one was paying any attention to me, and I could sit there on my stool at the end of the bar and observe everyone without worrying about some random stranger coming up and harassing me as I sipped from my glass of wine. Carolyn came back in a bit and inquired about food, and I told her I wanted the whiskey barbecue sliders and fries. Probably the least healthy thing on the menu, but I was starving and figured it didn't matter so much what I ate, as long as I got some fuel in my system.

When the food arrived, I ordered another glass of wine. Why not? I was having plenty of food to absorb the alcohol, and I could somehow sense I was in a safe place. How, I didn't know for sure—I might have possessed a magical talent to control the weather, but I definitely wasn't psychic. Even so, it felt okay to be there in Riverton, whereas I couldn't wait to get the hell out of Walden, despite the way Andrea had done her best to keep an eye on me and make sure nothing else untoward happened during my time there.

I chose to take my current sense of well-being as a good sign. While I'd never been one to look for symbols and portents, had never been the type of person who pored over her horoscope to see what the coming week might bring, I wanted to believe that the strange sense of belonging I enjoyed while sitting at the counter in Bar 10 was a good omen. If I hadn't felt like I fit in at all, I doubted I would have been quite as hopeful about looking for a job the next day.

Only time would tell if I was right.

The Wind River Casino's website allowed online job applications, but I thought I might have a better chance if I went there in person. I was all too aware of how my travels had begun to eat into the wad of cash in my wallet, and I knew I needed to start earning money again as soon as possible. Resolutely, I put aside all thoughts of the inheritance from my father; since I had no way of safely accessing it, that money might as well not have existed at all.

I printed out the Wind River job application at my hotel's "business center"—a couple of tables and a wireless printer—filled it out, and put on the most professional-looking of the outfits in my meager wardrobe: a dark cardigan over a white T-shirt, new dark jeans, and black flats. The ensemble wouldn't have gotten me in the door at a Fortune 500 company, but I hoped it would be adequate for a minimum-wage beverage server, which seemed to be the job opening that best suited my abilities. While I wasn't thrilled at the thought of having to circulate amongst the gaming tables and deal with either intoxicated or possibly handsy gamblers, I consoled myself with the hope that maybe at least the tips would be good.

It was a little before eleven in the morning when I presented myself at the casino's human resources office, which was on the north side of the building. The woman working there was clearly Native American—Arapahoe, probably, since that tribe operated the hotel and casino—and so were pretty much all the people I'd spotted on my way over who were working at the Wind River Casino in an official capacity. I recalled Carolyn's comment the night before about how almost everyone employed there was a member of the tribe and pushed back a surge of uneasiness. The hotel website had said that ninety percent of the employees were indigenous, but that meant ten percent weren't. I still had a shot.

And if this didn't work out, I'd go looking elsewhere. Riverton wasn't a big place by any stretch of the imagination, but I figured there had to be at least one or two restaurants there who needed servers. Or I could work as a cashier, although my few forays into retail had told me that I didn't like it much—you got dumped on by the public almost as much as you did when waitressing, but you didn't earn any tips to make the abuse a little easier to deal with.

"Applying for a job?" the woman behind the desk asked, and I nodded as I handed over my application.

"Yes. I was hoping you were still hiring beverage servers."

"Oh, we're always hiring those," she said. "I'm Leona Sanchez."

"Addie Wilcox," I replied, putting on a professional smile. Leona seemed friendly enough, her attire a mix of businesslike—button-up white shirt, dark slacks—and tribal, what with the gorgeous beaded choker she wore around her throat and the heavy turquoise jewelry on her fingers and her ears. But I knew I had to convince her that I was good material for the Wind River Casino, or I wasn't going to get very far.

"Nice to meet you." She glanced down at my

application and scanned it quickly, dark eyes moving over its contents. "It looks like you have a lot of serving experience."

I nodded. "Yes. I've been waitressing since I was sixteen."

"And you don't mind working as a bar server?"

"Not at all. I didn't see any openings for jobs at the casino's restaurants, so I wanted to apply for something that was the closest match to my experience."

Leona picked up a pen and made a note on my application, although I couldn't tell what exactly she was writing. "No, we don't have any of those positions available at the moment. However, one of our servers at the Red Willow restaurant will be going on maternity leave in a few more weeks. Would you be interested?"

Because of my perusal of the casino's website, I knew the Red Willow was the higher-end eating establishment there, and probably would offer a lot more in terms of decent tips. Except.... "I'm not sure I can wait a few weeks," I said. "I'd be happy to work as a bar server to start. Then you can see if you think I would be a good fit for the Red Willow."

"That's fine," Leona replied. "In that case, you can start tonight—the evening shift is from three-thirty to twelve, with a half hour for dinner."

Twelve midnight? Yikes. I'd never been much of a night owl, mostly because the waitressing positions I'd held in the past had been at diner-style places, the types of restaurants where the main meals were breakfast and lunch, and everything closed down at nine at the very latest. But I told myself I would adapt. It wasn't as if I had to coordinate my schedule with someone else. No, I was here all on my own.

And whose fault is that? crossed my mind, but I pushed the thought away. The last thing I wanted was to start brooding over Jake in the middle of a job interview, even if Leona was being pretty informal about the whole thing.

"Tonight would be great," I said, summoning a smile.

"Perfect. Come by around three—you'll need to watch the orientation video and fill out some paperwork, pick up your uniform, that sort of thing. Make sure you have your driver's license."

I nodded. "Do I need to bring anything else?"

"Just yourself, and a willingness to work hard." Leona extended a hand. "Welcome to Wind River."

Feeling a little dazed, I took her hand and shook it. "Thanks so much," I said. It wasn't until it sank in that I actually had the job that I realized how badly I'd wanted it. Just a little step, but something seemed to be going right for me at last.

Of course, the last time I'd felt that way, Randall Lenz had ended up on my doorstep, but I did my best to reassure myself there was no way he could possibly track down my current location. Not with the new identity the Wilcoxes had provided for me. At least, I had to hope that the name "Addie Wilcox" wouldn't ping an alarm somewhere. It was a calculated risk, but I knew there was no chance of getting another set of forged I.D. at that point. I wouldn't be setting up a bank account or buying a car or a house, and really, there was no reason why the federal government would have any reason to know anything about me until it came time to file taxes. April fifteenth was ten months off, which gave me plenty of time to figure out how to handle that particular situation.

Don't worry about that right now, I told myself. *Just focus on doing a good job and getting settled here.*

"See you at three," Leona told me, and I took her words as the dismissal they were, telling her I'd be back in a few hours.

After that, there wasn't much for me to do except get in my car and head back to the hotel… and to allow myself a small, cautious flicker of victory.

I was in Wyoming. I had a job. And with any luck, both Randall Lenz and Jake Wilcox would soon forget all about me.

9

IT FELT GOOD TO BE BACK AT WORK. AFTER getting poked and prodded by the staff doctor and pronounced fit to return to his regular duties—"just don't overdo it," Dr. Haley warned him—Randall Lenz hoped he could pick up where he'd left off. Or, since he couldn't precisely remember where he'd left off, at an approximate starting point that felt sensible to him.

Which meant doing his damnedest to discover what had happened during those blank hours and days when he couldn't remember much of anything.

Agent Dawson now sat with him in his office, laptop perched on her knees as she tried to help him reconstruct that missing time. However, he knew they were in for choppy waters when she said, "I'll do what I can, sir. But you weren't telegraphing all your movements, and all the available evidence suggests we've been hacked."

"'Hacked'?" he repeated, frowning at her. He'd spent the previous night at his own house, in his own bed, and the headaches that had plagued him ever since he'd awakened in that motel room in Kanab had finally subsided, but even though he felt materially improved, he knew he didn't want to be hearing that sort of troubling revelation from his assistant. "By whom?"

"I don't know, sir." She tucked a lock of pale brown hair behind one ear and frowned slightly. "All I know is that any trace of your movements after you left Kanab has been systematically erased. No gas or hotel receipts. No phone logs. Nothing. And since your laptop and your cell phone are missing, we can't use them to reconstruct your activities. We're flying blind, so to speak."

Lenz rubbed a finger against his temple, hoping the faint throb he'd just experienced wasn't his headache deciding to return. Had that been the faintest note of accusation in Dawson's voice, as if she thought deep down he should have done something more to protect his assets? No, he was imagining things. Lord knows he'd been beating himself up over the loss of his phone and laptop and Homeland Security I.D., even though he didn't know what he could have done to prevent those items from being taken. It was difficult to mount a defense when you'd been rendered unconscious for days on end.

"All right," he said. "But tell me what you do know."

She didn't precisely sigh, but he noted the way she pulled in a breath and was quiet for a moment, apparently gathering her thoughts. "I know that you went to fetch Adara Grant in Kanab, Utah, at approximately thirteen-forty local time on June fifth. I know that an unknown man named Jake interrupted the process, and during the ensuing altercation, Adara Grant's mother was shot. The recovery team came by soon after the gas explosion at the house, and you elected to stay in Kanab while you attempted to determine where Jake and Adara could have fled. It gets…muddy after that."

"Muddy" was not a word he wanted to hear right then. "But I didn't stay in Kanab."

"No, you checked out of the hotel there. However, the agency Taurus you were driving was found at that same hotel days later with an additional fifteen hundred miles on the odometer."

That was news to him. So, he hadn't been quite as abandoned in Kanab as he'd thought. Why hadn't the kidnappers left the car at the motel where they'd dumped him, instead of leaving it at the original hotel where he'd stayed? Some kind of twisted joke, or had they simply not wanted to make things too easy for him?

Lacking the opportunity to interview the bastards and find out for himself, Lenz guessed he'd never know the truth behind their actions. At this point, it probably didn't matter so much.

Time to focus on the important details. "So, I clearly did a decent amount of driving."

"Yes, but we don't know where. If there were any clues in the vehicle—tickets from parking garages, that sort of thing—whoever moved it to Kanab obviously removed them. There was a good deal of dirt in the tire treads, but it's consistent with the sandstone dust found in northern Arizona and southern Utah, so that doesn't help us very much."

All of this information was delivered in Dawson's usual brisk, matter-of-fact tone. Her expression was nearly blank as well, and yet Lenz thought he caught a worried flicker in her eyes as she looked up at him from her laptop's screen.

"I'm fine, Dawson," he said. "Haley cleared me."

"Yes, sir," she replied. "Only…your nose is bleeding."

Startled, he lifted a hand to his nostril, then drew it away. Blood had smeared itself across his fingers, not a huge amount, but enough to show him that something was wrong, especially since he wasn't someone who got random nosebleeds.

Feeling more irritated than worried, he reached for the box of Kleenex that sat on his desk and carefully blotted the blood. The second pass revealed far less than the first time he'd wiped it off, so it looked as though the nose bleed didn't intend to stick around for very long. Good; he had far more important things to worry about.

"It's nothing," he said, but Dawson's mouth pursed slightly.

From the looks of it, she wished she had the authority to tell him that it was definitely not nothing. However, since theirs wasn't the sort of relationship where she could chide him about not taking care of himself, she remained silent.

"Anything else?" he asked.

She shook her head. "Our analysts are looking into the source of the hack, but they haven't been able to find anything yet. Whoever's doing it, they're good. Really good."

"The Russians?"

"That would be the most likely scenario, but this doesn't feel like them. The removal of information is very surgical. The rest of the Project Daedalus files are untouched."

"That you know of," Lenz remarked, more unsettled than he wanted to admit at the notion of some outsider poking around in his agency's files. Those files contained information so sensitive, it would cause a national security crisis if it was ever made public.

It would also most likely result in the firings of everyone involved, not to mention congressional hearings and criminal investigations, but he considered those consequences secondary compared to the very real worry of having the general public discover that people with superhuman abilities walked among them.

"That I know of," Dawson agreed. "However, we've tightened security and changed our protocols. You've been issued a new username and password with your new laptop—the tech team is just finishing up prepping it and will have it to you in another hour or so."

"Good," Lenz said, although he didn't know whether there was really anything "good" about the situation. Yes, he needed a new laptop, and he supposed he should be glad that Dawson had gotten one set up so quickly, but he wasn't looking forward to memorizing a new batch of protocols. Not with the way his head currently ached.

Damn it, that headache hadn't been there a few minutes earlier. Haley had said that his symptoms and a few odd reddish marks which looked like healed burns on the soles of his feet made it seem as if he might have been struck by lightning, but that he couldn't find any other evidence of such an injury.

Under other circumstances, Lenz might have laughed in derision at the doctor's assessment. After all, the odds of being struck by lightning were exceedingly small. But when you were dealing with someone like Adara Grant, who seemed to attract strange weather phenomena the way a magnet might attract iron filings, then the idea of a strategically placed bolt of lightning wasn't quite so strange. However, if he had actually been struck, shouldn't his burns have still been raw and painful, rather than healed to the point where he wasn't sure he would have noticed them if Nicholas Haley hadn't called them out specifically?

Yet another mystery. For the moment, though, Lenz only wanted to focus on the problem at hand. His maladies—such as they were—weren't a big enough issue to distract him from his work.

"What's the status on Adara Grant?" he asked then, pushing aside his headache and the problem of the maybe-Russian hackers.

"Still missing," Dawson replied. "I reported to you that she'd opened several accounts under the alias 'Addie Wilcox,' and her last known location was Flagstaff, Arizona. However, those accounts remain untouched."

Had Dawson told him about that? The information seemed vaguely familiar, but only because he *thought* he should know it, not because he could actually remember any conversations they'd had on the subject. "How much is in those accounts?"

"Both the savings and the checking account have the FDIC-insured maximum of $200,000 each."

That was a hell of a lot of money for a supposed orphan from the back of beyond to have suddenly appear in her bank accounts. Where had it come from? "Origin?"

"We're trying to figure that out. Looks like a wire transfer from a numbered account, but we're having difficulty determining who set up that account in the first place."

Someone had wired Adara Grant four hundred thousand dollars. Who? And why? Nothing in her personal history indicated that she knew anyone with access to that sort of cash. No criminal record, no rich sugar daddy, nothing.

As he pondered that conundrum, Dawson continued. "We thought we had a lead on her vehicle—a metallic green Fiat 500X—but it turned out to be someone else."

"Where?" Lenz asked, his tone sharp with urgency.

"It wasn't hers—it didn't have paper dealer plates—"

"I don't care," he said. Maybe he was foolish to ignore what Dawson had told him, but he had that strange tickling at the back of his mind again, the itch of a hunch he couldn't ignore. "Tell me anyway."

"Santa Fe, New Mexico," his assistant replied, and he felt a surge of triumph.

"That's it. I'm going to Santa Fe."

~

Jake lay on the couch and stared up at the ceiling of his family room. The TV blared away in the background, tuned to a noisy and fairly horrible remake of *The Fantastic Four,* but he wasn't watching the movie for its quality. No, he had the television on because that way, the house didn't feel quite so empty.

All right, it wasn't really empty, because Taffy lay on the rug next to the sofa and watched him with worried eyes, but even so, he couldn't quite ignore the way the big Victorian house seemed to echo with Addie's absence. Stupid of him to think such a thing, when she'd only stayed there for a couple of nights, and yet...

...and yet, he knew this place would always feel wrong to him as long as she was gone.

Anger at Genoveva Castillo seethed in him, although deep down, he realized the Castillo *prima* had been handed an impossible conundrum. No matter which choice she made, she'd end up hurting someone. That she'd elected to shield Addie instead of helping him only spoke to the solidarity she apparently felt toward another witch. Or maybe she hadn't thought Jake's love was strong enough to justify the betrayal of such a trust.

It was, though. The ache of her loss thrummed through every limb, but it wasn't the same pain he'd experienced when Sarah died. Back then, he'd wanted to scream his rage at the universe, while at the same time he'd realized it didn't matter how much he railed against the capriciousness of fate, since it wouldn't change anything. He'd felt utterly helpless.

He didn't feel helpless now, though. He felt frustrated. Addie wasn't dead, only disappeared, and people existed in the world who could have helped him find her but had chosen not to.

Fine. He'd help himself.

After sitting up, he reached for the bottle of Kilt Lifter pale ale that sat on the coffee table and took a swig. It was strong and bitter, a suitable counterpoint to his mood.

Genoveva had said Addie was going someplace where she would be safe. To stay with another witch clan? That didn't make any sense to him; if she'd wanted the protection of witch-kind, she would have stayed in Flagstaff and allowed the Wilcoxes to look after her.

Which meant…what? That she'd gone someplace where there weren't any witch clans? Jake could see how she might want to avoid bringing any more attention to the witching world than she already had, but how could regular civilians possibly keep her safe from someone like Randall Lenz? The man was implacable, utterly without mercy, as far as he could tell.

Frowning, Jake dug his phone out of his jeans pocket and unlocked it, then called his brother. Since he'd swung by to pick up Taffy on his way home from Connor and Angela's place, Jake knew Jeremy was at his townhouse and not at Trident HQ. It appeared that even Jeremy was feeling a bit discouraged after the day's events; at any rate, he'd said he needed to take a break for the evening.

His brother picked up on the first ring, a sure sign that he was probably bored already and itching for something to do. "What's up, Jake?"

"You said there were no witch clans in Wyoming, right?"

No hesitation. "Yep."

"Genoveva said something about Addie going someplace where she would be safe, where the people there would have their own way of protecting her from the federal government. Does that sound like Wyoming to you?"

"It sure does." A pause, and then Jeremy added, "I assume you're running the problem through your deductive circuits because Genoveva wouldn't tell you anything actionable."

"Basically, yeah." When Jake had stopped to pick up his dog, he could tell Jeremy was full of questions, but he'd been so angry at Genoveva that he hadn't wanted to stop and chat. He'd known he needed to go home and try to ponder things on his own. The strategy seemed to have worked, or at least, he hoped he'd come up with a real answer to the question that had been plaguing him, that this wasn't all just wishful thinking. "But she let that little tidbit slip."

"We're talking about Genoveva Castillo here," Jeremy remarked, his wry tone not leaving much doubt as to what he thought of the Castillo *prima*. "I don't think she just 'lets' anything slip. I think she gave you a clue, but not too obvious a one."

"Her reasoning being that if I wasn't smart enough to figure it out, then I didn't deserve to find Addie?"

"Something like that, yeah."

How compassionate of her. But, as Jeremy had just said, it did sort of sound like the kind of thing Genoveva would do. Jake was silent for a few seconds, running through everything he knew about Wyoming…which admittedly wasn't much. Yellowstone, and prairies and mountains. And that TV show his father had liked so much, the one with the sheriff.

Longmire.

And as that particular detail clicked in his brain, Jake thought of something else, of several characters who had been key players in the show. Native Americans. There was a big reservation somewhere in Wyoming, wasn't there?

"A Native American tribe wouldn't be too cooperative with the federal government, would it?" he asked, and Jeremy chuckled.

"Probably not. I mean, they're sovereign nations, with their own police departments and all that. They're supposed to operate within the framework of the United States government, but I have a feeling if they get an opportunity to stick it to the man, then they're going to take it."

Right. It made a lot of sense, really. Go to ground in a place that didn't have any other witch clans, but surround yourselves with people who had no love for the federal government and definitely wouldn't go out of their way to offer its agents any assistance. Those tribes had their own power, a magic unlike the kind the witch clans practiced, but something that could be brought to bear in times of trouble.

"Then that's where she has to be. Hang on."

Jake got up from the couch and hurried over to the dining room, where he'd left his laptop sitting on the table. After opening it up and logging in, he went to the Chrome browser and did a quick search of Native American tribes in Wyoming. There were several, but the Shoshone and the Arapaho seemed to be the most numerous.

And the Eastern Shoshone and the Northern Arapaho were concentrated in the Wind River Reservation, which took up more than two million acres in the center of the state. Jake clicked on the link, saw there were several towns located near or within the reservation, the most populous being a place called Riverton.

A few miles south of Riverton was a large casino, just the sort of establishment where a girl who needed to get a job fast and had a bunch of waitressing experience might find some much-needed work.

You're jumping to conclusions, he told himself, trying to quell the excitement surging within him. Still....

"Can you check on a place called the Wind River Casino? Like, their personnel files?"

"You think that's where she went?"

"Possibly."

"Give me a few minutes. I'll get back to you."

The call ended there, signaling that Jeremy had hung up so he could go work his particular magic on the human resources database at the casino. Since his brother had managed to hack into government servers, Jake had no doubt that he'd be able to find what they were looking for.

And in fact, his phone rang again about ten minutes later.

"I'm in," Jeremy said, "but I'm not seeing any record of her."

"Maybe she used a fake name."

"Doubt it—they say right on their website that a driver's license or state-issued I.D. is required for employment. I'm pretty sure Addie wouldn't have had the time to get herself another fake I.D. But think about it, Jake—it's a long way from Santa Fe to the middle of Wyoming. Even if that's where she was headed, she wouldn't have had time to get settled and go looking for a job. She might still be on the road."

Right. In his eagerness to prove Addie really was where he thought she was, he hadn't even considered the logistics involved, but it was pretty doubtful that she would have gotten into town and gone looking for a job right away. She'd need a little time to settle herself. "So…what now?"

"I'd wait," Jeremy said, and Jake found himself shaking his head, even though he knew his brother couldn't see him.

"It's been two days. How long am I supposed to wait?"

"As long as it takes," Jeremy replied reasonably. "Besides, it's six o'clock at night. I suppose if you left now, you'd get to Santa Fe around midnight, but that's not going to help much, is it?"

"I could fly."

Jeremy let out a laugh that sounded suspiciously like a snort. "Wyoming's not exactly a hub. You'd have to go to Phoenix to get a puddle-jumper that'd take you to Jackson Hole—it's the closest big airport. And you'd still have a drive of a couple of hours from there."

Great. And here he'd thought Arizona was a big piece of nothing when it came to transportation. Obviously, Wyoming was even worse. "I could have Lucas fly me. That Piper of his can go that far, can't it?"

"Probably…if Margot would even let him go off on that sort of wild goose chase." A pause, during which Jake heard a clicking sound, probably his brother looking up something on his computer. "There's an airport just outside Riverton, but you'd still need to rent a car once you got there. Which you can't, because you don't have any credit cards to match your new 'Tyler' identity. No, the only logical thing to do is swap trucks. You can take mine, and I'll drive the Gladiator."

Right. Jake hadn't even considered that particular angle, but he realized that, while it had been necessary to scrub "Jake Wilcox" out of existence until they could get this mess with Randall Lenz and his agency straightened out, he was going to run into some difficulties managing simple tasks while operating under an assumed name. Still, he couldn't quite prevent himself from joking, "Sure. I know this is just your way of getting to drive my truck for a while."

"You got me," his brother responded, tone deadpan. "Just come on over, and we'll make the swap." He added, sounding resigned, "And bring the dog with you. Unless you were going to have Laurel watch her."

Which he could, he supposed, except that Laurel was currently renting Connor's former loft apartment in downtown Flagstaff, and the place wasn't really suitable for pets. The yard at Jeremy's townhouse wasn't big, but at least there was a patch of grass where she could go outside to go potty in between walks. "Thanks, man," he said. "I appreciate that. We'll be there in a few."

Jake ended the call, glad that Jeremy hadn't tried to continue arguing why it was a bad idea to go after Addie in Wyoming. If she was even there at all. He was only going on a hunch, but his instincts tended to be good, and even his much warier brother seemed to be in agreement that Wyoming was a good hiding place, for a variety of reasons.

Since he wouldn't be heading out until the morning, he didn't worry about packing anything except Taffy's bowls and treats, and the spare dog bed he'd bought just for instances like this one. The dog watched all these preparations with wary interest, as if she knew all too well what he had planned for her but was still a bit hopeful that maybe something a little more interesting than Jeremy's townhouse waited for her at the end of the trip.

"Not this time, girl," Jake told her, bending down to scratch her soft little head. "I need to get Addie back, but then when she's home in Flagstaff and things are back to normal, we'll all go on a hike or something."

This promise made Taffy's tail wag fiercely—she knew what a "hike" meant. While she couldn't keep up with the bigger dogs in really rough wilderness, she still loved to wander the numerous trails around town, smelling all sorts of new and exciting scents.

Since they were just going to the garage via the backyard, Jake didn't bother clipping her leash to her collar, but only stuffed it in his pocket before gathering all her supplies and heading out the door. The Gladiator was too high for her to jump inside, so after he'd set everything down on the back seat, he picked her up and put her in the passenger seat.

"No nose prints on the glass," he warned her, even though he knew the second they got started, her little wet nose would be pressed against the window.

In a way, focusing on the dog made it easier for him to ignore how badly he ached to get on the road right away, even though it was already almost seven o'clock and there was no way he could drive through the night without getting some rest first. No, Jeremy was right—he'd get started first thing in the morning, but anything earlier than that was madness.

When he turned the corner onto the street where his brother's townhouse was located, Jake saw that Jeremy had already pulled his big silver Ram truck out to the curb and had left the garage door open. He parked inside and got out, then went into the house through the door that led from the garage to the kitchen. To his surprise, Jeremy was loitering there rather than absorbed in his computer the way Jake had expected him to be. An open pizza box sat on the pale quartz-stone counter, a half-drunk bottle of Four Peaks brown ale nearby.

At the scent of the pizza, Taffy's tail started wagging furiously. Without bothering to greet Jake, Jeremy bent down and gave the dog a bite of pizza crust.

"That's one way to make her glad about coming to see you," Jake remarked.

"She's always glad to see me anyway." His brother bent down to feed Taffy another piece of crust, then patted her on the back. "I give her table scraps."

"So do I," Jake said, annoyed that his brother thought he spoiled the dog more than he himself did.

Jeremy shrugged. "There's more beer in the fridge. And you can have some pizza if you haven't eaten yet."

He hadn't, mainly because he'd been spending his evening brooding over Addie. His stomach grumbled, telling him that half a bottle of beer wasn't quite enough fuel to satisfy it.

From the way Jeremy's eyebrow tilted at an

ironic angle, he'd heard Jake's stomach rumbling but decided not to comment on it. Instead, he leaned over and pulled off another piece for himself.

The sharp, spicy smell of pepperoni was too much to ignore. Jake went over to the refrigerator to retrieve a beer, popped the cap, and then snagged some pepperoni pizza. The first mouthful was enough to tell him it was a damn good thing he'd decided to eat some dinner.

"Got you something else, too," Jeremy said, nodding toward an envelope that sat on the kitchen counter.

Mystified, Jake finished devouring his slice of pizza, then grabbed a paper towel and wiped his greasy fingers off before reaching for the envelope. Inside was a wad of cash.

It was his turn to lift an eyebrow. "What's all this?"

"Well, I doubted you wanted to leave an electronic trail by using your debit card at ATMs from here to Riverton," Jeremy replied. "So, I dug out some of my mattress cash for you. It should be enough as long as you're not gone too long...or don't do anything too crazy."

He supposed he should have thought of that. Trying to stay incognito was kind of a pain in the ass, when you got down to the actual logistics of the situation. "Thanks," he said, doing a quick mental count of the bills in the envelope. There was a little more than three thousand dollars in twenty-dollar bills shoved inside. Then he glanced up at his brother. "You really keep this much in your mattress?"

"Of course not," Jeremy said. "I have a safe. Never hurts to keep some cash around, just in case."

"I'd say this is a little more than 'some.'"

That remark only earned him a shrug. "I know you're good for it. And you don't really know how long you're going to be gone, do you?"

No, he didn't. Jake wanted to believe that all he had to do was drive to Riverton, find Addie, and plead his case, and she'd realize that there was no need for her to hide there in Wyoming when the Wilcoxes could shield her from Randall Lenz and his agents without any problem. However, he knew that particular pie-in-the-sky fantasy was just that—a fantasy. No, he'd probably have to fight hard to persuade the woman he loved that she didn't need to spend her life on the run. There was a lot he had yet to learn about Addie Grant, but he knew she was pretty good at digging her heels in if the situation warranted it.

Which was fine—he also had a stubborn streak a mile wide. The real trick would be seeing which one of them backed down first.

"Nope," he said simply in answer to Jeremy's question, without elaboration, and reached for another slice of pizza.

And because Jeremy was his brother, he didn't bother with a reply. Maybe just the faintest nod, as if acknowledging the fight Jake had ahead of him... and also indicating that, whatever happened, Jeremy had his back.

That was the beauty of family, wasn't it? Knowing they'd be there for you, no matter what?

All he had to do now was convince Addie that she was also part of this family...and that they'd be there for her, just like they would for any other Wilcox.

Otherwise, what was the point in having a clan?

10

I WAS RELIEVED TO LEARN THAT MY UNIFORM AS a bar server was pretty basic—just a white button-down shirt with the casino's logo embroidered on the left breast and black slacks. Since the place was run by Native Americans, I supposed I should have guessed that they wouldn't make their employees wear anything that exploited their heritage, but still, some of the nervous tension that had knotted my gut as I walked in through the employee entrance lessened as I finished changing out of my regular clothes in the restroom, pulled my hair back in a barrette, and stowed my belongings in the locker I'd been assigned.

There were a couple of other people in the employee lounge, all of whom looked like they must be Arapaho, or maybe Shoshone. They smiled and said hello, and I introduced myself, trying not to stammer over the "Wilcox" part of my assumed name, since I still wasn't used to thinking of myself as Addie Wilcox. No sign of any resentment that the new hire was a white chick, and I found myself relaxing that much more. I honestly hadn't known what to expect, but so far, everything seemed to be going okay.

A few minutes spent on paperwork—thank God for the fake driver's license and Social Security card that Jake's mysterious cousin Jasper had provided for me—and then I was ushered into a meeting room for my employee orientation. It was quick, just a short video about the casino and its history with the tribe, along with a few brief comments about the traditional dance exhibitions held there every Tuesday night, as well as upcoming poker competitions and other events. It seemed a little strange to me that they'd have dance exhibitions in a ballroom at a casino, but maybe the tribe had decided it was the best way to share their culture with the tourists.

Less than twenty-five minutes after I'd arrived, I was out on the floor, taking drink orders from the people who'd parked themselves at the slot machines and the gaming tables, getting drinks from the bartenders, and then bringing those drinks out to the patrons. For a Wednesday night, the place was pretty busy, but I was glad of that. As I'd learned on numerous occasions in the past, when I was busy, I didn't have much time to worry about what was going on in my life.

One of the bartenders was a few years older than I, and he kept trying to flirt with me as I ferried drink orders to and fro. Not in an uncomfortable way—I could tell he was one of those guys who was naturally outgoing and kind of a tease—but still, I had to keep coming up with ways to shut him down that didn't seem too rude. If my life had been different...if I hadn't met Jake and fallen in love with him...then I might have even encouraged Blake, since he was sort of cute and obviously someone who knew how to have fun no matter where he was or what he was doing.

But things weren't different, and although I'd told myself I needed to forget Jake and move on, that particular wound was still way too fresh for me to contemplate flirting with anyone else. I smiled and made evasive answers, until Jeannine, the other bartender, smacked Blake on the arm and told him to behave himself. After that, he was on his best behavior, but I could tell he was all too ready to start with the bantering back-and-forth again if I gave him the slightest encouragement.

All in all, the night passed far more quickly than I'd expected it to. Yes, I had to stifle a yawn here and there toward the end of my shift, but at least I wasn't worried about falling asleep on my feet or passing out face first into a tray full of gin and tonics. There was definitely something to be said for a job where you were moving all the time; I knew if I'd had to work those hours sitting at a desk rather than walking the floor of a casino, I would have passed out around ten o'clock.

And also thank God that Leona had taken pity on me and had given me the swing shift, rather than graveyard. There were people coming on duty just as I was getting my purse and other belongings out of my locker, and I wondered how many months it had taken them to get used to starting work at midnight and leaving at eight-thirty in the morning. I smiled at the people who smiled at me, nodded at those who didn't, and hoped that eventually I'd remember who everyone was. I'd met the two other bar servers who shared my shift, Tina and Desirée, and they'd seemed friendly enough, although we were all so busy that none of us had a chance to do much more than make a few introductions.

As I closed my locker and turned to head toward the exit, I found my way blocked by a man I'd never seen before. Clearly a member of the local tribe, he was older, maybe in his late sixties or possibly his early seventies, dark eyes bracketed by lines, iron-gray hair pulled back into an engraved silver ponytail holder.

"You're Addie Wilcox, the new hire?" he said.

His voice was deep, the words slow and deliberate, as if he carefully considered each one before pronouncing it—even when asking a simple question about my identity.

At once, my heart began to pound a little faster, although I tried to tell myself that I'd done just fine on my first day on the job, and that also there was probably no way someone who looked like this stranger could be working for Randall Lenz. Even so, my voice sounded shaky as I said, "Um, yes. Is there something I can help you with?"

He glanced around, but we were alone. The people who'd arrived to start the graveyard shift had already gone out into the casino, and those who'd gotten off at midnight had already hurried home— including Blake the bartender, thank God. "You seek to hide yourself among us, but there are those who will always know who you are."

A chill went over me, despite the cardigan I'd pulled on over my white work shirt. "Ex-excuse me?"

The stammered question earned me a smile. He had very white, very straight teeth. Dentures, or just a lifetime of eating good food without a speck of processed sugar?

"Come," he said, and gestured toward the meeting room where I'd watched the orientation video at the start of my shift. "We need to talk."

Frantically, I looked around the locker room,

hoping against hope that someone would come along and rescue me from my predicament. However, everyone else appeared to be gone or occupied elsewhere, and I had a feeling I was on my own. "I'm not sure—"

Another smile. He stepped away from me and went over to a bulletin board on the other side of the room, one that contained photos from various events and activities that appeared to have been held on the casino grounds. Pointing at one of them, he said, "You see this? That's me. I don't mean you any harm, Addie, but we must talk."

For a second or two, I hesitated, then decided it probably wouldn't hurt to walk over there and take a quick peek at the photo he'd just indicated. If nothing else, the bulletin board was that much closer to the exit, and besides, while the man who faced me looked trim and fit for someone his age, I still had a feeling I could outrun him if it came to that.

Clutching my purse strap, I sidled over to the stranger, then paused a few feet away but still close enough to get a good look at the photo in question. It showed one of the dance exhibitions I'd seen in the orientation video I'd watched earlier that day, only this event appeared to be much larger than the ones held in the casino ballroom and looked like it had taken place somewhere outside on the grounds. Standing in front of the dancers was the same man who stood next to the bulletin board now, only in the photo he was wearing full tribal regalia—I didn't know enough to even begin to guess whether it was Arapaho or Shoshone—instead of the chambray shirt and faded jeans he had on currently. The caption underneath stated, *Carson Archuleta, head of the Northern Arapahoe Business Council, opens the grand powwow, July 2018.*

"You're Carson Archuleta?" I asked.

He nodded. "Yes. We don't really have a chief these days, but I'm the closest thing to it." His dark eyes twinkled at me. "And harmless enough. I know these old feet can't keep up with yours, if you should choose to bolt." A pause, and he added in an undertone, even though there was no one else around to hear us, "I understand your caution. But I don't mean you any harm."

I'd heard that line before. This time, though, I had a feeling he was only telling me the truth. At any rate, I didn't sense caution shrilling along my nerve endings like electrical impulses through a power line, and so I thought maybe it would be a good idea to hear what he had to say. Yes, I was dog tired, but I didn't have to be back at work until three. I still had plenty of time to sleep.

"Okay," I said. "But I need to get home. It's been a long day."

Another glint in those dark, dark eyes, half-hidden by their heavy lids. "A hotel is not a home. But we'll leave that for another time."

Without saying anything else, he led me over to the meeting room and closed the door behind us. Worry flared at being shut in the windowless room with him, but since he didn't do anything more alarming than go over to the long table that sat in the center of the space and then pull out a chair, I told myself to calm the hell down.

Well, not that I wanted to get *too* calm. Not when it seemed obvious to me that he'd already figured out who and what I was.

"How did you know?" I asked, once we had both sat down.

He steepled his fingers under his chin and gave me a very direct look. Being on the receiving end of it made me think I had a pretty good idea why he was the head of the tribe's business council. His was the kind of stare that made you want to be on your best behavior.

"The magic of your people is different from the power that dwells in mine," he replied. "But there are those of us who can still sense it. Not all—or the people you worked with tonight would have been aware that there is more to you than meets the eye —but those of us who have walked the path of the shaman can tell when we encounter those who are born with the white man's magic in them. What is your gift, Addie?"

It never even crossed my mind to lie to him. "I can control the weather," I said simply.

"Ah." A nod as he absorbed that piece of information. Then he said, "It is a good gift, if used sparingly and with wisdom. You have learned this?"

I thought of the bolt of lightning that had struck Randall Lenz, the way his lean body had convulsed as the power of millions of volts of electricity shot through him. How the smoke had wafted up from his singed clothing, and his icy blue eyes had stared sightlessly at me for a moment before his lids dropped and he passed out completely.

There was also the matter of Arnie's damaged pickup truck, but for some reason, I didn't feel as guilty about that one, possibly because no one had actually been hurt, and the only real damage he'd have to deal with was paying the deductible on his car insurance. Also, the guy was a serious jerk.

Maybe I shouldn't have felt guilty about my attack on Randall Lenz, considering his plans for me, and yet I couldn't quite help myself. He might have been armed, but he still couldn't have had any real way of defending himself against such an assault.

"I'm trying," I said at last, and Carson tilted his head to one side, considering my words.

"That is good," he told me after a pause. "I would have doubted you if you had attempted to reassure me that you had all elements of your gift under control."

"But I'm supposed to," I protested. "That's how it works. Unfortunately, I sort of came late to the whole magic thing."

Another silence. He watched me for a moment, and I got the uncomfortable feeling that he was somehow able to look at me and know things he had no way of knowing. Not telepathy or anything so obvious, but more like…an instinct.

Or, as he'd said, a type of magic that was very different from my own.

"And you are still finding your way."

"Yes," I said. "But don't worry—I don't have any intention of using my powers at all. I'm trying to lie low."

He laid his hands on the tabletop and knotted his fingers together. Those fingers were adorned with silver rings studded with turquoise and onyx and coral, and heavy cuffs decorated with the same stones encircled his wrists. I wasn't used to seeing a man wear so much jewelry, and yet the impression was anything but feminine. No, there was strength in those hands, gnarled and sturdy as the roots of an oak tree.

When he spoke, his voice was quiet and firm. "And what has you hiding here, Adara Grant?"

Cold shivered through me. How had he known my real name? It wasn't as though I even possessed any identification which had that name on it, since I'd left my purse and everything else I owned behind when I fled the house my mother and I were renting in Kanab.

If Carson knew that particular detail about me, he must have known a lot more. However, as I met his steady gaze, I didn't see any condemnation or anger in his eyes, only a sort of acceptance.

Once again, I spoke the truth without hesitation. "Because there's a man who works for the federal government who wants me for my powers. He—he killed my mother. Not on purpose, I don't think, but I still have every reason in the world to stay far away from him."

"Ah." Again, just that single syllable, and yet it was enough to tell me that Carson Archuleta had absorbed my story and knew I hadn't embellished it, hadn't tried to hide anything from him.

For some reason, though, I felt as though I needed to explain myself further. "I thought—I hoped—that maybe I would be safe here. I don't have any connection to this place, so there's no reason to look for me in Riverton. But I don't want to cause any trouble. I can leave if you think it's best."

As I spoke those brave words, however, I couldn't help but experience a sinking sensation. If I left Riverton, where in the world was I supposed to go? Maybe I could find someone to forge a passport for me, and maybe I could get across the border into Canada. But would someone like Randall Lenz even give a crap about international borders? I already had the impression that he didn't care too much which laws he stepped on when pursuing someone who possessed the talents his agency desired.

"You will not leave," Carson said. Once again, his tone was firm. "We can offer you shelter here. As you said, there is no reason for this man to seek you out in this part of the world, and besides...." The sentence trailed off, and he released a breath, somehow looking more tired than he'd been just a moment earlier. "We cooperate with the government because we must, but there is no love lost between us."

"Thank you," I told him, even though those two small words seemed horribly inadequate to me. This man was willing to put himself and his people at risk in order to keep me safe, and I vowed to myself that I'd make sure no harm came to any of them. "I don't know what to say."

At once, the twinkle was back in his black eyes. "You don't have to say anything. Go back to your hotel and get some rest. Tomorrow is a new day, one that may bring you some pleasant surprises."

He rose from the table then, gave me a friendly nod, and let himself out. I continued to sit at the table for a moment, a little dazed at the realization that somehow, despite my worries, I was welcome in Riverton.

And pleasant surprises?

I thought I was about ready for something pleasant to enter my life.

The next day, I decided to get a late lunch at Bar 10 to fortify myself for my upcoming shift, since I didn't know any place else in town to eat and really didn't feel like experimenting. When I walked in, the restaurant was much less crowded than it had been the evening before. Carolyn smiled at me and waved, and I went ahead and sat down at the bar even though there were several open tables.

"What can I getcha?" she asked.

"Just an iced tea and a burger," I replied. Then, since I realized that subsisting on cheeseburgers and fries probably wasn't the way to go, I added, "But with a side salad instead of fries. I'm on my way to work."

"You got a job?" she asked, shooting me a delighted smile.

I could tell her reaction was genuine, that she really was glad that I'd been able to find employment so quickly. For some reason, that made me feel almost teary, that someone who was nearly a stranger would show such compassion for someone she hardly knew. "Yep," I said, willing my voice to remain steady. "I'm working as a bar server at the casino right now, but the manager thinks she might be able to slide me into a waitress spot at the restaurant in the near future, so things are looking up. Now all I need to do is find someplace more permanent to live than the Fairfield Inn."

Carolyn set my iced tea down in front of me and said, "Well, I might be able to help you with that."

"You can?" I asked, a little startled. It was nice enough to have encountered a friendly face and someone who looked genuinely glad to see me, but it wasn't as though I expected her to offer me a spot on her couch or something.

However, it turned out that wasn't what she had in mind. "Yeah—my sister has a little place she bought a while back and fixed up to use as an Airbnb, but she never got enough renters to make it worthwhile, and the ones she did get weren't all that concerned about keeping the place nice. So, she's decided to just use the house as a regular rental."

That sounded great, but…. "I was living with my mother before," I said. "Would your sister mind that I don't have any previous rental references?"

"Can she call your mother and talk to her?"

Not unless she uses a Ouija board, I thought. Keeping my voice steady, I replied, "No…she passed away recently. That's why I'm kind of on my own."

At once, the sparkle left Carolyn's hazel eyes. "Oh, hon, I'm so sorry. Tell you what—I'll put in a good word for you, and we'll see what happens. Tracy hasn't even started advertising it yet, but I think she'd be happy to have a nice person with a job in there."

"You can use Carson Archuleta as a reference," I blurted out, and she sent me a surprised glance.

"You know Carson?"

"He, um—he welcomed me to the casino last night, and we talked a little."

"That was nice of him." She paused, appearing to think it over. "What time do you start your shift?"

"At three-thirty."

She glanced over at the Budweiser clock on the far wall. One-forty, which meant I still had plenty of time before I had to be at work. "Let me text my sister. She should be able to show you the house before you have to get to the casino. And I'll get that order for your burger in so you have time to eat, too."

As I stammered my thanks, she pulled a phone out of her apron pocket and sent off a quick text, then stuck her head around back and relayed my lunch order to the staff in the kitchen. Just a minute later, her phone pinged, and she got it back out and gave a happy nod.

"Tracy can meet you at the house at two-fifteen. I'll write down the address for you."

"That's—that's amazing," I said, head reeling a little at how quickly all this was happening. True, there was no real urgent need for me to vacate the hotel right away, but having a place of my own would make my situation in Riverton feel much more permanent.

More real.

"Well, don't thank me yet," Carolyn said. "But I know my sister would like to have a nice, quiet single person in there." She lifted an eyebrow at me, mouth quirking slightly. "You're not a party animal, are you?"

"No," I replied, with such vehemence that she chuckled.

"That's what I kind of figured."

In short order, my burger and salad were ready. I ate quickly, but not so quickly that I couldn't allow myself to enjoy the food. And then I was out the door, where I hurried over to my car, entered the address Carolyn had given me into the nav, and was on my way.

The house in question actually wasn't that far, maybe a quarter-mile if even that much. It definitely looked adorable from the street, a square little clapboard-sided structure with a tiny front porch and a lawn so green it was almost blinding. As I got out of my car, a woman stepped onto that porch. She had the same bright red hair as Carolyn, and was tall and slim like her, too, so I assumed she must be her sister.

And sure enough, as I came up the front walk, the woman met me on the bottom porch step and stuck out a hand. "Hi, I'm Tracy."

"Addie Wilcox," I replied. I'd been mentally rehearsing introducing myself by that name, so it came out smoothly enough, without any hesitation. "Thanks so much for showing the house on such short notice."

"Hey, if I can get it rented without even having to advertise it, I call that a win." She grinned, and I noticed her eyes crinkled at the corners the same way her sister's did. They did look a lot alike, although Tracy's face was a bit more lined, and I guessed she must be the older of the two. "Come on in."

I followed her up the stairs and went inside. As the exterior had promised, it was very small, probably only about half the size of the house I'd shared in Kanab with my mother, with a teeny living room, even smaller kitchen, and a bedroom where there was barely space for a queen bed, one bedside table, and a highboy dresser. However, everything was new and neat and clean, the furniture in a relaxed cottage style, mostly neutrals with pops of red and bright blue. In fact, the kitchen had a little red retro-style refrigerator and matching microwave, and I sort of fell in love on the spot. I'd never seen a red refrigerator before.

"I love it," I said after Tracy had given me the tour—which took about five minutes, considering the size of the place.

She visibly relaxed, as if she'd been worried that I'd find some fault or another with the house. "Oh, great. Um…rent is six hundred a month, but that's with utilities included. You're working at the casino, right?"

I nodded. The rent would take a chunk of my earnings, but since I wouldn't have to pay for the utilities and I didn't have a car payment or credit card debt or anything else that would be a steady drain on my earnings, I thought I should be able to handle it. "Yes. I'm a bar server now, but I'm hoping to move up soon."

"That's what Carolyn told me." Tracy paused and glanced around. "So…I guess it's yours. We can just do month-to-month rent, unless you'd prefer a lease."

"No, month-to-month is fine," I replied. I supposed that meant she could raise the rent when-ever she felt like it, but on the other hand, if it turned out that I couldn't stay for very long, at least I wouldn't be breaking a lease in the process. "How much of a deposit do you need?"

"Oh, half a month's rent is fine. No need to be super-formal about it. And obviously, I'll pro-rate your June rent, so…." A pause as she pulled out her phone and made a few calculations. "That's seven hundred even to get started."

I actually had that amount in my wallet, just because I hadn't set up a bank account in Riverton yet, and I didn't feel safe about leaving all my cash in the hotel room's safe. Probably, leaving it in my purse and putting that purse in my locker at work wasn't the world's greatest idea, either, but no one had touched it the night before, so it seemed I didn't have much to worry about on that front.

As Tracy looked on, somewhat wide-eyed, I got out the cash and counted seven hundred dollars, then handed them over. "I don't have a debit card right now," I told her by way of explanation.

Luckily, she didn't ask any questions, only gave me a brass keychain with the Ford logo stamped on it and two silver keys dangling from the ring. "Front door and back door," she said. "The yard's on an automated drip and sprinkler system, so you don't need to worry about that. Trash can is on the side of the house. No garage, but there's a carport in back where you can park. And here's my number in case any emergencies pop up."

She recited her phone number, and I hastily entered it in my iPhone. Judging by the way her eyes widened again at the sight of that brand-new phone—and how she'd eyeballed my car earlier when I first drove up—she was probably wondering why someone who possessed such fancy gadgets was renting a teeny six-hundred-a-month house in Riverton, Wyoming. Unfortunately, I couldn't tell her the truth, and I couldn't think of a plausible story to cover the discrepancy, so about all I could do was hope she wouldn't ask any probing questions.

Which, to my relief, she didn't. Another thank-you, a cheery wave, and she was off, leaving me alone in my new house. I glanced at the clock on the mantel. Two-thirty. The casino was only five minutes away, so I figured I had sufficient time to run over to the hotel, pack my stuff, check out, and then come back to drop everything off before I had to be at work. Maybe it would have been smarter to wait until I was off my shift, but I didn't want to move into my new house in the middle of the night. I wanted it to be in broad daylight, just like anyone would who didn't have anything to hide.

That seemed to settle it. I went out to the porch and locked the door, then hurried over to my car. A brief backward glance over my shoulder to take a look at the house, and I was on my way.

If I ran into him, I'd have to tell Carson Archuleta all about that day's "pleasant surprise." I'd already started making a home for myself in a new place, just as my mother had taught me. Soon enough, I'd feel safe in Riverton…especially since I no longer had to worry about my "gift" causing any trouble.

And then maybe at some point, I could let myself forget about Jake Wilcox, about the family that had been mine for a few short days.

I should have known the universe wouldn't allow me to be that happy.

11

SHE'D BEEN HERE. RANDALL LENZ DIDN'T KNOW precisely how he knew that, but standing on the sidewalk in the middle of the Plaza at the heart of Santa Fe's downtown and gazing at the buildings that circled it made a strange tingle start somewhere at the base of his neck.

Or maybe it was only the man who'd just walked past and sent a curious glance toward him over one shoulder. The stranger was dark, obviously Latin in heritage, maybe in his mid-thirties, well-dressed. Why he should have looked over at Lenz, who stood there with a phone in one hand and a brochure in the other, playing tourist, he had no idea.

But the man who'd walked past him a moment earlier wasn't the issue here. Dawson had run through the databases of the local hotels, and no one named "Addie Wilcox" or "Addie Grant" had been registered at any of them, but she could have provided a false name. That's what he would have done. And although she'd done her best to thwart his plans and make his life as complicated as possible over the past few days, he certainly couldn't accuse her of being stupid.

Well, that was where good old-fashioned legwork came in. His assistant had sent him another still image off the security camera feed from the gas station in St. George where Adara Grant and her mysterious companion had been first spotted, and Lenz brought it up on his phone so it would be easily available when he went to the first hotel and started asking questions.

The closest prospect was an imposing pueblo-style structure half a block to the south and east. *La Fonda,* he reminded himself, a Santa Fe landmark. He had his doubts that Adara would have stayed anywhere quite so upscale, but he had to start somewhere.

He waited for the signal to change so he could cross the street, then began walking purposefully toward his destination. Although the sidewalks were crowded with tourists, people got out of his way as he approached. No eye contact, just a quick sidestep and occasionally a mumbled "excuse me." He'd long ago learned that a quick stride and a steely gaze separated a crowd like Moses parting the Red Sea, and so his progress to the La Fonda was quick enough, despite the throngs of June visitors choking the area around the Plaza.

Inside the lobby of the hotel, it was slightly less crowded, but not by much. He'd had the bad luck to arrive a little after three o'clock, just when everyone was trying to check in. And although he supposed he could have brandished his Homeland Security I.D. and gone immediately to the head of the line, he decided it was probably better not to be quite so conspicuous.

Some ten minutes passed before he was finally able to approach one of the clerks, a man around his own age, slight and dark, with touches of premature gray at his temples. "Homeland Security," Lenz said, and flashed his badge.

The clerk blinked, but he sounded calm enough as he asked, "How can I help you, sir?"

"Have you seen this woman?" He held up his phone with the image of Adara Grant on the screen, and the man's brows drew together as he studied the photo.

"Yes, I have," he said. "She checked out yesterday morning."

Perfect. "Can you pull up her reservation?"

"She didn't have one."

Now it was Lenz's turn to blink. A sign of weakness, but he hadn't been able to stop himself. "How could she have stayed here if she didn't have a reservation?"

"I—" The man hesitated, then glanced over at the woman who stood at the station next to his, as if doing his best to make sure she was otherwise occupied and not listening to their conversation. "We usually have a couple of rooms on standby in case one of our more prominent clients needs to put up a guest. The woman in that photo stayed with us on that basis. We never had her name."

Her identity wasn't an issue. Lenz already knew who Adara was; he just needed to know where she'd gone. "Who arranged the room for her?"

Another sidelong glance, and then the clerk leaned forward and said in an undertone, "Mrs. Genoveva Castillo. Her family has had a standing arrangement with the hotel for decades, from what I've heard."

He'd never heard the name before. Who was this Genoveva Castillo, and why was she offering favors to Adara Grant?

"I'll need Mrs. Castillo's address…please," he said, tacking on the "please" so the clerk would know it had been a courtesy and nothing more.

The man moistened his lips. "I—I'm not sure—"

"This is a matter of national security," Lenz said

smoothly. "Now, I can get that address myself, but it would be quicker if you did it for me. Your choice if you decide not to cooperate."

"J-just a minute, sir." The clerk typed something into his computer, then said, "It's 12 Gonzalez Avenue. That's not too far from here, off Palace Road."

Excellent. "Thank you. You've just made your country a little safer."

Lenz turned and strode away from the front desk, people giving way before him just as they had out on the sidewalk a few moments earlier. He'd left his rental car on a side street a couple of blocks away, and so it didn't take much time before he was back behind the wheel, the nav system guiding him to the address the clerk had provided. As the man had said, the house in question wasn't far away at all, less than a quarter mile distant. If time hadn't been of the essence, Lenz might have walked.

But he couldn't afford to lose any more precious minutes, and so he drove over to the Castillo residence, an imposing hacienda-style house behind a high adobe wall. Clearly, this Genoveva person wasn't lacking in wealth; it made sense that she would have a standing reservation at the La Fonda for any unexpected guests who might need a place to stay.

However, that still didn't explain how she knew Adara Grant. While it was true that she and her mother had lived in New Mexico for a time, they'd been in Tucumcari, which was far to the east of Santa Fe, close to the Texas border, and Truth or Consequences, hundreds of miles south from where he stood. As far as he could tell, they'd never even visited the state's capitol, had stayed put in the small towns that were their temporary homes and hadn't ventured very far before they picked up stakes and moved on to their next destination.

He found himself frowning as he let himself in through the gate of the house on Gonzalez Avenue, and did his best to smooth his expression. Although he doubted Genoveva Castillo would be terribly cooperative—not when she'd been assisting Adara Grant in her flight to wherever she was headed—he didn't see any reason to start things off on the wrong foot, so to speak.

The front porch was as heavy and massive as the rest of the house, the ponderous impression it gave lessened somewhat by an assortment of terra-cotta pots planted with cheerful pansies and petunias that had been placed in various strategic locations. Lenz pressed the doorbell, wondering what he would do if it turned out no one was home. After all, it was a weekday afternoon, a time when most people could be reasonably expected to be at work.

However, the door opened soon after the doorbell rang, and a tall man who appeared to be around thirty, dark and clearly Latino, looked out at him.

He seemed somewhat surprised to be confronted by someone wearing a suit and obviously on official business, but he still smiled and said, "Can I help you?"

"Agent Randall Lenz, Homeland Security," Lenz replied, showing his badge. "Is Genoveva Castillo at home?"

The man frowned slightly. "Can I ask what this is about?"

"You can ask." Without waiting to see if that remark had sunk in, he went on, "I need to speak to Mrs. Castillo. Official business."

A brief hesitation, and then the man said, "Come in, Agent Lenz."

He stepped out of the way so Lenz could enter the house. It was clearly very old, but immaculately maintained. Flowers bloomed in a vase on the round table in the foyer, but he didn't have much time to take in any details, because the man who had answered the door led him down a short hallway and into an enormous living room with a massive fireplace at one end and a series of windows that overlooked the gardens.

Sitting on the velvet-upholstered sofa in front of those windows was a dark-haired woman. She rose from the couch as he entered the room, and gave him a very direct look. "I am Genoveva Castillo. What is it you want, Agent Lenz?"

How had she known his name? He hadn't seen

the man take a phone out of his pocket or use an intercom or anything like that, so Lenz couldn't quite figure out how she'd become privy to that particular piece of information.

But then he supposed she must have overheard his conversation with the man who'd answered the door, even though he would have guessed they were too far away for their voices to be audible. He put the mystery aside and focused on the woman in front of him, somewhat surprised that she should be so young, probably around nine or ten years his junior. And extremely attractive as well, with lustrous black hair pulled up into an elegant twist at the back of her head, large dark eyes, and a full mouth enhanced by a light coating of lipstick.

He realized he was staring and said, "Did you recently put up a guest at the La Fonda Hotel?"

"I have used the hotel for out-of-town visitors," she replied, a response that didn't exactly answer his question.

"A clerk there said you had a young woman stay the other night in one of the rooms reserved for special patrons like yours. This woman, actually."

He pulled his phone out of his pocket and approached Genoveva so she could see the image of Adara Grant on its screen. For the briefest moment, her gaze slipped past him and went to the man who'd escorted him inside. Her husband? Probably;

they made a good pair, both tall and slim and handsome, Hispanic like so many of Santa Fe's residents.

But then she looked down at the screen, and her mouth turned up in a slight smile. "Ah, I can see why there might be some confusion. As a matter of fact, I did have my cousin Elisa visiting briefly on her way to Taos, and she does resemble this woman. But they're not the same person."

Just a little too convenient that she'd have a relative who so closely resembled Adara Grant. He asked, "I don't suppose you have a photo of this 'Elisa,' do you?"

"Actually, yes, I do." She glanced across the room to her husband, who'd remained standing a few paces away. "Eduardo, would you mind going to my office and fetching me the family album? The one with the green cover—I think I left it on the side table."

"Of course," he replied. "Just a minute."

He headed back out to the hallway, presumably to get the album she'd requested. Genoveva's dark gaze flicked back to Lenz. "I'm afraid I'm not being a very good hostess," she said, her smile now almost apologetic. "Would you like to sit down, Agent Lenz? I can get you some lemonade, or would you prefer iced tea?"

"No, I'm fine," he told her.

Most women her age would have blinked or at least appeared slightly flustered at such an outright refusal of their hospitality. Genoveva, however, only nodded and remained standing as well, hands placed on her hips, that same faint smile playing around her lips. He knew nothing about her, and yet she definitely had the air of someone who was comfortable in her own position, and most likely used to having other people do as she asked.

Well, he supposed that quality wasn't so strange in someone who obviously possessed a good deal of wealth. Was it hers, or had it come from her husband? Judging by the way she'd sent him to get the photo album and he'd acceded to her wishes with nary a protest, Lenz had a feeling the money— and the power—were all Genoveva's.

Poor bastard.

Eduardo returned, a large green photo album in his hands. However, he was smiling as he handed it over to his wife, and there was no mistaking the warmth in her gaze as she thanked him, their eyes meeting for a moment in the sort of look that was almost uncomfortable to watch.

Someone else might have thought, *Get a room,* but Lenz only stood silently as Genoveva leafed through the photo album and then paused. "Here's a photo of my cousin Elisa," she said. "She's the one in the middle. You can see why the clerk at the hotel might have been a little confused."

He stepped over to her and looked down at the picture she'd indicated. It showed a trio of young women, all of whom appeared to be in their early twenties, dark-haired, pretty. The one in the center of the group had a smooth oval face and wide blue eyes, a contrast to the dark eyes of her two companions. She was smiling broadly—an expression he'd never seen on Adara Grant's face—but even so, he could see how closely this Elisa resembled her, although there were minor points of difference. Adara's hair was dark brown, while Elisa's was nearly black, and Adara's chin slightly more pointed, her mouth not quite as wide. Still, if he hadn't spent hours scrutinizing Adara Grant's countenance as it stared up at him from the various file photos they'd collected on her, he had to admit he probably wouldn't have noticed those subtle differences.

And if he had been unable to distinguish such fine details, then he very much doubted the clerk at the La Fonda would have detected them, either. Probably, the man had interacted with this Elisa person for a moment or two at the very most, if even that much. After all, since she'd been staying there as Genoveva Castillo's guest, she wouldn't have had to provide a credit card or a driver's license to check in.

"Yes, they are remarkably similar," Lenz agreed. A sudden thought occurred to him, and he asked, "Your cousin has already checked out of the hotel?"

"Hours ago," Genoveva replied. "I'm sure she's

already in Taos by now. But if you think you need to speak to her, then I can give her a call."

For a moment, he considered calling her bluff— if it was even that. She seemed completely calm and assured, and certainly displayed none of the tells he might have expected from someone who was lying to a federal agent. Maybe she was just that good a liar, but he doubted it.

No, it seemed much more likely that he'd been following the wrong lead. "No need for that, ma'am," he said. "It was an honest mistake, but I'm sorry to have bothered you."

"No bother. I'm always glad to help."

Those words were accompanied by another smile, one that didn't flicker. Lenz nodded and said, "I'll just show myself out."

"Have a good day, Agent Lenz."

He returned the sentiment, tilted his head in acknowledgment toward Eduardo Castillo, and then went down the hall, through the foyer, and out onto the porch. Once there, with the warm breeze ruffling his hair, he looked back at the house with narrowed eyes, then shook his head.

Time to start inquiring at the other hotels. He had a suspicion that it would all be a wasted effort, except he still couldn't shake the feeling in his bones that Adara Grant had come through Santa Fe. Why here, and where she'd gone afterward, he didn't know.

He was beginning to wonder if he'd ever find out.

~

Jake's cell phone rang at a little past three o'clock, just as he was passing a Utah town on Highway 90 with the crazy name of Panguitch. Who or what a Panguitch was, he had no idea; he was just glad that soon he'd be on I-15 and able to get up to a decent cruising speed of seventy-five miles an hour.

A glance down at the screen told him it was Connor calling, and for a second or two, he wondered if he should ignore the phone and let the call roll over to voicemail. For all he knew, Jeremy had decided to rat him out to the *primus,* and Connor was reaching out to tell Jake he was on a fool's errand and that he needed to turn around and come straight back to Flagstaff.

However, issuing commands really didn't seem like Connor's style, so after a brief hesitation, Jake picked up the phone. Technically, he should have patched it through the truck's Bluetooth system, but he'd been in such a hurry to get on the road that morning, he hadn't bothered to do much of anything except double-check the adjustment of the mirrors and the seat. Jeremy had already threatened him with bodily injury if anything should happen to his truck, but Jake very much doubted anything was going to go wrong. He'd hit some clotty traffic here and there, but on the whole, everyone on the roads seemed pretty well-behaved. Besides, the big Dodge Ram wasn't even two years old yet, and barely had ten thousand miles on the odometer. Jeremy was just being paranoid.

"Hey, Connor," Jake said, sending a couple of quick glances to either side at the traffic surrounding him to make sure there weren't any state troopers or local cops lurking nearby who might feel inclined to give him a ticket for ignoring the hands-free law. "What's up?"

Connor sounded less than amused. "'What's up' is that I just got a call from Genoveva Castillo."

"Really? Why?"

"Agent Lenz just paid her a visit. Somehow, he managed to track Addie to Santa Fe."

Shit. Trying to sound calm, Jake asked, "Genoveva didn't tell him anything, did she?"

"Of course not. She fobbed him off with some story about having a cousin who looked just like her, and he bought it."

"*Does* she have a cousin like that?"

"No. It was some sort of an illusion she cast on a family photo album she had lying around. Luckily, he didn't seem to see anything strange about her story, and he left. After that, he went around town, trying to track Addie down, but according to Genoveva's spies, he didn't have any luck. He left after that—I guess a private jet picked him up at the Santa Fe airport."

Jake reflected that the spy network of a witch clan definitely surpassed any modern surveillance systems. No matter what might be going on in a clan's territory, there was generally someone around to witness it and pass the information along. "So, we're in the clear."

"No, 'we' are definitely not in the clear. Genoveva was just a little pissed off to have her home invaded by someone from Homeland Security, but I talked her down."

"Then, no harm, no foul."

Connor let out a gust of a breath. "Jake, you can't act like this is no big deal. You know we're all about avoiding outside scrutiny. If we've suddenly got federal agents crawling up our asses, then it's a problem."

Although he supposed he could see why Connor might view the situation that way, Jake thought it was far more useful to look on the bright side. "Only if they find something…which they won't. You just said that Lenz left Santa Fe empty-handed. I assume he didn't have any other leads to follow."

"No, because Jeremy made sure to scrub the local traffic-cam footage of all data involving Addie."

Which Jake had already known would happen, but it was good to have confirmation from Connor, just the same. "Then Lenz is back to square one, while I'm already more than halfway to Riverton."

"About that...."

"What?" Jake asked, his tone sharpening. "It's a little late to order me to turn around."

"You know I don't 'order' anyone to do anything." Connor paused for a second or two, then went on, "No, it's just that you need to tread carefully when you get where you're going. For one thing, you don't even know for sure that Addie will be there at all. And second—well, you may not exactly be greeted with open arms by the local tribe. Things are pretty chill between the Navajo and the Wilcoxes, but that's because we've been living side by side for almost a hundred and fifty years. But there aren't any witches in Wyoming, and they might not be too happy to have you show up and start wagging your dick around."

"I'm not going to be 'wagging my dick,'" Jake retorted. Seriously, did Connor think he was a complete moron? "I'm just going to find Addie. I don't plan to stay there any longer than I have to. And I'm fine with explaining that to any tribal elders or whoever it might be that has a problem with me being there."

"Okay, okay," Connor said, obviously guessing that his cousin wasn't too thrilled with being treated like a total rube who didn't understand the delicate nature of the situation. "Just wanted to make sure we were on the same page." He hesitated again before asking, "Have you figured out what you're going to say to Addie?"

"Working on it." Which was only the truth; there'd been a lot of empty miles along Highway 89 where he didn't have much else to do with his time than mentally rehearse the speech he wanted to deliver to Addie, the one where he was loving and persuasive and also completely understanding of the reasons why she'd left in the first place. Whether any of those artfully crafted sentences would actually stick in his brain once he saw her face to face, he had no idea.

"Okay. Just one more thing."

"What?" He was coming up on the turn-off for Highway 20, which he needed to take to meet up with I-15 and head north along his intended route, and he really didn't need Connor distracting him at some critical juncture.

"It might not mean anything, but Genoveva told me something sort of odd. She said when she first met Randall Lenz, it was almost as though she felt the tingle she always gets when she meets a new witch or warlock, but then it was gone so quickly, she wondered if she was imagining things."

That was weird. Not that he thought of Genoveva Castillo as the sort of person to rattle easily, but she must have been off-balance by having a federal agent in her home. Jake knew that when he'd first encountered Agent Lenz, he sure as hell hadn't experienced anything like that telltale "tingle," and he guessed that Addie would have said something to him once he'd explained to her what it felt like to meet someone of witch-kind for the first time.

He said as much to Connor, who responded, "Yeah, that was sort of what I figured. It would be one thing if you'd never met the guy, but...."

"Well, we all did, didn't we?" Jake said. "I mean, we were all at the cottage with him after Addie zapped him with that lightning bolt, and none of us felt anything."

"Right. I almost forgot about that. Yeah, it must have been something going on with Genoveva. Anyway, I'll let you go. You're still planning to drive straight through to Riverton?"

"Yep. I've got about six hours left—and I'm just about to get to my turn-off, so I need to go."

"No worries. Good luck with everything."

Connor ended the call there, and Jake set the phone back in the cupholder. That little tidbit about Randall Lenz was sort of strange, but not anything they probably needed to worry about. No, the far more important detail was that he'd already gotten on a plane and was headed back to Virginia, and therefore was someone else's problem...at least for the time being.

The next few miles needed Jake's full concentration, because Highway 20 turned out to be pretty damn twisty as it cut through the hills on its way to I-15, but in less than half an hour, he was on the interstate and headed north. The higher speed limit lifted his spirits; eighty miles an hour made him feel like he was quickly eating up the distance between himself and Addie.

If she was even in Riverton at all. He knew he was currently making a pretty big leap of faith, but he pushed any doubts out of his mind. It was all going to be fine.

As he was approaching the outskirts of Provo, figuring he'd stop to refuel there and take a bathroom break, his borrowed truck stalled as he was cruising along in the fast lane at just a hair over eighty. Cursing, he took his foot off the gas and pressed the "Start" button, hoping that might reset things. But the Ram didn't respond, only continued to lose speed. He had power—the dashboard displays and stereo were still working—but the engine appeared to be dead in the water.

Luckily, traffic wasn't so thick that he couldn't manage to guide the damn thing over to the right shoulder, where he drifted to a stop. After putting on the hazard lights, he got out his phone and his Triple-A card, and dialed the 800 number. They promised a tow truck would be out to pick him up in less than twenty minutes, which gave him plenty of time to call Jeremy and bitch him out.

"Your goddamn truck died on me right in the middle of I-15," he said without preamble when his brother answered the call.

"And that's my fault?" Jeremy responded, sounding unruffled. "I just had it serviced a month ago. It's fine."

"Well, it's not fine now. I'm sitting on the side of the interstate outside Provo, waiting for a tow truck."

A pause, and his brother said, "Hey, at least it died somewhere close to civilization. It could have been worse."

True—the truck could have croaked somewhere off Highway 89 in the middle of nowhere—but Jake was in no mood to be pacified with platitudes. "I don't have time for this," he growled.

"Cool your jets, dude. I'm sure the local dealership will get you fixed right up."

Probably, but how long would that take? It was already past four-thirty; by the time the tow truck showed up and took the crippled Ram to whatever Dodge/Chrysler/Jeep dealership was closest, he'd be lucky to slide in under the wire and get it logged in before the service department closed for the day.

However, he didn't bother to point all that out to his brother, since Jeremy could tell time as well as anyone else and probably had already realized that this little delay was going to force him to stay overnight in Provo...if he was lucky. If whatever had happened to the truck was major enough, he could be stuck there for a few days.

But then Jake glanced up into the rearview mirror and saw the tow truck approaching, and figured that was his cue to hang up before his bickering with Jeremy devolved any further. "Tow truck's here—gotta go," he said briefly, and ended the call.

To his relief, the driver was entirely professional, and got the crippled Ram truck hooked up and ready to roll right away. In less than ten minutes, Jake was in the service office at the local Dodge dealership and doing his best to explain the situation. Luckily, no one questioned why he was driving his brother's truck, or why they had two different last names, although he'd been prepared with a cover story if it had turned out to be necessary.

Most likely, the main reason why he wasn't grilled about the whole thing was because it turned out that model year of truck had been recalled for the very same mechanical problem which had left him stranded on the side of I-15. Why Jeremy hadn't gotten the damn truck fixed, Jake didn't know, although he guessed that he probably hadn't gotten the recall notice due to his move—he'd bought the truck while still living at home, nearly a year before his purchase of the townhouse where he currently lived.

"We should have you back on the road sometime tomorrow afternoon," the service tech, a guy named Adam, told him. "Sorry about the inconvenience."

"It's okay," Jake said, even though of course it wasn't. But it wasn't Adam's fault the truck had crapped out on him—and, as Jeremy had pointed out, better for it to have died near civilization than any of the boondocks he'd driven through on Highway 89 before reaching the interstate. "Don't suppose you know if there are any nearby hotels."

"There's one across the street," Adam replied. He was probably about ten years older than Jake, with light brown hair that was already thinning and the kind of fair skin that turned ruddy with too much exposure to the sun and wind. "A Wyndham something-or-other. Anyway, you can walk over there and see if they have any rooms available. If not, we've got Uber—you should be able to have one take you to a different hotel if this one doesn't work out."

"Thanks," Jake said, hoping the hotel across the street would have something for him and that he wouldn't have to search any further. At least if he was staying this close, then he could be at the dealership right away as soon as the work on the truck was finished.

Adam nodded, and repeated his reassurance that someone would call when the truck was ready. Jake headed out, took a quick glance around, and then went to the nearest light so he could use the crosswalk to get to the other side of the street. Traffic was thick on University Avenue, the thoroughfare that went past the dealership, and he knew he didn't dare jaywalk. Or rather, while he knew his own telekinetic power would allow him to shove a marauding car out of the way if necessary, he doubted that putting on such a display in the middle of Provo's rush hour was a very good idea.

It turned out the hotel did have a couple of rooms available, so he checked in—paying cash, and using the same story about waiting on his debit card that he'd given the front desk clerk at Treasure Island in Las Vegas—and then went upstairs to his room. No point in really unpacking; he dropped his duffle bag on the luggage rack in the closet, dug out his toiletry kit and put it in the bathroom, and then wondered if five-thirty was too early to go in search of dinner.

Probably. However, he figured he could at least try to figure out where to grab something, so he got out his phone. He'd just unlocked it when it began to ring.

Jeremy again.

"Good news," he said, speaking quickly, as if he wanted to make sure Jake wouldn't have a chance to say anything. "She's there."

Despite his annoyance with his brother, Jake

experienced a surge of relief. "Addie? She's in Riverton?"

"Yep. I figured I'd start checking around, see what kind of surveillance they've got in town. Which turns out not to be much—they don't even have traffic cams—but of course, the local casino has cameras everywhere. She's working there."

"At the casino?" That news startled him. All right, he supposed he should have guessed she would start looking for work wherever she landed, but he hadn't thought it would happen so quickly. Then again, she'd told him she'd been working as a waitress in Kanab, so she probably wouldn't have had too much trouble finding a position.

"Yeah. Wind River Casino. Looks like she's a bar server—you know, the people who bring you drinks while you're playing the slot machines or whatever."

Jake did know—not because he made a habit of gambling, which had never been his thing, but because he'd gone with Sarah one time to the Twin Arrows resort and casino, located about twenty miles east of Flagstaff, just so they could check out the place. Being a bar server looked like hard work, but it was honest enough, and he figured the tips must be pretty good.

"And that's why you don't need to stress about the truck," Jeremy continued. "She has a job, which means she's probably not planning to go anywhere. And now you know exactly where to find her."

"But that means Lenz might be able to find her, too."

"Maybe, but how's he going to know where to look? We already had a pretty good idea of where she might have been headed. Lenz doesn't have that kind of information. Right now, he doesn't know where she is. I'm not saying he couldn't eventually track her down, but he's not going to do it right away."

Jake hoped his brother was right. And while he guessed that yes, Addie appeared to have already put down some roots in Riverton, that didn't mean she might not bolt if something spooked her. He still was going to get on the road as soon as that damn truck was ready to roll.

"True," he said, but his tone sounded grudging even to himself. "Even so, after the way he found her in Flagstaff, I'm not going to take anything for granted."

"Not saying you should," Jeremy replied. "Just don't give yourself an ulcer, okay? And call me tomorrow once you're back on the road."

If I'm back on the road, he thought darkly, but he didn't bother to utter that pessimistic notion out loud. He'd already been dogged by enough bad luck over the past few days; he wasn't about to give fate an open invitation to rain more crap on his head.

Hope for the best and prepare for the worst... and he sincerely hoped that "worst" was just the truck breaking down, and that nothing even more terrible was lurking in the near future, just waiting for the chance to derail his plans that much further.

"I'll call," he promised, and left it there.

At the moment, there wasn't much else he could do.

12

I didn't run into Carson during my next day's shift—I had a feeling he didn't make a habit of hanging around the casino, and had only been there so he could speak with me in private—but I still was far more cheerful than I'd been the day before. Already, I found myself falling into a rhythm, starting to recognize a few patrons who were obviously regulars. I had my own feelings about gambling, about people spending money they quite possibly didn't have on an activity that seemed frivolous at best to me, but I knew it wasn't my place to comment or judge. No, I just tried to smile and be friendly, to make sure I got everyone their drinks in a timely manner. And actually, about half my customers weren't drinking alcohol at all, but iced tea or sodas or sparkling mineral water.

It also felt good to know that I wouldn't be

going home to a hotel room after work, but to a real house. For the first time in my life, I had a place all to myself, something that was truly my own. Okay, I was renting, and so technically, the house belonged to Tracy, and yet simply knowing the place was all mine made a little thrill go through me. The night before, I'd slept better than I had since I'd left Kanab, even better than I had at Jake's house, despite how comfortable the bed in his guest room had been.

But I didn't want to think about Jake, or about what might have happened between the two of us if I'd stayed in Flagstaff. The reason I was coping at the moment was because I'd allowed myself to put him away, to lock all the memories of the time we'd spent together in a hidden little compartment somewhere in the back of my mind. Otherwise, it would all have hurt too much, and with the rest of my life beginning to look up, I didn't want to let that pain in. I had to hope that sooner or later, my interlude with Jake would begin to fade, like a piece of newspaper left out in the sun, and eventually it wouldn't have any more power over me than the blurred and faded newsprint of a story that might once have held some relevance but could no longer inflict any wounds on my psyche.

Blake was a lot more subdued that second night; I didn't know whether Jeannine had once again told him to behave himself, or whether maybe word had gotten around to Leona that he was showing just a little too much interest in the new bar server than was strictly professional. Either way, while he seemed friendly enough and definitely got my drinks prepped quickly, he didn't appear too inclined to try engaging me in conversation.

And I told myself that was fine. While I hoped that one day I'd be ready to try romance again, I knew I shouldn't be in any hurry. And even if I'd wanted to jump right in with someone new, I knew it wouldn't have been very smart to enter into a relationship with someone who was a co-worker. If things didn't work out, it could be awkward, to say the least.

Eleven o'clock rolled around, and I allowed myself a grateful sigh. Once again, my shift had passed more quickly than I could have hoped, but no matter how well work might have been going, after spending almost eight hours on my feet, I was ready to call it a day, go home and have a snack, and crash for the night before getting up to do it all over again the next afternoon.

I'd just brought a couple of rum and Cokes to a pair of older ladies who seemed determined to sit at the slot machines until the witching hour when I heard a voice I thought I'd never hear again.

"Addie."

Thank God the tray I held was empty, or I probably would have spilled drinks all over the floor.

Jake Wilcox stood a few feet away, watching me. His cheeks and chin were covered with dark stubble, as if he hadn't bothered to shave since I'd fled Flagstaff, and he wore a leather jacket over a T-shirt and jeans. Looking at the chiseled symmetry of his face, the thick dark hair that made me want to run my fingers through it, I wondered how I'd ever thought Blake the bartender was cute.

Somehow, I managed to respond, even though my hands shook and my heart had started to pound like I'd just run a marathon. "J-Jake? What are you doing here?"

Those dark eyes never left mine. "I could ask you the same thing."

Shit. I clutched the plastic tray I held, hoping that might ease the trembling in my fingers, and glanced around. No one seemed to be paying any attention to me, but I still had almost forty-five minutes left in my shift. I couldn't stand there and have that particular conversation with him. Not on the floor of the Wind River Casino.

"I'm off at midnight," I said, my voice almost preternaturally calm. "We can talk then."

He hesitated, and for one awful moment, I feared he might try to make a scene. But then he appeared to realize that attracting attention in such a public place was the last thing he should do, and he gave a reluctant nod. "I'm not much on gambling, but I can hang."

Actually, I had a better idea…or at least, an idea that didn't involve Jake Wilcox loitering on the casino floor and making me even more distracted than I already was. "Why don't you go and wait at my place?" I said. "It's only five minutes from here."

That suggestion earned me a pained look. "What, you have a 'place' already?"

"Well, I didn't want to spend the rest of my life at a Fairfield Inn," I shot back, and he appeared to relent.

"Okay, fine. Where is it?"

I told him the address, and he nodded, not bothering to put it in his phone. Maybe he thought it was safer that way.

Actually, I was inclined to agree.

"I'll be there a little after midnight," I promised him, and after another pause, during which my already thumpy heart decided to speed up in worry, he shrugged.

"Okay. I'll see you then."

To my relief, he turned and headed for one of the exits, and I told my heart I was way too young for a thrombosis. Trying to act natural, I picked up a couple of drink orders and went back to the bar.

"Who was that guy?" Blake asked, straight black bars of brows drawing together. So much for acting casual; right then, he looked as if he could have cheerfully picked up a bow and arrow and shot Jake right through the heart.

"A friend," I said, and left it there, hoping Blake would get the hint.

Of course, he didn't. "I thought you were new in town."

"I am," I replied. "He's a friend from where I used to live."

"Oh."

"Anyway," I went on in quelling tones, "I need a greyhound, a vodka rocks, and a shot of Cuervo gold."

Blake's eyes narrowed, but to my relief, he didn't push it, only said, "Okay. Give me a minute."

I waited while he prepped the drinks, then took them to my waiting customers. Right then, I didn't know whether to be relieved that the casino didn't have any visible clocks—the management obviously didn't want the patrons to know how many hours they were spending at the slot machines or the blackjack tables—or glad that I couldn't tell exactly how much time was passing.

But pass it did, although by the time midnight finally arrived, I thought I might dance out of my skin from sheer antsiness. I hadn't bungled anything too badly during the last forty-five minutes of my shift, although I almost gave a teetotaling 7-Up-drinking older couple the pair of seven-and-sevens that were supposed to go to the man and woman playing slots down the next aisle. They assured me it was fine, but I still told myself I needed to get my act together. This early in my tenure at the casino, I simply couldn't afford to make any mistakes.

I wished Jeannine a good night—Blake had already disappeared, thank God—and hurried out to my car. The night air was cool, with a fresh wind blowing out of the north, carrying with it the scent of dry grass. Like so much of this part of the country, Riverton was waiting for the arrival of the summer rains to wet down the prairies and fill the creeks and waterways.

However, I couldn't distract myself with thoughts of the weather and the time of year, not when I had Jake waiting for me back at the little house I'd just rented. I would have been asking myself how he'd managed to find me, but when you had someone like his brother Jeremy on your team, a lot of what might have seemed impossible became downright easy.

At least, I hoped Jake was in town because Jeremy was just that good at tracking down the seemingly untrackable, and not because I'd left a trail behind me that anyone with half a brain could have discovered. Otherwise, I might have Randall Lenz on my doorstep in the not-too-distant future.

That thought made a shiver go down my spine, although I tried to reassure myself that Genoveva would never have given my position away. Besides, if Agent Lenz actually knew where I was, he would have been in Riverton already. I had enough to deal with at the moment; manufacturing fake crises when I'd just had a real one dropped in my lap seemed like an extremely bad use of my time.

Maybe it was a good thing that Jake and I had seen each other first at the casino, if only because having to behave ourselves in such a public place had taken some of the rough edges off such an encounter. As I drove, I wished I had a longer commute, just because that would have given me more time to get my thoughts in order. I supposed I should have come up with a plan for just such an eventuality, but I'd hoped he wouldn't be able to find me at all, or, even if he'd managed to track me down at some point, enough time would have elapsed that it might have given us the perspective we needed to approach the situation like rational adults.

But he was clearly angry, and that frightened me. Not because I feared he would lash out and hurt me physically—maybe I didn't know him well, but I still knew Jake wasn't that sort of person—but because I simply didn't have enough experience with romantic relationships to know how best to manage his anger. My mother and I had bickered, of course, just like almost any mother and daughter might from time to time. This wasn't the same thing, though…not at all.

I turned onto my street and slowed so I could pull into the driveway and park the Fiat in the carport out back. There was a big silver pickup truck in front of the house, and I thought it looked vaguely familiar. Had I seen it parked out in front of their headquarters by Wheeler Park? Maybe it was Jeremy's, and Jake had borrowed it for this particular road trip. Actually, that particular arrangement made sense, considering how conspicuous that Jeep Gladiator of his had turned out to be.

A light showed in the front window; obviously, Jake had already let himself in. That was one handy thing about being a witch or a warlock—you didn't have to worry about loaning someone your house key, since they could use their innate magical powers to get inside.

I took a breath, then another, and made myself get out of the car and walk toward the front door. It would have been faster to come in through the back door, which opened into the kitchen, but I thought it might be playing dirty to suddenly appear in the opposite direction from where Jake was expecting me to arrive.

When I opened the front door, I saw him sitting on the couch, looking down at something on his phone. However, he glanced up as soon as I entered the house, then shoved his phone back in his pocket. A glass of water sat on a coaster on the coffee table. He must have noted the way my gaze moved in that direction, because he said quickly, "I got myself some water. Hope that was okay."

"Of course," I said, an automatic reply. Not that I was going to begrudge him a glass of water. Honestly, since I hadn't gone to the store yet, it was about all I could offer a guest anyway. I set my purse on the little table next to the armchair and then went and sat down, my hands in my lap.

"It's nice," he said next. "The house, I mean."

His tone was almost surprised, as if he hadn't expected me to land on my feet quite so easily. I could have pointed out that I had tons of experience starting over in new places, but I also had to admit I had sort of lucked into my current living arrangement.

"Thanks," I replied, and decided I might as well leave it at that.

It was so hard to sit there and make myself look at him. I wanted to hang my head, to start blabbing apologies for why I'd left him like that, no letter, no goodbye, no nothing. He was so damn handsome… but also tired, shadows under his eyes, fine chin covered in stubble.

I'd done that to him.

He spoke then, voice quiet but also hard, unyielding as the granite peaks that had loomed on either side of the highway as I drove through Colorado. "So, do you want to explain yourself? You take off in the middle of the night, no discussion, not even a goddamn note. Did you think I didn't deserve even that much consideration?"

I winced, my fingers digging into the arms of the paisley-patterned chair where I sat. "I didn't want to hurt you—"

"But you did. And you had to have known how it would look, disappearing like that."

"I know." I swallowed a breath and wished I'd gone to fetch myself a glass of water. My throat felt dry and scratchy as sandpaper. I told myself to be strong, to face him and be honest. He deserved that. "I was scared, Jake," I said, making myself look at him, forcing myself to acknowledge the pain in his expression. "After—after seeing how Agent Lenz found me, I knew if I stayed in Flagstaff, he'd just keep coming after me. I couldn't put the rest of you in danger like that."

"We took care of Lenz," he shot back, voice almost a rasp. He reached for his water and took a swallow. "We scrubbed his memories, dumped him back in Kanab. As far as we can tell, he still doesn't know what happened to him."

"Jeremy's tracking him?"

Jake nodded. "Yeah."

"Has he quit?" I asked then. "Given up on me and moved on to the next project?"

Silence then. A muscle in his jaw twitched, giving me the only answer I needed.

"So, he hasn't quit."

A long pause. At last, Jake responded, "No. He went to Santa Fe, but even though he was able to figure out that Genoveva Castillo had put you up at the La Fonda, she stonewalled him, and, as far as any of us can tell, he's back to square one. He doesn't know you're here."

"Then running away worked."

His gaze met mine, eyes dark, unreadable. I might have been looking at the face of a stranger right then, rather than a man I'd laughed with, cried with, who'd kissed me in a way that made me think I'd never want to kiss anyone else. Voice flat, he said, "Running away never works, Addie. Sooner or later, all the things you don't want to face will eventually catch up with you."

A bitter laugh escaped my lips before I could hold it back. "What, then? You think I'm supposed to confront Agent Lenz and what…kill him? Because that's the only thing I can think of that'll keep him from coming after me."

"I didn't say that."

"What's your solution, then?"

Jake's fingers knotted together. I could see the muscles standing out on his forearms, see the tension in his entire body. "I don't know," he said at last. "But I know we're much better off facing this together than you being here in the middle of nowhere with a bunch of strangers who have no reason to offer you any help if the worst should happen."

A day earlier, I would have been inclined to

agree with him. After my conversation with Carson Archuleta, however, I knew I wasn't quite as alone in Riverton as Jake thought. Would he believe me if I told him that?

"I'm not completely on my own," I said quietly. "The head of the local tribe basically said he'd have my back if Randall Lenz or any of his goons came sniffing around."

That piece of information seemed to surprise Jake, judging by the way his eyebrows lifted slightly, but he didn't try to tell me I must be mistaken. Instead, he sat there for a moment, considering my words.

"That was kind of him," he said after a pause. "But even if they're willing to help, those people aren't your family. You've got family who're willing to look after you. Why is it so much harder to accept their assistance?"

Because they are *my family,* I thought then. *I'm too personally involved, even if I haven't met most of them yet.* But to think I could put Angela and Connor in danger, or Laurel, or Jeremy or Joanna or any of those hundreds of Wilcoxes who were bound to me through blood, in harm's way? I didn't want to contemplate what Randall Lenz might do to any of them, if he were to find out they'd done their best to hide me from him…if he somehow managed to discover that they, too, possessed unique and valuable gifts.

No, better to stay safely far, far away.

"They've already done enough," I replied, suddenly feeling exhausted, realizing I just didn't have the emotional or physical stores of energy to deal with all this after a long shift at the casino. On top of that, my body hadn't adjusted to its new schedule yet, and clearly thought I should have been in bed by that hour. Right then, I was just bone tired.

Jake's expression hardened. "Do you think *I've* already done enough?"

"I…I don't know. I don't know what you expect me to do!" I burst out then, my fragile calm beginning to shake apart. "I'm tired and I'm scared, and I just want to sleep for a hundred years. Maybe then this will all be over by the time I wake up."

My hands were shaking, fingers trembling as I tried to push a lock of hair back behind one ear. At once, Jake got up from the sofa and came over to me. To my surprise, he knelt on the rug in front of the chair where I sat and took my hands in his, holding them tightly so I could feel how warm and strong his touch was. Just that sensation, so familiar even though we'd only held hands a couple of times, was enough to send a shudder of need through me.

"I'm here, Addie," he said, voice low and earnest. "How could you think I would let you go without a fight?"

"Is that what this is?" I whispered. "A fight?"

Jake shook his head, expression now one of frustration. "No. I don't want to fight with you. But you have to understand—" He stopped there, mouth tight.

Somehow, I got the feeling that there was something else going on than just our personal differences. "I have to understand what?"

"It's not just you," he replied in an undertone, almost as if he was worried that someone might be listening to our conversation, although we were utterly alone in the house and—if the dark windows in the homes on my street were any indication—anyone in the immediate vicinity was long since asleep.

I stared at him, not sure what he meant by those words. Usually, that sort of comment was followed by, *it's me,* and yet I had a feeling that hadn't been his intention.

"Jeremy got into Lenz's laptop, and then into the servers at his agency," Jake went on. "Lenz has been collecting specimens like you for at least three years now, maybe longer."

"'Like me'?" I echoed, a dawning horror wakening inside as I began to realize what he must have meant. "Other weather-workers?"

"No…other witches and warlocks. Their talents seem to range all over the place, from what we can tell. But he has them locked up at a facility somewhere in Virginia."

"'Them,'" I repeated, forcing the unwelcome word through my reluctant brain. "How many?"

"Fourteen."

Fourteen. Fourteen people being held like lab rats, or guinea pigs. I still didn't know exactly what Randall Lenz planned to do with me once he had me in custody, and I was pretty sure I really didn't want to know. "That's…terrible."

"I know. And the reason I'm telling you this is that you need to understand that what Lenz was doing…it wasn't personal. You were just another specimen to add to his collection. So, I have no reason to believe that he won't give up after a while and go looking for the next witch or warlock who pops up on his radar."

In a way, that theory made some sense. On the other hand…. "And I'm supposed to be glad about that?"

Jake's fingers tightened on mine. "No, of course not. But I wanted you to know it's not like he's Ahab and you're the white whale or something."

Despite the grimness of the situation, I couldn't help smiling at that particular metaphor. "Gee, thanks."

"You know what I mean."

And yes, I did. Or at least, I thought I understood what Jake was trying to say to me. While Lenz wanted me in his zoo—or whatever you wanted to call it—I certainly wasn't his sole target. "So, what…I'm just supposed to ride this out until he moves on, and then I can go back to Flagstaff and pretend none of it ever happened?"

"I'm not saying that." He let go of my hands and stood up, brushing at the knees of his jeans. "What I am saying is that you should be able to look forward to a time when he isn't a concern anymore."

I wanted to believe that. At the same time, I couldn't help feeling a bit disgusted with myself for being all right with the idea of Agent Lenz locking up more witches and warlocks…as long as I was no longer the target. But obviously, I wasn't okay with it—I just didn't know what the hell I was supposed to do to help those poor people who were already his captives.

Jake reached out and pushed a lock of hair away from my face, and I wanted to weep at the tenderness of the gesture. What had I ever done to deserve a guy like him?

"It's okay, Addie," he said. "It's going to be okay."

"Is it?" I asked, more because I needed some kind of reassurance right then—even if it might turn out to be false—than because I actually thought the situation could get better.

"I found you, didn't I?"

I nodded, not trusting myself to speak.

"I want to kiss you," he said quietly. "Is that okay?"

Probably not. Or rather, even though I knew that reopening any intimacies between us was fraught with its own set of problems, I just didn't have the strength right then to say no. I wanted to feel his lips on mine, his arms around me. It had been easy to pretend I could forget him and move on when I didn't have him around, but now he was there, just inches away, I knew that had been a fool's dream. Right then, he felt as inevitable as the sun rising in the east every morning.

I whispered, "It's okay."

He bent and touched his mouth to mine, gently at first, barely a brush of lips against lips, and then our mouths opened and we were tasting one another, bodies pressed together, the kiss deepening with an almost feverish intensity. Oh, God, how I'd needed this. In that moment, I understood that I couldn't live without Jake. We were still so new to each other, and at the same time, we seemed to understand the other person in a way that only came after years in a relationship together. You could call it witchy chemistry, or fate, or plain old-fashioned lust. I didn't know; I only knew right then that I might as well tell the earth to stop spinning than tell myself I could live without Jake Wilcox. Both statements would have been equally untrue.

Eventually, he pulled away, gaze earnest as he

stared down at me. I wasn't sure what to say. If he stayed much longer, I knew where this would end up—the two of us together in my bed. Maybe that wouldn't have been such a bad thing. At the same time, though, I wanted that first experience with him to be special, not when I was tired and worried and not sure where all this was going to end up.

"You can sleep on the couch," I blurted out, and his eyes crinkled in amusement.

His voice, though, was serious enough as he replied, "I think the first time I stay here, I want it to be someplace other than the couch…if that's all right."

"It is," I said, in a way relieved that he also understood where all this was going. Not that night, maybe not the next, but soon.

"Good. And it's okay—I have a room at the Fairfield Inn."

Irrelevantly, I wondered if he'd gotten the same room I'd vacated only a day earlier. "Okay," I said. "I have to work tomorrow," I added. "But I don't start until three-thirty, so we can meet for lunch. And then I'm off Sunday and Monday, so that'll give us some time."

Time for what, I didn't specify. I had a feeling he'd be able to figure it out, though.

And, to my relief, he didn't tell me I should ask for the next day off, or make noises about my having to go to work. Maybe he was thinking to himself that it was better to let it go for now, that acting as though my job wasn't important would probably be the best way to get me to dig in my heels all over again.

He bent and kissed me once more, a gentle kiss this time, just his way of telling me good night. "Pick you up at eleven-thirty?"

"Sounds perfect," I said.

A smile, one that made my knees want to melt, and then he went to the door. "See you tomorrow," he told me, and let himself out.

Well, that seemed to be that. For all my trying, it didn't seem as though I could quite get Jake Wilcox out of my life.

13

RANDALL LENZ STARED AT THE PSYCHIATRIST, face impassive, even though what he really wanted to do was tell the man this was an utter waste of his time and that he was going to walk out.

"It's natural to experience side effects from an extended fugue state," Dr. D'Onofrio was saying, voice almost too precise, as though he thought if he enunciated everything clearly, even a dunce like a federal agent should be able to understand what he was talking about. His hazel eyes looked muddy behind the frameless glasses he wore, and his thinning dark hair was speckled with gray. And he was a good five or six inches shorter than his patient, a discrepancy he didn't like very much, if the way he'd quickly asked Lenz to take a seat was any indication. "Your assistant said you've been having headaches. And there was a nose bleed?"

"One," Lenz said shortly. "My allergies were acting up."

Actually, he didn't have any allergies, had always been almost supernaturally healthy, but it was a harmless enough lie. Anything to get him out of there and back to his duties.

He had to quell a flare of irritation at Dawson, even though he knew his assistant had only reached out to management because he'd made the mistake of mentioning that he couldn't quite get rid of the headaches he'd been experiencing for the past few days. She knew the headaches were unusual, and that particular symptom, combined with the nose bleed and a higher-than-average level of irritability, had probably made her think he needed to be checked out.

Although he didn't quite want to admit such a thing, even to himself, he knew he'd come back from his trip to Santa Fe in a very bad mood. He'd been so sure he would catch up with Adara Grant there, and instead he'd been stonewalled by a woman ten years his junior who acted as though she was queen of the world and everyone around her had been put there merely to carry out her commands. All right, that description probably wasn't quite fair, but he had to admit to himself that Genoveva Castillo had rubbed him the wrong way.

And he also had a gut feeling that she'd been lying to him about Adara Grant, but he was damned if he could figure out how or why. The whole situation felt to him as if some vitally important connection existed between all the interested parties, something he should have been able to figure out but which kept eluding him nonetheless. That was what frustrated him the most; he was used to being in control, and ever since his path had crossed Adara's, it felt as though he'd been shoved onto a runaway train, one with no conductor and a set of tracks that were about to lead him straight over a cliff.

He knew there was absolutely no connection between all the subjects currently held at the facility outside Alexandria. Lenz and his staff had thoroughly investigated all of them—their family connections, their academic and work histories, every single aspect of their lives. About the only thing they had in common was that all of them had been adopted or had been brought up in the foster system, but both those situations were common enough; he himself had been adopted as an infant. At any rate, if there was some overarching thread that bound them all together, he was damned if he could figure out what the hell it might be.

D'Onofrio ruffled through the papers on his desk. "Have any of your memories from those missing days resurfaced?"

"No."

"Dr. Haley said you'd suffered some unusual

burns. Do you think they might be connected to the headaches?"

Lenz narrowed his eyes at the other man, feeling a surge of satisfaction as the shrink quickly looked away rather than try to maintain eye contact. "Doubtful. Anyway, they're not burns—Haley only said they *looked* like burns. They could be something else."

"Such as?"

"I don't know," Lenz said, tone even, although he felt as though he was spitting the words out from between clenched teeth. "I didn't spend six years in medical school. You tell me."

Dr. D'Onofrio straightened in his chair, although his gaze still wouldn't quite meet that of his patient. "I'm not a diagnostician, Agent Lenz."

You're not much of a psychiatrist, either, Lenz thought, but he remained silent. This was all procedure, just another stupid hoop he had to jump through to prove he was fit to be at work and in charge of his department. "If there's nothing else, I have a lot of work to do."

More shuffling of the papers on the shrink's desk, which Lenz guessed was a delaying tactic, nothing more. "It might be a good idea to take some leave—"

"Unacceptable," he cut in. "I've already missed enough days as it is. I'm rested and ready to work."

This declaration was met by a slight lift of an eyebrow. However, D'Onofrio didn't protest, only wrote something down on the papers in front of him, then closed the folder. "All right," he said. "I have my reservations, but your cognitive functions don't seem to be impaired and your symptoms, although somewhat troubling, don't seem to be interfering with your work. You're cleared for regular duty—but if the headaches get worse, or you notice you're not sleeping well or are more irritable than usual, let Dr. Haley know immediately so we can run some more tests."

Privately, Lenz swore to himself that he'd swallow an entire bottle of ibuprofen before he admitted to anyone that his headaches were in any way debilitating. He needed to stay on the job because he didn't dare miss one clue, one tiny piece of data that might lead him to Adara Grant's current hiding place. However, he only replied, "Of course, doctor. Can I go now?"

The shrink hesitated, but he seemed to realize that Lenz's request was only courtesy, and he was going to leave whether or not he was given permission. "Sure, Agent Lenz. Have a good day."

He doubted that was going to happen, but he responded with a nod and a similar platitude, then got up from his chair and left. Since the man wasn't officially with the agency and worked as an outside consultant, his offices were located several miles away from the facility where Lenz's division was housed.

As usual, traffic in D.C. was hellish, but about twenty-five minutes later, he pulled into the parking lot of the nondescript campus where he spent most of his waking hours. After scanning his new I.D. badge and dropping off his laptop case in his office, he went to the small room where Agent Dawson and her counterparts were housed. She sat at her workstation, gaze flickering over a series of images scrolling on her screen.

At his approach, however, she turned and said, "Still no sign of the green Fiat 500X we believe Adara Grant was driving."

While he'd expected as much, he couldn't help experiencing a flare of annoyance. The vehicle was distinctive enough that it should have been fairly easy to detect, even on Santa Fe's crowded streets. And although the city didn't have cameras at every intersection, there were still enough of them that at least one should have picked her up.

"Hacked?" he asked, trying not to sound as irritated as he felt.

"I'd say that's the most reasonable explanation, although if that's what we're dealing with, the hacker is very skilled. There aren't any detectable skips or jumps in the footage, which is what usually happens when frames have been deleted."

"No idea who's doing it?"

She shook her head. For the first time, he noted the dark circles under her eyes, signs of weariness that the glasses she wore couldn't quite conceal. "No. We're working on it, but...."

But it could take time. And, in the end, although discovering the identity of the person or persons who'd been able to hack what was supposed to be an unhackable system was important, it wasn't as important as locating wherever Adara Grant had gone to ground.

"Then we need to move on to facial recognition and see if we can locate Ms. Grant that way," he told Agent Dawson, and she let out a breath.

"That's going to take time."

"I know. Which is why we should have been on it yesterday. I'll be in my office."

Dawson didn't bother to protest, only turned back to her keyboard and began typing in the order.

Since he knew she was on top of the situation, Randall Lenz went to his office and shut the door, and allowed himself to rub his temples, willing the headache that had begun to throb there to go away. Dawson was right—the movies and TV shows made facial recognition seem like a magic ticket for locating a person, but it wasn't quite as easy as that. The algorithms were always being massaged and improved, and yet they still could only work with what they were given. Quality of surveillance cameras varied widely, and if his quarry was out in some boondock with equipment from the early 1990s or worse, then the system might not be able to detect a match even if an image of Adara Grant actually came across its servers. Also, there was the sheer volume of data to be processed, hundreds of millions of images from cameras mounted in shopping centers and in grocery stores and on street corners, in office buildings and car repair shops and restaurants.

If they were really, really lucky, something might turn up in the next week. And even if it did, there was no guarantee that the woman in question would have stayed put. After all, one thing Adara Grant was really good at was moving around.

A needle in a haystack would be easy compared to the task ahead of him.

At the moment, it felt more like looking for a mote of dust in a sandstorm.

Jake told himself that he shouldn't be so nervous about meeting Addie for lunch, that he'd done the really heavy lifting the night before when he confronted her at the casino and at the house she was renting. Still, he didn't want to screw this up. While he was relieved that she hadn't sent him packing, had even shared a kiss with him...a kiss that made him realize all over again how much he needed her in his life…he wasn't so blinded by that one success to forget she hadn't made any promises beyond this lunch meeting.

But at least his brother had been right about one thing—while the delay in Provo had been annoying, losing a day of travel hadn't made much of a difference. Addie had a job and a house…he wanted to know how the hell she'd managed to land someplace so nice within a few days of arriving in town…and clearly, she didn't have any plans to go anywhere.

Well, at least not any time soon.

He parked Jeremy's truck at the curb and walked up to the house. Now, in broad daylight, he noticed that the white paint on its clapboard siding was fresh and bright, as were the deep red accents on the shutters and the front door. As someone who'd been involved with a lot of renovations on old houses in the recent past, Jake could tell a good deal of effort must have been expended to maintain the home in such good condition.

Convincing Addie to leave this place might turn out to be harder than he thought.

Don't borrow trouble, he told himself as he climbed the porch steps. *She wouldn't have kissed you like that if she wasn't ready on some level to come back to you.*

Then again, he could be misreading her signals. Maybe she'd given him that kiss as her way of saying goodbye. But no, that didn't make sense. If she'd intended to send him packing, why even bother to have lunch, or inform him that she didn't have to work on Sunday and Monday?

He knocked on the door, and Addie opened it almost immediately. The night before, she'd had her hair pulled back in a ponytail to keep it out of the way while she worked, but now it lay glossy and smooth over her shoulders, which were bared by the sleeveless blouse she wore. Its dark emerald hue intensified the green in her eyes, and right then, he thought she was quite possibly the most beautiful woman he'd ever seen.

"Hey," she said, her voice almost breathless, as if she had hurried to answer his knock.

He wouldn't flatter himself by thinking that the sight of him took her breath away...even though her appearance had pretty much done the same thing to him.

"Hey," he replied. "I hope you have some advice on where to eat, because I didn't see much on the drive over here."

She grinned. "Luckily, I do. Come on in—I need to grab my purse."

Jake stepped inside and took a quick glance around as she went through a door that must have opened into the bedroom. The little house was even more appealing with bright daylight pouring in through the open windows and warming the shiny oak floor. His cousin Laurel would definitely have approved of the decor, which was neutral without being dull and had pops of red and blue here and there to liven the overall look.

"How'd you find this place?" he asked Addie when she reentered the living room.

"The bartender at Bar 10—her sister owns it. Actually, that's where we're going for lunch, so maybe you'll get to meet Carolyn. I'm not super-familiar with her schedule yet."

Maybe not, but it seemed obvious to Jake that Addie had done a pretty good job of making connections here in Riverton. Well, considering the way she'd moved around so much, she probably was used to learning the ropes in a new town. In a way, he was relieved to hear she planned to take him to a place where she already knew someone. If she'd been trying to hide their connection, wouldn't she have suggested lunch at a restaurant where they could be incognito, so to speak?

"Well, it'll be great to meet her, if it turns out she's there," he replied easily, figuring it was best to keep things casual and friendly for the moment. He had a feeling Addie wouldn't be very thrilled with him if he tried to get too intense during this lunch date, not when she had to be at work in a few hours.

That reply earned him a smile. They headed out to the front porch, where she locked the door with the key, even though he knew good and well she could have used her witch powers to secure it. But he realized there was an older couple sitting on the porch of the house next door, watching them as they left, and probably she'd wanted to make sure she didn't do anything that looked too out of the ordinary.

She glanced at the silver Ram truck parked at the curb. "What happened to the Gladiator?"

"Jeremy and I swapped. I thought it was probably safer to drive something a little less…memorable."

"Good call."

They got in the truck, and she directed him to head back out to Main Street. Once they'd turned the corner and were cruising along, he asked, "Do you always have an audience when you're coming and going from your place?"

Her nose crinkled in confusion, and then she let out a chuckle and said, "Oh, you mean the Schuylers? I think sitting on the porch and watching the world go by is their main entertainment. At least, they're always out there when I leave for work, although even they've packed it in by the time I get home."

There was nothing but rueful amusement in her tone, and yet he had to wonder if it bothered her to be working such crazy hours. Probably better not to ask, not when they seemed to be getting along so well.

"Then I'll try to make sure I don't do anything that would attract attention."

"Thanks—I appreciate it. My first day there, they kept giving me the hairy eyeball, like they were expecting me to bust out with a huge party or something."

That mental image made Jake smile a little. "Oh, I'm sure you could fit a whole five or six people inside your living room."

"If they all knew each other really well," she replied, full mouth quirking. The amusement left her face in the next moment, however, and she said in a very different tone, "I'm not sure what I'm supposed to do about you being here, Jake."

"Don't 'do' anything," he told her, his tone still casual. The last thing he wanted was to get all hot and heavy with an in-depth discussion right before they got to the restaurant. "Or actually, do tell me where I'm supposed to turn, since I have no idea where I'm going."

A quick flash of a smile, there and gone too quickly, but at least he could tell he'd managed to lighten the mood a little. "Turn right up there," she said. "It's easier to park on the side street."

He did as she'd directed and made the turn onto a small lane that bordered a block of commercial buildings. All the parking spaces closest to the corner had already been taken, so he parked a little farther down. As they got out of the truck, Jake could feel his pulse accelerate slightly. Why, he wasn't really sure, unless it was just the idea of possibly meeting this Carolyn person, of having her judge him. It seemed fairly obvious that she was an ally of Addie's, or he doubted that she would have told Addie about the possibility of renting a house from her sister.

The entrance to the restaurant turned out to be tucked into an alleyway. They went inside, and he asked, "How'd you even find this place?"

"One of the girls who works at the Fairfield Inn told me about it," Addie replied. She flashed a smile and offered a wave to the red-haired woman working behind the bar, who must have been Carolyn. Since she was busy pouring drinks, the bartender couldn't do much more than lift a hand in greeting, but Jake still noticed the way the woman's gaze paused on him, startled, and then approving in an appraising kind of way.

That first hurdle apparently cleared, he felt a bit more relaxed as he followed Addie to the last available booth and sat down across from her. She handed a menu over to him. "I've only eaten here three times so far, but everything I've had has been good, so you're probably safe ordering whatever you like."

"Good to know."

The menu offered a wider variety than he'd been expecting, so Jake perused it with some interest, glad of the chance to take a mental breath and relax a little. He was surprised by the wine and beer selections, seeing several he would have liked to try, but then he reminded himself that Addie had to go to work after their lunch. Drinking probably wasn't a very good idea, even if he would have appreciated the chance to take the edge off.

A waitress—a woman around Carolyn's age, probably in her late thirties, with bleached hair and too much mascara—came by to take their drink orders. With a mental sigh, Jake asked for an iced tea, and Addie requested one as well.

That business handled, she leaned against the back of the booth, glanced around, and said in an undertone, "So...how *did* you manage to find me?"

"Process of elimination."

Her eyebrows lifted as she picked up the paper napkin from where it sat on the table in front of her, then set it on her lap. "That's a heck of a process, to be able to find one person in the middle of a country as big as this one."

"Well, I had a few ways to narrow things down. Just because of the way Wyoming is like Utah...." He paused there and watched her for a few seconds, waiting to see if she would understand the reference. Her extraordinary eyes lit up in comprehension, and she offered him a nod. "Anyway, I figured there couldn't be too many places where you could have gone. And then when I factored in Genoveva's hint—"

"So, she did rat me out after all?"

Since Addie sounded amused, Jake figured she was joking…mostly. "I wouldn't call it that. More like…she made a comment that could have been taken a number of different ways, but when Jeremy and I put it together with what we already knew about Wyoming…well, that helped us make an educated guess."

He had to stop there, since the waitress had returned with their iced teas, and they needed to order some food. As much as he would have liked to be more leisurely about the whole process, he knew his time with Addie was finite, that after lunch he'd have to take her home so she could change and get ready for work.

Once they'd put in their food orders—a Greek pizza for him and a Cuban slider for her—he went on, "It was still a leap of faith. Jeremy thought I was nuts, and Connor read me the riot act about marching into tribal territory without any real game plan, but…." Jake let the words trail off, acutely aware of how Addie's gaze was fixed on him, those gray-green eyes of hers so shimmering and deep, he thought he could easily drown in them. "You're worth it, Addie. If it had turned out you weren't here, I would have come up with a different plan and tried again."

"Jake, I—" She pulled in a breath and fidgeted with the napkin in her lap. Looking down, she said, "You're making this really hard for me."

Which meant she was already fighting with herself. He couldn't allow himself to feel triumphant about that, not when she was in such obvious mental anguish. "I don't want it to be hard. But I also know I could never have forgiven myself if I hadn't tried to find you. I understand why you did it —really, I do—but all I can do now is tell you the same thing I told you last night. Running away doesn't solve anything."

She reached for her iced tea and plucked the slice of lemon off the rim, then squeezed it into the glass. A delaying tactic, probably, but Jake made himself sit quietly and swallow some of his own drink, waiting to see how she would respond.

After sipping some tea, she said in almost a whisper, "I know that. But—but I was so scared. I'm still scared, Jake. We both know that Randall Lenz isn't messing around."

"No, he's not," Jake agreed. "But I also know that he doesn't have a clue who or what he's dealing with. Because it's not just witch clans"—his voice dropped as he uttered that loaded phrase, and he took a quick look around, but no one seemed to be paying any attention to the two of them—"it's people like my brother, who can use his talent to hack whatever systems need to be hacked to keep you hidden, and it's people like Connor and Angela, who were able to go into Lenz's head and remove any inconvenient memories. The guy may be a federal agent, but it's pretty hard to defend yourself against people with those sorts of abilities."

Addie gave a reluctant nod. "I understand that, but—"

"But you think because he found you once, he can find you again."

Another nod.

"He's looking, but with Jeremy covering for you, he's not going to be successful a second time."

Her gaze lifted from the napkin she'd been fussing with in her lap, and he could see the worry clearly in her wide, beautiful eyes. "You sound so confident."

"It's because I am." Without his brother, circumstances might have been very different, but as things stood, Jake was pretty sure that Jeremy could keep Randall Lenz off the trail for as long as it took.

However, Addie still didn't appear convinced. Her fingers tapped against the side of her glass of iced tea as she said, "And…what? Is Jeremy going to be forced to keep babysitting my digital footprint until Lenz gives up?"

Jake had to smile slightly at that description of her current predicament. "It's not exactly 'babysitting.' Don't ask me to explain exactly what he does —algorithms or something—but he sets up mechanisms to seek out certain sets of images and make sure they're scrubbed from any public or private databases. Basically, once they're operating, he doesn't have to do much more than update the parameters every once in a while. It's not like he's hunched in some windowless basement, perpetually scanning video feeds for any signs of your presence."

Her mouth quirked. "No, I've been there, so I know the Wheeler Park house isn't what you'd call 'windowless.'" A pause before she asked, "But does it have a basement?"

Because the place was old, it had been built with one. However, since the home's square footage was more than adequate to their needs, he and Jeremy and Laurel hadn't done anything with the basement except store some empty boxes and a few other odds and ends down there. He said as much to Addie, who accepted that description and appeared ready to let it go.

Before either of them could say anything else, however, Carolyn the bartender approached, clearly taking advantage of a gap in the lunchtime crowd to come over to their table so she could meet Addie's friend.

To his relief, Addie didn't look at all worried or nervous, but only said, "Hey, Carolyn. This is my friend Jake—he's visiting from Arizona."

Damn. He'd forgotten to give her his cover identity of Tyler Greene, but at least she'd been fairly vague, had only provided a first name and the name of an entire state, rather than introducing him as Jake Wilcox from Flagstaff, Arizona. It could have been worse.

Carolyn's gaze was steady, appraising, but once again, Jake thought he could detect some approval in her hazel eyes. He supposed he should have been glad of that, while at the same time, he found himself vaguely amused to have her so clearly judging him. What would have happened if she'd found him somehow lacking?

Then again, he thought he should be glad that Addie had already found friends and protectors here in Riverton. Even if he hadn't managed to locate her, she might have been okay.

But he had found her, and he was going to continue to do what he could to convince her to come back to Flagstaff with him. Even if the people of Riverton had welcomed her with open arms, this still wasn't her home. She had family waiting for her in Arizona.

"Hi, Jake," Carolyn said. "Nice to meet one of Addie's friends. Are you in town long?"

Good question. He hoped not, even though what he'd seen of Riverton so far seemed nice enough, a small, pretty town with a river flowing through it, framed by far-off mountains. There were far worse places where Addie could have ended up.

"A few days," he lied, figuring that such an

answer was vague enough not to cause too many problems for him or Addie. "I'm on my way to Yellowstone to meet some friends."

Yet another lie, of course, but it explained why he was in Riverton by himself.

Apparently, Carolyn found his story plausible enough, since she nodded and said, "Oh, yeah, we get a lot of people coming through here on their way to the park. Nice time of year for it, too." A quick glance over her shoulder, as if to check to make sure no one was waiting for her at the bar. To Jake's relief, a man and a woman in their late forties, both of them wearing Yellowstone T-shirts and looking like the tourists they clearly were, had sat down there in the bartender's absence, and were now looking around, obviously wanting to order some drinks. Carolyn offered Jake and Addie a rueful smile, and said, "Well, no rest for the wicked. Nice meeting you, Jake—enjoy your lunch."

She headed toward the bar, and while he didn't quite release a sigh of relief, he was glad he wouldn't have to keep fabricating stories to hide his real reason for being in Riverton.

Addie apparently hadn't missed the shift in his expression, because a faint smile now played around her full mouth. "It's okay, Jake—I can tell she liked you."

"Well, thank God for that," he replied as he reached for his iced tea.

"I have a feeling she wouldn't like you as much if she knew why you were really here, though."

"Are you going to tell her?"

"Of course not." Addie swirled her straw through her iced tea, playing with the slice of lemon floating in the tall glass. "I'm not that stupid."

"You're not stupid at all."

Her brows pulled together for just the slightest moment. But then he watched her shoulders lift, even as she asked slyly, "You didn't think I was stupid for bailing out the way I did?"

"Stupid? No." Jake paused for a second, allowing himself a quick glance around to make sure no one was listening—especially Carolyn. But since the woman was preoccupied with taking orders from the tourists who'd just seated themselves at the bar, and everyone else in the vicinity appeared consumed by their conversations and meals, he figured it was safe enough to add, "Hurtful, maybe."

At once, Addie's face went still. She let go of the straw and placed her hands flat on the tabletop. Voice a murmur, she said, "I didn't mean to hurt you."

"I know you didn't. Otherwise, you would've thrown me out last night. But we still need to get this whole thing figured out."

She was silent then, watching him with something that almost looked like fear in her eyes. What was she afraid of? That she wouldn't have the courage to tell him to get lost...or that she would?

"I know," she said at last. "It's just my head is telling me one thing and my heart is telling me another, and I don't know which one to listen to."

Without stopping to think, he reached out and laid his hand on top of hers. Her fingers were cold, even though it was warm inside the restaurant.

"Always listen to your heart, Addie," he told her. "It was my heart that led me here."

For a long moment, she didn't respond, only sat there with her fingers unmoving beneath his hand. Eventually, however, those fingers twined themselves around his and gave them a gentle squeeze. She looked up, and something in her gaze made his heart want to skip a beat.

"I'm glad," was all she said, but he somehow knew in that moment she'd reached an inner decision, even if she hadn't yet acknowledged it even to herself.

Right then, Jake knew everything was going to be all right.

It was hard to leave Jake at my place and go to work that afternoon. But even though I realized I'd reached a decision as I sat there at our table at Bar 10, I hadn't yet made him any promises. If nothing else, I needed to work my shift so I wouldn't leave anyone in the lurch.

He said he'd hang for a while, and then go out and explore Riverton while daylight held. And actually, he told me he'd be fine with going back to his hotel room, but I'd replied that I wanted him at my place when I got home from work, even though it wouldn't be until after midnight. No arguments from him, only a promise that he'd be there, even if he was snoring on the couch by the time I returned.

"I'll make sure to take off my shoes first, though," he promised me, an amused glint in his dark eyes.

Was it fair for him to be so absolutely adorable? I knew I probably should have hardened my heart and let him know it wasn't safe for me to go back to Flagstaff with him, and yet, I realized I didn't have that kind of courage. The kiss we'd shared the night before was the only evidence I needed to prove we were meant to be together. I'd run away in the middle of the night without talking things over because I'd known that otherwise, he probably would have been able to dissuade me from leaving town in the first place.

Whatever this bond was between us, it was stronger than anything I'd ever experienced before. Maybe that should have scared me. I supposed it did, a little. At the same time, though, it made me feel a bit better about the situation. After all, was it really my fault that I didn't have the strength to fight something so completely overwhelming?

I gave him my spare house key—just in case the Schuylers were hanging around when he got there and might have noticed if he let himself in the witchy way—and said I'd be home around twelve-fifteen or so. When Leona had put me on swing shift, I hadn't really argued, mostly because I'd just needed a job—any job—and since I hadn't planned on having much of a social life anyway, it hadn't mattered what kind of hours I worked. In that particular moment, though, knowing that I wouldn't be getting back until the middle of the night made me chafe at my current schedule.

Still, there wasn't much I could do about it. I tried to sound casual as I told Jake goodbye, but he saw right through that ploy. He bent down and kissed me, a thorough, lingering kiss that sent thrills to every nerve ending and made me want to push him down on the couch for a good old-fashioned make-out session. However, I didn't have time for that, so I had to settle for returning the kiss for a minute or two before I pulled away.

"I have to go," I said, knowing how breathless I sounded. "I'll see you after midnight."

"All right, Cinderella," he replied with a grin.

About all I could do was shake my head and make myself go out the back door, then climb in my Fiat and head to work. In the parking lot, I had to waste a minute repairing the damage he'd done to my lip gloss, but that was okay. If nothing else, sitting in the car and carefully reapplying gloss, then smoothing my hair, allowed me to get my thoughts centered. I didn't want to show up acting all flighty and distracted. Mine might not have been the most important job in the world, but that didn't mean I wanted to screw things up, either.

Because it was a Saturday, the casino was packed. Actually, the hustle and bustle provided its own strange form of relief, just because I was so busy that I didn't have much time to think about Jake Wilcox and the problem he presented. Oh, not that I thought he himself was the problem, more that I had to somehow get my head to understand what my heart wanted. It would be safer to stay in Riverton, but the arguments he'd presented for returning to Flagstaff kept rattling around in my head, even as I ran back and forth from the bar, carrying all those gin and tonics and Jack and Cokes and the various assorted mixed drinks the people who'd descended on the Wind River Casino kept ordering. Clearly, they were bound and determined to have a good time, even if the house odds kept them from going home with much more money in their pockets than when they'd gotten started.

What if it really was possible for Jeremy's computer talents to keep Randall Lenz out of my life permanently? It seemed like far too much to hope for, but I had to admit that I was new to magic and all the ramifications of witch-kind's various talents. Shouldn't I trust what Jake had told me, that I honestly had nothing to worry about?

I thought of Flagstaff, of the tall peaks that towered above the town, the darling downtown section where Jake had taken me to taste wine and have dinner. The way I'd been utterly at home in his house, despite the sexual tension I'd already felt sparking between us. His adorable little dog, who I assumed was probably being watched by Jeremy while Jake was out of town. Laurel's friendliness, and the way Connor and Angela had welcomed me to the family. And let's not forget the generosity of my brother, who'd apparently handed over half of his inheritance without blinking an eye.

How could I think it was possible to turn my back on all that? I'd made the attempt, but in retrospect, all I'd done was make things harder for everyone. I should have stayed and talked it over with Jake, should have let him explain why I was allowing my worry and my fear to run away with me.

Well, I couldn't change what I'd done, but I could allow myself to consider a future where I wasn't always in hiding, always looking over my shoulder.

Luckily, none of that woolgathering got in the way of my work. I fetched and carried, and although I caught Blake giving me the side-eye a couple of times, as if he had somehow guessed I had a lot weighing on my mind, he didn't ask any questions, probably because he was just as busy as everyone else on shift that night.

However, the thought of packing it up and leaving town also made a pang go through me. Leona had given me a job, and it didn't seem right to bail out on her after only working for a few days. No, it wasn't as if I'd been hired after a lengthy candidate search or anything like that, but still, my mother had taught me to follow through with my commitments. I didn't like being a flake.

And then there was the house. Tracy had offered it to me on a month-to-month basis, so she obviously hadn't been too concerned about locking me into a lease, and yet she probably hadn't thought there was any chance of my pulling up stakes when I'd only been around for a week or so. Of course, I'd pay for the full month's rent—if I went back to Flagstaff with Jake, money definitely wouldn't be an issue anymore —but even if Tracy didn't ask too many questions, I knew Carolyn would want to know what the hell I was doing, especially after she'd suggested me as a possible renter for her sister's property.

Damned if I did, damned if I didn't.

Despite those internal equivocations, I knew deep down that my heart belonged to Jake. Exactly how we'd work all this out, I wasn't sure, but we'd come up with some sort of solution.

I hoped.

Eventually, midnight rolled around. I counted up my tips and couldn't help being pleased—I'd pulled in nearly two hundred dollars that shift. Maybe I really didn't need it, not with millions waiting for me in Flagstaff, but it still felt good to know I'd earned those two hundred bucks through hard work and nothing more.

I didn't linger, though, only said my goodbyes to

everyone and headed out to my car. In my mind, I kept rehearsing what I wanted to say to Jake. Should I lay it all out on the line as soon as I got home, or should I wait to have a real talk in the morning when we were both more awake?

Either option had its own pitfalls, unfortunately. Probably, it was best to see how Jake was doing when I got there. If he was sleepy and tired, then I'd let it go until we were both in better shape to have a meaningful conversation. After all, I had the next two days off. It wasn't as though we wouldn't have plenty of free time to discuss what should happen next.

That all sounded very rational, very mature. Whether I'd be able to refrain from blurting out to a sleepy Jake that yes, I did love him and this had all been a horrible mistake, I didn't know for sure.

After I got home and quietly let myself in through the back door, I walked into the living room, only to find Jake passed out on the couch, an afghan pulled up to his chin and the TV still playing, showing some kind of infomercial for a not very appealing-looking pillow. And although I couldn't quite prevent a stab of disappointment from going through me, at the same time, I had to grin at the picture he presented right then, his dark hair sticking up against the couch cushions, sock feet peeking out from below the edge of the afghan, which wasn't quite big enough to fully cover up someone as tall as he was.

I definitely didn't have the heart to wake him, not when he was dead asleep like that, a faint snore drifting from his mouth every once in a while. Instead, I got another blanket from the linen closet and spread it over him, then went into the bathroom and quietly washed my face and brushed my teeth, and slipped into my bed.

Maybe it was silly of me, but I felt somehow safer knowing that Jake Wilcox slept out in my living room.

The next morning, he was awake when I emerged from my room. His eyes met mine, and he looked almost sheepish.

"Sorry I passed out like that," he said. "I guess I was more tired from the drive than I thought."

"No biggie," I assured him. "It was pretty late. And I have to admit, that couch is really comfortable."

His hand rubbed the back of his neck. "Mostly. I think I got a crick."

He looked so adorable right then, with his mussed hair and the dark scruff of several days' growth of beard on his cheeks and chin, that I had to keep myself from grinning. I didn't want him to think I was smiling at his discomfort, after all. "Well, let's see if some coffee will help."

Immediately, his expression brightened. "You just said the magic word."

Yes, coffee did have its own magic. I bustled about in the tiny kitchen, glad that Tracy had first set the house up as an Airbnb, and so it was already equipped with pretty much anything we could need for breakfast, including creamer in the fridge and some frozen waffles in the freezer. I suggested those to Jake, and he nodded, relief clear in his face.

"Eating something here definitely sounds better than going out for breakfast in town."

I lifted an eyebrow as I leaned against the counter. Before I left my room, I'd pulled on a T-shirt and yoga pants, and brushed my hair and pulled it back into a ponytail. That seemed safer than wandering around in my jammies, and so I didn't feel too nervous about letting Jake see me first thing in the morning. It wasn't as though we hadn't spent a night together before, although this time, just like when we'd shared that hotel room at Treasure Island, absolutely nothing had happened.

Maybe if I was lucky, I might be able to correct that lack in the next day or so.

"Worried about getting the third degree from someone else?" I teased him, and he sent me a sideways glance.

"Maybe," he allowed.

"Not much chance of that," I said as I got a couple of mugs down from the cupboard and set them on the counter. "Seeing as Carolyn is the only person I know around here."

"What about your landlady? The people you work with?"

"Well, okay," I replied. "But Tracy doesn't work at any of the local restaurants, and obviously, I wouldn't drag you over to Wind River...even though I've heard they've got a great breakfast buffet."

The magic word "buffet" made Jake prick up his ears. "Oh, really?"

"I thought you weren't much of a breakfast guy."

He raised an eyebrow, one corner of his mouth lifting in something that might have been the beginnings of a smile. "Buffets are different. Maybe tomorrow?"

Actually, that sounded like it could be fun. Luckily, the breakfast buffet was served every morning, not just on Sundays, so it wasn't as if I had to worry about missing our one and only chance to go out for brunch. "Sounds like a plan," I said, then lifted the carafe from the coffeemaker and poured a good measure into each of the waiting mugs.

I remembered that Jake liked his black, so I took his mug of coffee over to him after I poured a little creamer in mine, and sat down on the armchair by the couch. He'd already folded the blanket and the afghan and set them neatly on one arm. Taking the mug from me, he asked, "What do you want to do today?"

Honestly, I hadn't thought much about it, since I'd been so preoccupied with brooding over what I needed to say to him. In the back of my mind, though, I'd toyed with the idea of doing some exploring around the area. When I came to Riverton, I'd been focused on finding work and a place to live, and I hadn't done much more than go to work and come home, although I had at least located the most convenient gas station and grocery store. Neither of those spots was exactly what you could call picturesque, though.

"Explore, maybe?" I suggested. "I haven't really gotten out and about yet, and there's some beautiful country around here."

"That would be fun," Jake said, then added, "As long as my brother's truck doesn't betray me again."

"'Betray' you?" I repeated, not sure what he was talking about.

He sipped his coffee and offered me a rueful smile. "Oh, there was a recall Jeremy didn't know about, and the damn thing died on me just outside Provo. Cost me a whole day while I waited for them to fix the truck, but the guys at the Dodge dealership swore up and down that it's fine now and shouldn't cause any more trouble."

"Well, we could drive my car," I told him. His comment about his problems with the borrowed truck had answered one question for me; in the back of my mind, I'd been wondering why he'd showed up in Riverton three days after I fled Flagstaff, even though from the way he'd talked, it sounded as if he'd come after me almost as soon as he realized I was gone.

Jake tapped his fingers against the side of his coffee mug. "I'd feel better taking the truck. You don't have to drive too far in this part of the world before you can get into some rough terrain, and even though your Fiat has all-wheel drive, it's not the same thing as having a four-wheel-drive truck."

No, I supposed it wasn't. If Jeremy's truck had been given a clean bill of health, then I supposed it was safe enough to drive on that day's outing... wherever it turned out to be.

"Sure," I said. "Let me get my laptop, and we can figure out what sounds like a good day trip."

He nodded, and I fetched the computer from where I'd been charging it on a side table in the bedroom. After perusing the local offerings—and there were more than I'd expected to find—we decided to drive through the Wind River reservation and go visit what was supposed to be Sacagawea's gravesite. We settled on that particular outing not just because some of the driving tours we'd found encompassed days of travel and hundreds of miles, but also because I thought it might be safer to stay on tribal land whenever possible. Yes, Jake had sworn that Jeremy's algorithms were working in the background, carefully scrubbing me from every bit of security and traffic camera footage out there, and yet I thought it never hurt to take a few extra precautions.

Because there was only one bathroom in the house, we had to take turns in the shower and so weren't out the door until almost ten-thirty. That was all right, though; it wasn't as if we had any particular schedule we needed to follow. Mostly, this was just about spending the day together.

And I was fine with that.

Because it didn't sound as if there were many places to eat along the route we'd chosen—well, except the casino, and we'd decided against going to the buffet—Jake and I stopped at the Smith's grocery store on Main Street and loaded up at the deli, and bought a little biodegradable ice chest to carry everything. Just being at the store with him was more fun than I'd expected, and I wondered what it would be like to go shopping together in Flagstaff, buying stuff for the house as we planned meals together.

Which I had to admit was getting ahead of myself just a wee bit. I knew Jake wanted me to go back to Arizona with him, but he hadn't made any comments about cohabiting. Understandable, since we'd only known each other for a few weeks, and yet....

I wanted to share his life, share his house. And I had a feeling he wanted the same thing, only he was doing his best not to push me. After all, I hadn't even said anything to him about the change of heart I'd experienced after realizing that I didn't want to spend another day away from him, away from the life I'd briefly glimpsed in Flagstaff and now knew I wanted so desperately.

"But I want to take you out to dinner tonight," he said as he stowed the ice chest on the back seat in the truck's extended cab. "There has to be someplace to go besides Bar 10."

"Of course, there is," I replied, my tone mock-severe. "Riverton isn't just a wide spot in the road. There are lots of restaurants here. I know there's a steakhouse because I've passed it a couple of times while coming and going."

This piece of information seemed to reassure Jake, because he flashed me a smile and said, "A steakhouse is perfect. We'll go there. I'm sure all the driving and exploring we have planned will work up a decent appetite."

"Because all the food we just bought couldn't possibly be enough to hold us."

His grin only broadened. "Oh, that's picnic food. I'm talking about a steak dinner."

About all I could do was chuckle as I fastened my seatbelt. "Okay, Jake. Whatever."

He didn't reply, only backed the truck out of its parking space and drove west on Main Street—aka Highway 26—heading out of town. It wasn't too long before we were out on the open prairie again, golden-brown fields of dry grass extending for mile upon mile on either side of the road. The land out there felt impossibly vast, the sky overhead a vault of clear, clear blue with only small puffs of clouds here and there to break up the sapphire expanse.

We were both quiet as the miles rolled away under our wheels, and that was just fine. Once again, I thought of how comfortable I felt around Jake, as if we'd known each other all our lives rather than a few short weeks. I thought he sensed that connection as well; there was a lot we needed to talk about, and yet it was as if we'd both reached a mutual agreement not to discuss anything while we were on the road, other than a comment here and there about the route.

Eventually, we reached the turn-off for Highway 287, which would lead us south and west toward Fort Washakie. I didn't notice much of a change in the landscape at first, but as we traveled south, things grew greener, and I saw the shape of a mountain range off in the distance, rising above the rolling land beneath. Another half hour or so, and we were following the nav as it led us to the cemetery, one that was still in use by the Native American tribes who'd lived on this land for hundreds of years.

"It's so colorful," Jake murmured as we walked quietly through the cemetery grounds. "I guess I wasn't expecting that."

I'd never been in a Native American cemetery before, either, and so I was also a little surprised by the bright flowers on the graves—both real and made of paper—the strings of beads and brightly painted statues that adorned the resting places of their loved ones. In a strange way, I felt comforted by the display, by the obvious signs that none of these departed souls had been neglected.

Of course, because of my surroundings, I couldn't help thinking about my mother's grave in Kanab, so far from Ohio, where she'd been born. Exactly a week had passed since her funeral, a funeral I hadn't known was taking place until it was already over...a funeral I couldn't have attended even if I'd been told about it. Were the flowers people had brought to her gravesite still there, or had they been cleared away once they'd begun to fade?

I didn't know. I assumed that Jeremy could get footage of her grave for me, since he'd captured images from the funeral by using one of the cemetery's security cameras. What difference did it make, though? I could risk everything by going there and laying flowers on her grave, but doing so wouldn't bring her back.

"Hey," Jake said, his hand slipping into mine. "Are you all right?"

Suddenly, I realized tears had started to slide down my cheeks. "I'm fine," I replied, and reached up with my free hand to wipe those betraying tears away. "Thinking about my mother. I suppose being here in the cemetery just brought it all back."

He pulled me close and held me, not saying anything, only doing what he could to reassure me with his presence. And it did feel good to have him there, to know he loved me and would have turned back time if he could in order to prevent my mother's death.

That wasn't his talent, though. All either of us could do was try to find our way forward from where we currently stood.

And clearly, even though I'd been worried and preoccupied and focused on other things, that sudden upwelling of tears had taught me that my grief was still very real, very near. It lurked beneath the surface busyness of my life, just waiting for that one sound, that one scene, that one scent, to remind me how the woman who'd been my whole world was now gone forever, and no matter what magical talents I or the other members of the Wilcox clan might be able to command, none of them were powerful enough to bring her back.

Jake murmured into my hair, "I should have thought of that. I don't know what I was thinking, bringing you to a cemetery."

"It was my idea, too," I told him, then pulled away so I could look up into his face. Contrition was clear in his dark eyes, along with worry that our day together had been spoiled. "And I'm okay. Really. I just—it just catches me off guard sometimes. Let's go find Sacagawea's grave, okay?"

For a few seconds, he didn't respond, only stared down at me, obviously looking for signs that I wasn't quite as all right as I professed to be. What he saw must have reassured him, because after that pause, he nodded and said, "Sure."

Hand in hand, we walked amongst the gravestones until we found the memorial we were looking for—a tall headstone not too far from a small log cabin. It was engraved only with the date of her death, probably because Sacagawea's exact birthdate hadn't been known. At least that wouldn't have been an issue with my mother's headstone, since the people who'd taken care of the service would have been able to get that information from her driver's license. Had they been surprised to learn she wasn't even forty-five yet? She'd been so young when I was born, and still looked younger than her mid-forties when she died. Probably, most people would have thought she was ten years younger than her true age, except that she couldn't be that young and have a daughter in her middle twenties.

"Sacagawea was really young when she went with Lewis and Clark," Jake said, speaking in a low, respectful tone. "I remember that from my high school history class. She would have been barely old enough to drive if she lived now, but she was able to guide those men across hundreds of miles of wilderness."

That revelation made me feel like a bit of a slacker, even though I knew the early 1800s were an utterly different world from the one I lived in. "I'm glad people still remember her and what she did for this country."

Because bouquets of wildflowers lay on her grave, recent offerings from those who'd made their pilgrimage here. Clearly, Sacagawea hadn't been forgotten.

I hadn't brought any flowers, but there were some daisies growing wild nearby. I went over to the nearest patch and plucked one, then took it over to the memorial stone and laid the cheerful little blossom on the ground in front of it.

"Do you want to see the statue?" Jake asked. "I think I see it over there."

He pointed toward a monument that appeared to have been placed toward the rear of the cemetery. I gazed at it for a moment, then shook my head.

"No. We've found her grave, and that's enough. I doubt the statue really looks like her anyway."

One eyebrow lifted, as if he was surprised that I'd decided against visiting the monument after driving all that way, but he didn't protest, only said, "Sure. If you're hungry, I noticed a campground as we were driving in. We could probably find some-place there to have our picnic."

I told him that sounded like a good idea, and we made our way back to his borrowed truck. Sure enough, there was a small wooded spot about a quarter-mile from the cemetery, and we were able to park not too far from the picnic area, which had concrete tables and benches. There were people seated at some of the other tables, and kids playing noisily on the grass, but that was all right. In a way, I was glad Jake and I didn't have the place to ourselves. We'd have to talk about inconsequential things rather than witch clans or the relentless Randall Lenz or any of the other weighty topics that had occupied my mind recently.

Instead, we talked about the casino and River-ton, about the weather and where Tracy had found that insanely cute red refrigerator for the house I was renting. Nothing that couldn't be overheard, nothing that would seem out of place for a couple spending their Sunday exploring this part of the world and sharing a picnic lunch.

When we were done, we packed up our things

and went back to the truck, and from there, we slowly wended our way back to Riverton, eventually ending up at the Three Sisters flea market, a crazy hodgepodge of more miscellaneous stuff than I thought I'd ever seen collected in one place. Jake bought me a silver and turquoise bracelet to go with the earrings he'd gotten me in Williams, and I talked him into letting me get him a big silver belt buckle worthy of a rodeo champion.

"I'm going to look like an idiot," he said as he resignedly slid the buckle onto his belt and snapped it in place. However, he smiled as he spoke, so I knew he was teasing me a little.

By that point, we were back at the house and the hour was going on six-thirty, although at that time of year, the sun still blazed brightly and wouldn't sink below the horizon for another two hours. I put my hands on my hips and surveyed the effect of the belt buckle against his faded jeans and dusty work boots.

"I like it," I announced. "Makes you look like you belong here in the wild west."

"Flagstaff isn't the wild west?" he returned, dark eyes dancing with amusement. "You should hear some of the stories about what the Wilcoxes got up to when they came to the Arizona territories in the late 1870s."

I could only imagine. And yes, I supposed Arizona was just as wild west as Wyoming, especially when you took the whole Tombstone/OK Corral thing into account, but Tombstone was a long way from Flagstaff. "Well...." I hedged.

He came over to me and pulled me against him. Luckily, I wasn't wearing a belt, so we didn't clink or anything, but I could feel its hard shape against my belly and found myself wondering if something else was hard a bit lower down.

Blood rushed to my cheeks. Where the hell had that come from? Okay, I wasn't blind enough that I could ignore the mounting sexual tension between the two of us, something that had been building all day, but....

In an entirely different tone, he said, "Do you want me to stay here?"

For a second, I could only blink up at him as I took a step back, not sure what he was asking. Then the meaning of those words began to sink in. "In Riverton?"

"Yes."

His question had come from so completely out of left field, I blurted the first thing that came to mind. "Can you even do that? I mean, I thought witches and warlocks couldn't just pick up and move wherever they wanted."

"You did."

Well, that was true...sort of. "I got permission from someone, though."

Since I'd told Jake about my meeting with

Carson Archuleta and how he'd told me it was all right for me to stay here in Arapahoe territory, I didn't have to explain myself. Jake said, "Maybe you could get permission for me, too."

That was an eventuality I hadn't considered. Was it even possible for Jake to leave his clan and settle down someplace far from Wilcox territory? "I couldn't make you leave Flagstaff," I protested.

"If that's what it takes to stay with you, then I'll do it," he said, his voice firm and quiet. "You need to know that, Addie." A pause before he went on, "We're not playing here, are we? I mean, we've had a pretty perfect day, and I thought—"

"We're not playing," I cut in. I reached out and took his hand in mine. "When I ran—I thought I was doing the right thing. But I know the right thing is being with you."

He pulled me close and kissed me, and heat sang through my veins all over again. Maybe I was making a huge mistake, but he was right about one thing.

To be happy, I had to follow my heart…and Jake was what my heart wanted.

No matter what.

15

IN THE PAST, RANDALL LENZ HAD ALWAYS enjoyed writing reports. They were a way to revisit the accomplishments of the recent past and remind him that, while the day-to-day duties of his work could sometimes feel tedious, when looked at in broader strokes, the work he was doing appeared to be paying off quite well.

Not this week, though.

The headache was back, but he ignored the bottle of ibuprofen tucked away in his desk drawer. He kept the thing locked up, but what if someone noticed how many tablets he'd consumed over the past few days? He'd have to explain himself to Dr. Haley—or worse, to the agency's consulting psychiatrist. No, thank you.

As Lenz had expected, the agency servers had

been chewing through footage from a vast array of security cameras across the country, but so far, they hadn't caught a single glimpse of his quarry. Whether that was because she'd disappeared into a cave or because her mysterious benefactor continued to quietly remove any incriminating images before they made it to the agency's watchful eyes, he didn't know. Most likely the latter, and even though he'd talked to all of the analysts who worked for him, impressing on them how important it was to track down the individual or organization responsible for the breach, they'd all but thrown up their hands in defeat.

Only Dawson was brave enough to say what the others were thinking.

"I have no idea who it is," she'd told him just the evening before, her blue-gray eyes shadowed with weariness. "But they're really good. It's like— it's like someone running their fingers through water, and us trying to figure out whose fingers those are when they've left no trace behind. It might as well be magic."

Magic. Lenz had wanted to scoff at her, but he'd noted once again how tired she looked and decided to let it go. She was working as hard as she could, and he couldn't expect much else from her, not without pushing her to the point of collapse, which wouldn't be good for anyone involved. He needed his best analyst, even if she wasn't currently giving him much to work with.

He leaned back in his office chair and shut his eyes. It was late on a Sunday night, and even Dawson was at home. Of course, the agency had staff 'round the clock, but only a few people were on duty at that hour, and Lenz knew he didn't have to worry about anyone walking into his office and spying him in a moment of weakness. Not unless they had something truly important to report, anyway, and if that were the case, he doubted anyone would remember that he'd been resting his eyes for a few minutes.

If only that goddamn headache would go away.

In the back of his mind, a niggling fear had begun to grow, one that whispered he must have suffered some sort of irreversible brain damage during those lost hours the week before. Most of the time, he could ignore it, but with his temples throbbing and the ache feeling as though it was going to make his skull implode sooner rather than later, it was hard for him to entirely dismiss the notion that something really was horribly wrong with him.

It probably would have helped for him to get a decent night's sleep, but he'd never been very good at that. Several of his exes had given up on staying overnight at his house, claiming that he was restless all night, and sometimes spoke and moaned as if in the grip of some nightmare, even if he could never recall what it was.

Most likely, he still suffered the same nighttime disturbances, but since his last serious relationship had ended several years ago and he'd decided in the intervening time that he didn't have room in his life for anyone, he'd had no one to tell him that he cried out in the darkness like a man hag-ridden.

The shrink would probably have a field day with that little detail. Good thing Lenz had no intention of divulging it to anyone.

He went back and scrolled through his notes on his conversation with Genoveva Castillo, hoping against hope that he might have overlooked something, even the tiniest slip that would betray her connection to Adara Grant. But, just as with all the other times he'd studied his write-up of their encounter, he couldn't find a blessed thing.

Fingers through water, indeed.

If only any other likely candidates had presented themselves. Then he could have back-burnered the troublesome Ms. Grant for the time being and focused on someone who might have been a little less difficult to acquire. Unfortunately, despite the agency's ceaseless scanning for those whose patterns didn't fit the norm, nothing else had come up. The universe had apparently decided that she was to be his one and only quarry.

So be it. He knew he wouldn't give up.

Sooner or later, she'd make a mistake. And then she would be his.

Jake could tell Addie was still a little rattled by the offer he'd made her earlier, but he didn't regret saying those words. Honestly, he was sort of kicking himself for not considering such an option from the very beginning.

It was only tradition that decreed witches and warlocks should live in their respective clans' territories. A very old and settled tradition, true, but Addie already had permission to stay in Northern Arapahoe territory indefinitely, it seemed, so why not ride along as her plus-one?

He liked what he'd seen so far of Riverton; it was a small town, true, without a lot of Flagstaff's amenities, but the country was beautiful, and he had a feeling land would be, if not cheap, at least a lot less expensive than the immediate area around his own hometown. They could buy some acreage, build a house, maybe take up ranching or something else that would provide cover for their Wilcox clan income and Addie's sizable inheritance.

Pie in the sky? Maybe; Jake knew he was making a lot of assumptions, foremost among them that this Carson Archuleta, the tribal elder who'd allowed Addie to stay in Riverton, would be okay with a warlock coming along and hooking up with a self-exiled witch…and maybe starting their own witch family in the not-so-distant future.

"You look like you're a million miles away," Addie said as she reached for her glass of wine.

"Not that far," he replied. They'd come to dinner early, partly because all that roaming around in the fresh air had stimulated their appetites, despite the big picnic lunch they'd shared at noon, and partly because the steakhouse closed at eight on Sunday nights and they didn't want to be forced to go somewhere else. "Just to the land around Riverton. I was wondering what a ranch might go for around here."

Her eyebrows lifted. While he found her beautiful at all times, he had to admit that she looked especially stunning that night, with her dark brown hair falling against her bare shoulders and the silky green blouse she wore awakening all the greenish tones in her jade-hued eyes. "You want to be a rancher?" she asked, sounding genuinely surprised.

"Well, I'll have to do something with myself if I relocate here, won't I?"

"You're really serious about that?"

"Dead serious."

She flinched slightly at that reply, and he cursed himself for his choice of words. But he couldn't take the comment back—not without calling even more attention to what he'd just said—and so he forced himself to continue.

"I honestly think it's the smartest thing to do… if the local tribe is okay with us setting up our own little colony here."

Glass in hand, she settled against the back of her chair and sent him another questioning look. "So, now we're a colony?"

Damn. He really was stepping in it this evening, wasn't he? And Jake knew he couldn't blame his verbal gaffes on the wine, either, considering he'd drunk less than half a glass so far. But, in for a penny—

"Maybe eventually. I mean, if we're together—"

A chuckle as she appeared to take pity on him. "Okay, I get it. You want lots of little Wil…erm, kids running around."

"Well, not *lots,* lots," he told her, figuring he should do his best not to scare her off completely. "Two seems like an acceptable number."

"Yes, I suppose so." Her lips twitched, and she lifted her glass to take a sip, obviously doing her best not to laugh out loud at his discomfiture. "So, you want to stay in Riverton and buy a ranch and have two point five kids and a white picket fence. Am I missing anything?"

"I don't think so," Jake replied. "I mean, I already have a dog."

"What about the part where you make an honest woman of me?"

He stared at her for a few seconds before he realized what an utter hash he'd made of things. There he was, talking about kids and ranches and dogs, and they hadn't done anything except share a few kisses. He hadn't told her he loved her. He definitely hadn't asked her to marry him. It had been so amazing to spend this day with her and to reestablish their connection that his brain had just sort of skipped ahead to what it viewed as the logical next step.

"Well, that, too…if you'll have me."

Her gaze met his. Good thing they had a quiet table off in a corner, or anyone intercepting that glance might have gotten scorched by the need in her eyes, a need matched by a terrible hope, as if she'd never truly thought the day would come when someone might ask her to be their partner in eternity. Which was what he was attempting to do, even if he'd done his best to stumble over himself and make it sound as if he didn't know what the hell he was doing.

Voice pitched so low that he had to lean forward to hear her words, she said, "This is kind of nuts, isn't it? I mean, you just got into town the night before last. And before that, I'd thought I would never see you again."

"I thought the same thing," he replied. "But I found you. That has to mean something."

"It means a lot." She lifted her glass of wine and took a sip, then put it back down on the cloth-covered table.

"I'd expected you to be angrier," he told her then, and wondered if he should have kept his mouth shut.

Once again, her mouth looked as if it wanted to smile…but it didn't. "I'm kind of surprised I wasn't. I think I was just more shocked than anything else. Anyway, you seemed angry enough for both of us."

"I did?" So much for trying to keep a rein on his emotions.

"Not in a scary way," she said quickly. "Just…I could tell you were upset with me. And I can see why, even though I thought I was doing what was best for both of us."

He had to ask. "Do you still feel that way?"

Another of those direct stares. He loved that about her, loved that she would meet his gaze and not try to look away or deflect just because it would have been easier to do so. "No. I want…I want to be with you. However we make that work. Even if it means eventually going back to Flagstaff, with all the risks that might entail."

She looked as if she wanted to say more, but their waiter came by then with the steaks they'd ordered. After thanking him and letting him know they were both fine and didn't need anything else for the moment, Jake said quietly, "I don't think being in Flagstaff is as risky as you think it is. But, like I said, I'm fine with being here."

"What if Connor tells you that you have to go home?"

That possibility had crossed his mind, but Jake thought it was probably a long shot. "He's not a king, Addie. He can't order me to do stuff."

"He can't? I kind of got the impression that we all had to do what the *prim*—what he tells us to do."

Technically, that was true. In any witch clan, if the *prima*—or *primus*—laid down the law, then it was the clan members' duty to act according to their wishes. And Addie's father, Jackson Wilcox, had definitely run the clan that way. But Connor was cut from different cloth, and Jake very much doubted he would try to enforce his power as *primus*. He might try to persuade the two of them that it wasn't safe for them to be on their own so far from Wilcox territory, and he might enlist Angela to add her two cents to the discussion, but in the end, it wasn't as though he would send his lieutenants to find them and throw them in witch jail or something.

"This isn't the Dark Ages," Jake said.

"Maybe not, but…." Addie let the words trail off, then shrugged. "You have a lot more experience with this sort of thing than I do, so I guess I'll just have to take your word for it. And in the end, I suppose it doesn't matter where we are as long as we're together."

Exactly what he'd been hoping she'd say. He'd come to the same conclusion, but it still heartened him to realize he wasn't dreaming all this, that she wanted the same things he did.

"Yes," he said, then made himself smile. "But now we'd better eat our steaks, or they'll get cold."

This was only the literal truth, so she nodded and picked up her fork and steak knife, and he did the same. A few minutes passed as they helped themselves to medium-rare steak and loaded baked potatoes and grilled asparagus. The food was better than he'd expected, and Jake chided himself inwardly for thinking once again that a little place like Riverton, Wyoming, couldn't have decent food. No, it wasn't Criollo or Brix or The Cottage, all favorite restaurants of his in Flagstaff, but he thought that a guy could definitely get used to eating steaks like these.

And once their conversation resumed, Addie guided it to safe topics like their plans for the next day, and whether they should attempt to make a real dinner in her tiny kitchen. Jake said that sounded like fun, and promised to do any chopping and slicing and dicing.

"It's probably the only thing you can really trust

me with," he told her ruefully. "I'm the kind of guy who can burn water. Well, unless I'm barbecuing something, but I don't think I saw a grill at your place."

"Nope—Tracy did a good job of outfitting the kitchen, but there's no barbecue." Addie poked a spear of asparagus with her fork, lifted it to her mouth, and chewed delicately. "And I'm not the world's greatest cook or anything, but even I can manage a pot of spaghetti."

"And garlic bread?" Jake asked, knowing he sounded like a kid asking for his favorite dessert. But he loved the stuff, even though he tried not to eat it too often.

"Sure," she said, smothering a smile. "And salad, too, so we're not being completely decadent."

Actually, he thought that being completely decadent sounded like fun, although he didn't protest the salad, only murmured his assent and then reached for his glass of wine.

Speaking of dessert—they decided to split a piece of chocolate fudge cake, and finished off their meal just a little before eight. Feeling virtuous that they'd gotten out of the restaurant before its official closing time, Jake guided Addie to the truck and then went around to the driver's side. Even at that hour, twilight still lingered and the landscape wasn't entirely dark. Despite the glow around the world's edges, he could see the great, glittering mist of the

Milky Way arched overhead, and craned his neck to get a better look.

Addie followed his gaze. "I don't think I'll ever get tired of that sight," she said quietly. "It makes me glad that my mother almost always had us living in small towns where the streetlights weren't bright enough to drown out the stars. I don't know how people in big cities manage."

Neither did he. Flagstaff was a medium-sized town, but it was a designated "dark sky" city, meaning the city planners had taken pains to ensure that whatever light it gave off wasn't enough to interfere with local star watching.

And he noticed how she'd mentioned her mother easily, without the slight hesitation that usually entered her voice whenever she spoke of Lyssa Grant. He hoped that was a good sign; it was natural for Addie to have been confronted by her grief all over again when the two of them entered the Native American cemetery that afternoon, but maybe the healing process was continuing on levels he couldn't necessarily always detect.

"Well, it doesn't look as if we'll have to worry about living in a big city," he remarked, and she smiled, eyes nearly as bright as the stars that sparkled overhead.

"No, probably not."

They both climbed into the truck, and he pointed it toward Addie's little rented house. By that point, he'd come and gone from the place enough times that he knew how to get there, and he pulled up into the driveway and parked behind her Fiat in the carport, which was already starting to look dusty from having to sit out all day with not much protection from the elements.

Now that the time had come to walk her back inside, a strange diffidence stole over him. In his mind, he'd been imagining how he wanted their day together to end—and, if the signals she'd been giving were any indication, she felt the same way—but he couldn't be completely sure. If she decided she wanted to wait, of course he wouldn't protest, and yet he'd still be disappointed.

And possibly also slightly relieved. After all, it had been years for him. Not that he didn't think he could rise to the occasion, so to speak, but he wanted their first time together to be perfect.

Maybe she was feeling some of the same hesitation, because she was quiet as she led him inside and then locked the door behind them. After setting her purse on the kitchen table and draping her lightweight cardigan on the chair next to it, she turned around and said, not quite meeting his eyes, "Do you want some water? I don't have much else, but—"

"Water is fine," he said quickly. It was a good idea, partly because getting water to drink would give them something to do, and also because their waiter, while attentive otherwise, hadn't been quite as proactive about filling their water glasses as he might have been.

"Okay." She got some glasses out of the cupboard and filled them from the tap; her fridge, although cute, didn't have a dispenser in its door or any of those modern conveniences. After handing a glass to him, she took a sip, then blurted out, "This is awkward, isn't it?"

He'd been thinking pretty much the same thing, but he still felt relieved by her honesty. "It doesn't have to be. I just wanted to make sure you got in the house safely—I can go back to my hotel after this."

"No," she said at once. After taking another swallow of water, as if she needed it to fortify herself, she went on, "I want you to stay, Jake. I want…I want to be with you. If that's okay."

If it was okay? Of course, it was okay. He'd never wanted anything more in his life.

"I'd like to stay," he said quietly.

"Good."

She set down her glass and laced her fingers in his, then pulled him close. Their mouths met, and he tasted the sweetness of her lips, the faint tang of the wine they'd drunk with dinner. Need pulsed through him, all the awkwardness of just a moment earlier gone as if it had never existed. Her body, slender and yet lush at the same time, pressed against him, warm and utterly inviting.

And there were her eyes glowing up at him, telling him she wanted this just as much as he did.

"Let's go," she whispered, and led him from the living room.

What could he do except follow?

16

I WASN'T LETTING MYSELF STOP TO THINK. NOT with the way my blood seemed to race through my veins, not with how my fingers attacked the buttons on Jake's shirt as if they had a mind of their own. I knew I had to keep going, because otherwise, I'd lose my nerve.

I didn't want to do that. Maybe I'd lost my mind, but I wasn't going to let doubt or worry or fear stop me from being with him. From the moment he'd first kissed me, I'd known deep down it would come to this. I could run away, but I couldn't hide from the connection between us, which felt like a living thing. Denying it was impossible.

Surrender seemed the only option.

His body surprised me with its perfection. Or rather, I'd guessed he would be gorgeous, but those abstract imaginings couldn't come close to the reality of his smooth, sun-tanned skin, or the taut, sculpted muscles of his arms and chest and stomach. I trailed my fingers over his bare chest and heard him make a sound halfway between a gasp and a sigh, as if even he hadn't really been expecting to react so strongly to my touch.

Once again, our mouths met as we tasted one another, breaths mingling, bodies pressed together. His fingers fumbled with the hem of the blouse I wore, and I pulled away long enough for him to draw it over my head and drop it to the floor. Then he moved on to the hooks at the back of my bra, and released them so it could fall to the carpet and lie next to my blouse.

Maybe I should have been embarrassed or shy to be so exposed before him, but with hot blood surging through me and a deep pulse of need throbbing at my core, I was far beyond modesty. I wanted him to look at me like that, dark eyes glittering with desire, his obvious lust more of a turn-on than I'd ever believed something like that could be.

His head bent, and he took my nipple into his mouth. Oh, dear God, it felt so good that I couldn't do anything except let out a moan, fingers digging into his shoulders as that pulsing core of desire at my very center seemed to grow hotter and more needy.

Then he was pulling me to the bed, where we

both fell down on the quilt. He pushed it out of the way so the cool sheets could touch my bare skin. In the next moment, he was undoing my jeans and then yanking them down, along with the panties I wore underneath. His fingers slipped into me, gentle but strong, and I let out a moan so loud, I wished I'd had the forethought to close the bedroom window.

After that, however, rational thought was pretty much gone. All I could do was lie there and revel in the new and exquisite sensations shivering their way through my body. I wouldn't lie; I might have been a virgin, but I'd touched myself before, stealing precious moments when I was alone in the house to do my best to give myself some kind of relief. However, those rushed, half-guilty interludes couldn't begin to compare to the sensation of Jake Wilcox's deft, sure fingers touching me in exactly the right place, letting me know that I wouldn't have to wait very long for the climax.

Even though I could feel the orgasm approaching, it still took me by surprise, surging through me with the force of a summer monsoon storm. I cried out, then raised a hand to my mouth to muffle the sound, my body shuddering as it rippled along every limb, nerve endings singing with the energy of a climax unlike any I'd experienced before.

Jake held me until my breathing quieted, then placed a gentle kiss on my temple. "I guess I wasn't moving too fast after all," he said, but although the words could have sounded flip, they didn't come across that way, not with the gentle caress of his tone.

"Not too fast," I responded, my own voice breathy and husky. My heart still pounded, but in a good way. "That was…incredible."

His lips touched mine. "Oh, darling…we're just getting started."

I couldn't help but smile. "Damn straight."

That time, it was my fingers reaching for the button of his jeans, undoing the crazy belt buckle I'd bought for him earlier at the flea market. It made a heavy metallic clank as I dropped his discarded pants off the side of the bed, but I barely paid attention. No, my gaze was caught by the large bulge in the black boxer briefs he wore.

Again, no time to hesitate. I slipped my fingers under the waistband of his briefs and pulled them down. A little gasp escaped my lips at the sight of him, but I reminded myself that fortune favored the bold, and I reached out and wrapped my hand around his shaft.

That time, he was the one who gasped. I slowly moved my hand up and down, hoping I was doing it correctly and wasn't exposing myself for the complete amateur I knew I actually was.

It didn't seem as if Jake had any complaints, because a moan escaped his lips, and he sank down onto the pillows as though he could no longer support his own weight. I knew better than to stop, and continued to caress him, reveling in the exquisite sensation of the silky skin that overlaid his rock-hard erection.

His breathing quickened, but after a moment, he laid a hand on top of mine. "You need to stop there," he said, his voice ragged. "Or I'm going to come."

"You say that like it's a bad thing."

He rolled over, pinning me beneath him. Breath hot against my neck, he whispered, "Oh, I want to. But I'd rather be somewhere else when it happens."

"What…like on the living room couch?" I asked innocently, and he chuckled.

"You know exactly what I mean."

Oh, yes, I did. I didn't have a chance to respond, though, because he'd begun to kiss his way down my body—pausing for a moment to give my breasts some extra attention—and then paused between my legs. Was he really going to…?

Yes, he was.

I arched my back as his tongue touched me, my fingers digging into the sheets. Just being stroked by him had been amazing, but this—this was utter heaven. All the heat and sensation in my body seemed to be focused on the exquisite center of pleasure at the core of my being, throbbing with desire, with the realization that I was now thrall to its needs and could do nothing except allow myself to be swept away, to focus all of myself and my consciousness into that one pulsing point of pure pleasure.

Another orgasm exploded through me, so intense that I thought I saw shooting stars when I shut my eyes. I gasped and gasped, doing my best to pull some much-needed oxygen into my lungs. Jake pressed his lips against my belly, kissing his way upward this time until our mouths touched. I tasted my musk on his lips and trembled again, thinking of how he'd managed to bring me to such heights, to the kind of exquisite sensation I hadn't even imagined was possible.

And I could feel him pressing against my leg, hard. He was so close….

"I need to get a condom," he said, and I blinked at him, the words not quite processing. He smiled down at me. "I know we're both safe. But I'm not sure risking pregnancy is a very good idea right now."

Of course. I knew that. And yet—and yet, I hated the thought of having even the world's thinnest condom separating the two of us. I wanted to feel him in every way possible.

"If you have to," I told him. "But…I wish you didn't."

He paused for a moment, face still so very close to mine. "There might be another way…."

"What?"

"It's a charm the McAllister witches have been using for generations. They call on Brigid—the goddess—to keep them from conceiving. I guess they've been teaching it to my Wilcox cousins."

I supposed if you accepted the reality of witches in the world, then you also had to accept there could be other forces out there as well, ones that might be called gods and goddesses, for lack of a better term. "This charm works?"

"I think so. At least, Laurel says it does."

Well, if Laurel claimed that it worked, then I was willing to give it a try. I wanted this first time with Jake to be utterly perfect, and that meant fore-going a condom…since I had a witchy alternative that sounded much more appealing.

"What do I have to do?"

"After…well, afterward, you just say, 'Blessed Brigid, now is not the time. Bestow your blessings elsewhere.'"

The charm was almost deceptively simple. "That's it?"

A flash of white teeth in the darkness as he grinned. "That's it."

"Perfect."

We kissed again, bodies pressed together. This time, I could feel him moving closer, could feel him pushing against my entrance. I tried not to tense, because even though I wanted this more than anything else in the world, I knew the first time could hurt a little, and I didn't want to mar our perfect moment by wincing in pain.

"Ready?" he whispered.

"Yes," I said. "Oh, yes, Jake."

Whether it was because I was truly ready for him, or because those stories about first-time pain were an exaggeration, I didn't know, but it definitely didn't hurt as he slipped inside me. No, I was only overwhelmed by the sensation of being closer to him than I'd ever been to anyone in my entire life. We began to move together, our bodies finding their rhythms as he pushed deeper into me and I wrapped my legs around him. Yes, that was utterly perfect, the connection between us deepening as well, feeling almost like a live thing. The entire universe might have been only the two of us, the sound of our breaths blending, the heat of his flesh mingling with the warmth of mine.

Yet another climax began to build in me, a slow, rolling wave that grew and grew as he moved faster and faster. This time, he was the one who cried out first, hips slamming against mine when he came, his seed a sudden heat in the very center of my body. A moment later, the orgasm swept through me as well, and I let out a moan, clinging to him, riding it out, waiting until the very last shimmer of ecstasy had flowed through my limbs before I allowed myself to fall limply against the cushions.

I needed to say the charm…and I would. But I needed to tell him something first.

"I love you, Jake Wilcox," I said.

"And I love you, Adara Grant," he replied.

We slept in each other's arms, and when I woke up the next morning, it seemed the most natural thing in the world to kiss Jake softly on the cheek, and to watch his eyes open and then warm with desire as he turned and faced me. Without speaking, we reached for one another, hands moving over the other person's body, each of us coming alive to the day and the strength of the connection between us. Still in silence, he sank into me as I welcomed him, welcomed the perfect sensation of him filling all the empty spaces I'd carried within me for too long.

Afterward, we shared the shower, which was surprisingly big for a house so small. In the daylight, I could get an even better look at all the magnificent planes and angles of his body, could sink to the floor of the shower enclosure so I could take him in my mouth and return the favor he'd given me the night before.

Eventually, though, we were out and dressed, smiling at each other while the coffee brewed. I remembered that we'd discussed going to the break-fast buffet at the casino, but I was hungry, and went ahead and got a box of frozen waffles out of the freezer.

"Sure you don't want one to tide you over until brunch?" I asked, even as I let myself get a good look at him in all his early morning glory, hair still damp, dark scruff serving to highlight the strong lines of his jaw rather than obscure it.

"Okay," he said. "I guess I have worked up kind of an appetite."

I grinned at him and popped a pair of waffles into the toaster oven, then went to the cupboard to get us some mugs for our coffee. "Still want to eat in tonight?"

A gleam went through his dark eyes at that particular question. "Oh, I definitely want to…eat in."

I tilted my head and shot him what I hoped was a properly scolding look. "Is that all you can think about?"

"No," he responded. "It just all I *want* to think about."

Well, I couldn't give him too much grief over that, not when my own brain seemed perfectly happy to keep replaying some of the key moments from our encounter the night before…and the one that had followed this morning.

"Fair enough," I said blithely as I got out the carafe of coffee and filled both our mugs. "Still, I suppose we should think of a couple other things to do today."

"Well, brunch," Jake said. "And we'll need to go to the store if we really are going to attempt a spaghetti dinner here tonight."

Right. Trying to put together something decent in such a tiny kitchen would be a challenge, but I agreed that it would be better to have a cozy dinner at home, especially since we were going out for brunch. "True, but that isn't exactly going to take all day."

"We can do more exploring. Wander around. It looks like it's going to be another nice day."

That it did. I didn't pretend to know much about the weather in this part of the world, but so far, it seemed as if June felt somewhat the same as it had in Colorado and New Mexico, sunny and warm, with no sign of any storms. We should take advantage of the sun while we could.

"Sounds good," I said. "Maybe head south this time? The area around Lander looked kind of interesting when I drove through."

Jake agreed that sounded like a good plan, and after we had our coffee and breakfast waffles, we headed out to the store to get supplies for our evening dinner. By the time we'd brought everything back to the house and stored our supplies in the fridge or the cupboards, it was almost noon, as good a time as any to go out for brunch. Just as I'd promised him, the spread was huge and varied, and I wondered privately whether I'd even have room for a spaghetti dinner after eating what felt like my weight in bacon and made-to-order omelettes and a dizzying array of sweet rolls and other breakfast pastries.

But we worked a lot of it off by wandering the trails around Lander. And probably some more in sheer nervous energy, because I reached out to Carson Archuleta and let him know what Jake and I were planning. To my infinite relief, he only said Jake was welcome to stay with me in Wind River for as long as he liked, and that he hoped we would both be very happy there.

By the time we got back to the house around six, I was already starting to feel hungry again. We poured ourselves a glass of wine to fortify ourselves for dinner prep and got to work, with Jake slicing and dicing peppers and onions for me just as he'd promised, while I sautéed some ground beef for the sauce and set a big pot of water to boil for the pasta. I didn't have a cookbook, but that sort of thing wasn't necessary when you could look up literally millions of recipes on the internet, and soon enough, I had what promised to be a very tasty sauce gently simmering on the stove.

I had Jake set the table while I prepped the garlic bread, and, despite using a new recipe for the sauce and working with a kitchen I didn't know very well, by the time seven o'clock rolled around, we had what looked like a pretty creditable spaghetti dinner laid out. He poured us more chianti after we sat down, and lifted his glass to touch mine.

"To another perfect day," he said. His dark eyes shone as he gazed at me and added, "Then again, I think pretty much every day with you is perfect."

My cheeks flushed, but I made myself look straight at him. I needed to accept his compliments, not try to ignore them or pretend they couldn't possibly be true. "And it's perfect being with you."

He sipped some of his chianti and set down the glass. "I like this place. I think we can make it home."

"It's a little small," I said, giving a quick glance around the combo living/dining room where we sat.

His lips twitched. "Not this house," he replied, "although I'll admit it's pretty cute. I just meant Riverton and the general area around here."

Even though we'd already discussed the eventuality of making the Wind River area our home, an unwelcome swirl of unease went through me. "You're sure? It seems like it's a big deal to give up your clan, just for me."

"You're not 'just' anything, Addie," Jake said. He reached across the table and placed his hand on mine. "Where you are, I'm home. I feel that more strongly than ever now."

Home. Yes, that was exactly how I felt with

Jake. Like I was at home, the sort of secure, welcoming home my mother had done her best to provide for me but had never really managed to make a reality. It wasn't her fault...no, it was the fault of my magical talent, which had forced us to be perpetually on the move. All the same, my entire youth and young adulthood, I'd always been just a little off balance, a little uneasy, since I'd always known that it didn't matter how comfortable I might feel in a place—sooner or later, something would happen to compel us to run away to the next temporary haven.

"I feel it, too," I murmured, and he squeezed my fingers gently before releasing them so he could pick up his fork.

"Then it's settled. I'll need to go back to Flagstaff briefly, though, to get some stuff worked out."

"'To Flagstaff?" I echoed, trying not to give rein to the worry that wanted to flood through me. "Why?"

To my relief, he didn't look annoyed by the question, even though I'd feared as I asked it whether I was coming off as far too needy. "Well, for one thing, I need to get Jeremy's truck back to him and pick up mine. But don't worry," Jake added quickly, "I know that Gladiator is way too conspic-uous to bring to a place like Riverton. While I'm in Flagstaff, I'll trade it in for a Wrangler. There's millions of those on the road, so I doubt it'll attract too much attention."

I had to agree that was probably a better solution. At the same time, though, I experienced a pang of guilt at forcing Jake to give up his beloved truck. It didn't seem fair.

But if the world had taught me anything, it was that a whole bunch of things in it weren't exactly fair. Anyway, this wasn't something I'd asked Jake to do, but a decision he'd come to on his own, so I didn't see the point in arguing with him over it.

"Okay," I said, and picked up my glass of wine and took a sip.

"And I have to get Taffy, obviously," he went on, "and see if I can get someone to house-sit for me while I decide what to do with the place. And move some money around, and break the news to my parents."

I hadn't even thought about that part. Most of our discussions had revolved around the clan in general and not Jake's immediate family in particular. Possibly because I was so unmoored, with both parents gone, I'd almost forgotten that he had a mother and father—and grandparents—who naturally wouldn't be all that thrilled to have him announce he was leaving Flagstaff and moving two states away.

"They're going to hate me," I said morosely, and once again, he reached over and touched my hand.

Despite my current worry, I couldn't ignore the thrill even that small caress sent through my body. It still amazed me, the way I reacted to him.

"No, they won't hate you," he told me. "I'll explain the situation, and they'll understand. My parents are cool—you would like them."

Since they'd raised someone like Jake—and his brother Jeremy, although I had to admit he was more difficult to know—I couldn't really argue with that statement. At the same time, another wave of guilt washed through me. It seemed as though I should have asked to meet Jake's parents during the time I spent in Flagstaff, but he'd never broached the subject, and frankly, I hadn't thought to ask. Things between us then had been very new, and it hadn't felt like we'd reached the point in our relationship when it was necessary for me to do the whole "meet the parents" thing.

"I wish I could have met them," I said, and he offered me an encouraging smile.

"I'm sure you will at some point. We can have them come visit after we get settled here. I'm sure if Carson Archuleta is okay with having me living in his territory, then he won't object to a family visit."

Probably not, especially since that was all it would be—just a drop-in by Jake's parents to finally get to meet me and see where their son had ended up. If we found the right property, we could be settled fairly quickly. I allowed myself a brief daydream of showing them around Jake's and my new house, complete with acreage and maybe something fun like goats. Just a chance to live like normal people…a nice young couple that no one would ever suspect of being a witch and a warlock hiding out from the federal government.

"That sounds like a great idea," I said, and was rewarded by his brilliant flash of a smile.

"Well, we'll bring it up once we get settled," he replied. "And when I'm in Flag, I'll move some money around so we have enough liquid assets to purchase property when we do find something. I know Connor will make sure to do the same thing for you."

I wasn't sure whether I shared Jake's confidence, but I had to admit that he knew my half-brother far better than I did. "Well, if that's how it shakes out, then we should use my money to buy a house. I mean, you must have a lot tied up in your place in Flagstaff, and if you don't sell it right away…." The words trailed off as I tilted my head at him. "How *did* you afford that house, anyway? I mean, I know you said everyone in the clan gets a stipend, but that's still not enough to buy a house like that, is it?"

"Not usually," he said. Judging by the way he leaned against the back of his chair and smiled slightly, I guessed I hadn't touched on a sensitive topic, and I allowed myself an inner exhalation of relief. "It was priced really low because it belonged to a couple of relatives who wanted to downsize to a townhouse after they retired. Also, the Wilcoxes are kind of unusual in this, but everyone also gets a one-time cash payment when they decide to buy a house. It's a quarter-mil per person, and Sarah and I pooled ours to buy the place, so…that's why I could afford it."

He said the words so blithely, as if it was no big deal. A quarter million dollars, handed out to everyone in the clan when it came time to become a homeowner. Just how much money was the Wilcox family actually sitting on? It had to be millions and millions, and my head fairly swam at the thought.

My stupefaction must have been obvious, because Jake went on, "Remember, the clan's been in Flagstaff for generations, investing in land and mineral rights, that sort of thing. We have tons of investments and a huge portfolio. And we also have people like my cousin Lucas, who kind of helps things along."

"Lucas?" I said. I didn't recall Jake mentioning him before. "Is he a stockbroker or something?"

"No," he replied with another grin. "His talent is luck. He passes along tips on things, and they always pan out. When the market crashed in 2008, he told the clan money managers to pull everything out of stocks and put it in T-bills and other low-risk investments instead. So, we didn't lose any money—and we also made a lot from buying up distressed properties and then selling them at big profits once the economy rebounded and housing prices went back up."

Luck. There was a hell of a talent. Once again, I wondered why the universe had decided to inflict my particular "gift" on me, although I had to admit it really wasn't so bad now that I had a grip on it, thanks to Joanna's tutelage.

I hadn't missed the part where Jake had mentioned how his fiancée had contributed to the purchase of his home, but I decided not to mention it. After all, he'd already told me that they'd bought the place together, and although I didn't know how they'd worked it out and wasn't going to ask, I guessed that she must have had a will or some other bequest which stated that Jake should inherit the house if anything happened to her.

"Sounds like it's a pretty good deal to be a Wilcox," I said before picking up a forkful of my neglected spaghetti.

"Most of the time, it is. Not that we haven't had our issues over the years, but it's been pretty smooth sailing lately."

Well, except for wiping the memory of a government agent and dumping him in an anonymous motel room in Kanab, Utah. Luckily, it didn't seem as if that particular exploit had come back to bite anyone in the ass.

Not yet, anyway.

Although I'd resolved to remain cheerful about the situation, I couldn't quite prevent myself from letting out a small sigh. "And yet you're still willing to leave all that behind."

"To be with you, Addie," Jake said, his tone quiet but intense. "You're worth it."

I had my doubts about that, but I didn't want to argue. Clearly, Jake's mind was made up, and I had to admit his solution did seem to be the best one. By that evening, I'd been in Riverton for almost a week, and I hadn't seen hide nor hair of Randall Lenz, or anyone who looked even remotely like a government agent. Whether it was luck or Jeremy's superior hacking abilities or a combination of the two, it appeared as though I truly had given my pursuer the slip.

"I'll make sure you never regret the decision," I said then. This time, I was the one who reached out, and Jake's hand slipped into mine, warm and reassuring.

"I never will. Wherever you are is where I want to be. And this will be a quick trip—no more than four days at the most."

Four days sounded like an eternity, but I knew he needed enough time to handle all the necessary business in Flagstaff, and it was a very long drive, even if he decided to brute-force it and do the thirteen-hour drive in each direction in a single day, rather than break it up the way I had when traveling to Riverton.

"I'll be here," I assured him. "And I'll be back at work the whole time, so I'll have something to keep me busy."

"See?" he said. "It'll work out. It always does."

I told myself I believed those words. After all, after so many years of misfortune, I was ready for my luck to change.

17

THE THOUGHT FORMED FULLY IN HIS HEAD, SO solid and real that it was almost as if someone had spoken the words in his ear, even though he was alone in his office.

You need to go back to Santa Fe.

Randall Lenz scowled and rubbed his temple, even though—at that particular moment, at least— he didn't have a headache. Still, he thought he'd prefer a migraine to random voices in his head.

He reached for the lukewarm cup of coffee sitting on his desk and took a swallow, trying not to grimace at the taste of the bitter liquid. Government funding up the wazoo, and yet no one around there seemed able to produce a decent cup of coffee.

Frown deepening, he put the coffee back down and considered what the voice had told him. And no, it wasn't really a voice, *per se,* but a thought so solid and real, it might as well have been spoken out loud.

Why Santa Fe, though? That particular lead had turned out to be a complete dead end. He could only imagine Genoveva Castillo's reaction if he should turn up on her doorstep again. No, he didn't have any reason to fear her, but his research had told him she was a woman with some power in her community, and if she should voice a complaint to her congressperson or one of New Mexico's senators…well, that wouldn't be a very good look. The agency did its best to fly under the radar and avoid attracting attention. If one of its program directors was accused of harassment, that might invite closer scrutiny of its activities…which might then result in an investigation into exactly where it got its funding.

However, returning to Santa Fe didn't necessarily mean he would have to speak to Ms. Castillo. On his last trip, he'd been in and out so quickly that he hadn't spent a lot of time poking around, other than making inquiries at the downtown hotels. He hadn't seen the point, not when there were no more leads to follow, no video footage to substantively prove that Adara Grant had even been in the city at all.

But something was tickling his mind, and Lenz knew it was never a good idea to ignore one of his hunches. Sometimes they took a while to come to fruition, but they almost always paid off one way or another.

And, for the moment, no one was auditing his expenditures, so it wasn't as if he had to justify the cost of yet another trip to New Mexico. He picked up the phone and put in the request, and was told that a car would take him to his waiting jet at Hyde Field, only three miles away.

No need to pack; the go-bag he kept in his office at all times was waiting just for this sort of occasion. He got up from his chair and went out to Dawson's workstation. As usual, she had her eyes glued to the monitor in front of her, slender fingers flying across the keyboard.

"Did you find something?" Lenz inquired as he paused behind her office chair.

"I'm not sure yet," she replied, not looking away from the monitor.

As far as he could tell, she was shuffling back and forth between two frames of a video that looked as if it had come from a gas station security camera. An odd flicker came and went on the screen so quickly, he wasn't sure whether he'd actually seen anything at all, or whether his eyes were playing tricks on him.

"Did you see that?" Dawson asked.

"Yes, I think so." He glanced down at her, noting the way her teeth had caught on her lower lip as she stared at the image. It wasn't the first time he'd seen her bite her lip in such a way, and the unconscious tic almost always signaled that she was focused so intensely on something, she didn't even know what she was doing. "What do you think it is?"

"Not sure…but I'm starting to wonder if it's a breadcrumb our hacker left behind."

"An artifact from something he tried to scrub?" Lenz inquired. The possibility sent a spark of excitement through him, even though he had to admit that the evidence involved appeared to be flimsier than parachute silk.

"Maybe. You see?" She touched her finger to the screen, where that same strange blur was frozen in place. It almost…

…well, it almost looked like a person. A slender person, with what might or might not have been long dark hair falling down their back.

Adara Grant was slender, with dark brown hair that hit just below where her bra strap would be.

He knew he was reaching, and yet….

If the image really had been scrubbed in some way, who else would the hacker have been trying to erase? Lenz supposed it was possible that he'd also used some sort of randomizing program to hack into the security feeds of various locations around the country, just to throw any investigators off the track, but such a possibility seemed a bit far-fetched.

No, it made a lot more sense that, good as he

was, he'd made a mistake here. A very small one, a little bobble that probably would have escaped notice under most circumstances. But Dawson had eagle eyes, and she'd been obsessing over Adara Grant's disappearance almost as much as Lenz had.

"Where is this footage from?"

"Alamosa, Colorado. It's about forty miles from the New Mexico border."

New Mexico. And here he'd already ordered a plane to take him to Santa Fe. His hunch might have been a little off, but it had been sending him in the right direction.

"What's around Alamosa?"

Dawson minimized the still shot from the video footage with its strange blur and brought up a map of the western half of the country. From what Lenz could tell, it didn't look as though there was much of anything around Alamosa. It was a wide spot in the middle of Highway 285, and obviously more than a hundred miles from Denver.

Still….

Something had been telling him he needed to head back to that part of the country. While he doubted Alamosa had been Adara Grant's final destination—if that blur on the surveillance footage was even her at all, and not some artifact from a glitchy camera—he knew in his gut that she must have gone that way as she left Santa Fe. Because yes, Genoveva Castillo's story about her lookalike cousin notwithstanding, he also knew without knowing how he knew that Adara had been there in the capital city before heading out to…wherever she intended to go. Someplace where she could hide herself, could lie low and hope that she'd done enough to keep any pursuers off the scent.

Denver made some sense, simply because it was often easier to lose oneself in a big city than in a small town in the middle of nowhere, but if it had been her destination, her route didn't make a lot of sense. It would have been simpler for her to take I-25 east and then north, rather than follow Highway 285 directly out of Santa Fe and then be forced to cut over on another small highway to reach the Mile-High City.

Unless she had wanted to avoid the interstate, for whatever reason. Another way of trying to lie low? Possible; the interstate had more traffic cameras than the smaller "blue highways."

"When was this video taken?" he asked.

Dawson pulled up the image again. The time stamp in the lower corner told him it had been shot on June ninth. A whole week earlier.

Hell. That much time elapsed could have put Adara Grant anywhere in the country. Or even the continent, although Lenz reminded himself that she didn't have a passport and therefore would be somewhat constrained in her movements.

And yet….

He somehow knew she was still somewhere in the West, hadn't turned right at Denver and continued on I-70 until she reached the East Coast and disappeared into its sprawl. For one thing, although Adara and her mother had moved around a lot, they'd pretty much stayed in the mountain states—Wyoming and Colorado, Utah and New Mexico. There was no evidence at all to suggest they'd ever gone back to Ohio, Lyssa Grant's home state, or anywhere farther east than that. Likewise, they'd never traveled farther north than the southern part of Wyoming, or farther west than Kanab.

For good or ill, people tended to stick with what they knew, repeating the same patterns that had become embedded in their lives over the passing years. Lenz was not a gambling man, but he would have bet a sizable amount of money that Adara hadn't ventured too far afield.

"Is there an airport near Alamosa?"

Dawson typed away, then nodded. "One right in the town, sir. San Luis Valley Regional. It'll handle your jet, no problem."

Perfect. He'd take the car to his waiting plane, and instruct the pilot to fly to Alamosa rather than Santa Fe. While he still didn't believe Adara Grant would be waiting for him there, he knew he would be that much closer to her.

And then…

...well, and then, he'd just have to wait for a sign and hope his luck would continue to hold.

Jake couldn't quite avoid holding his breath as he passed the city limits sign for Provo, but the borrowed truck he drove didn't give any indication that it intended to cause the same problem it had on his outward bound journey. Still, he stopped there for gas and a quick bite, knowing he was going to push on to Flagstaff no matter what. He'd left Riverton at seven in the morning, giving a sleepy Addie a quick kiss before grabbing his things and heading out. With minimal stops—and no car trouble—he figured he'd be home by nine that night at the latest.

You'll need to stop thinking of it as "home," he reminded himself as he pulled back onto Interstate 15. *Riverton is going to be home now.*

That thought sent a pang through him, even though he'd only been telling Addie the truth when he'd said that home would be anywhere she was. Still, he'd never known anything except Flagstaff, and had honestly never expected to make a life for himself anywhere but there.

But circumstances had intervened, and he'd make the best of it. Riverton was a pretty town— lots of wide-open spaces, plenty of opportunities to hike and explore. It wasn't as if he had to worry about finding a job, although he supposed at some point he'd probably need to do so, if only to keep people from wondering how the two of them were staying afloat with no visible means of income.

First things first, though. He'd be getting in too late to talk to his parents, but that conversation would need to take place the next day. And although they'd never been anything but supportive of him and the choices he'd made in his life, he could only imagine some of the arguments they might offer to prevent him from relocating to Wyoming.

You barely know this girl....

A warlock stays with his clan, no matter what....

Bring her to Flagstaff—we can protect her....

That last argument would probably be the hardest to counter, simply because Jake had thought pretty much the same thing. But after what had happened to her mother, Addie simply couldn't be budged on that point. She'd already lost family to Randall Lenz, and she was damned if she was going to allow that kind of misfortune to happen to anyone else.

And who could really blame her for thinking that way?

Jake cut over on I-70 so he could pick up Highway 89 and continue toward Flagstaff. He'd gone back and forth with himself over the route, just because he didn't like the idea of having to drive through Kanab. However, in the end he'd decided to take the risk, mostly because he didn't want to waste the time it would take to go the long way on I-15 through Las Vegas and down to I-40, but also because more than a week had elapsed since Randall Lenz had been dumped there, and Jake very much doubted the agent would have hung around in Utah any longer than he absolutely had to. No, he was probably all the way across the country, back at his agency's headquarters in Virginia…and hopefully, he'd stay there for a good long time. With Jeremy's algorithms effectively erasing any evidence of Addie's presence, it wasn't as though he'd have any leads to follow anyway.

By the time Jake reached Flagstaff's eastern outskirts, the long day had finally bled into twilight, the sun gone behind the horizon. Although he was dead tired by that point, he didn't mind the coming of darkness; this was territory he knew well. In fact, he couldn't help smiling a bit as he passed the turn-off that led to his cousin Joanna's house, and he uttered a silent thank-you to her for the help she'd given Addie. No matter what else happened, at least they no longer had to worry about her weather-working powers getting out of control and attracting unwanted attention.

He'd texted Jeremy when he stopped for gas in

Page, so his brother knew he would be coming by to pick up Taffy. No worries that it was already past nine o'clock—Jeremy usually worked until at least one or two in the morning, and Jake was already feeling guilty enough about leaving the dog behind in Flagstaff that he didn't want to wait until the next morning to retrieve her.

Since Jeremy was already expecting him, he only gave a peremptory knock and then went ahead and let himself in. As soon as he walked in the door of his brother's townhouse, Taffy was there, tail going a mile a minute, dancing around him and making little whining noises in her excitement. Jake bent down and picked her up, and couldn't help grinning as the dog licked his face like a kid going to town on an ice cream cone.

"All right, all right," he said with a laugh. "You're going to lick my face right off."

"Not much chance of that," Jeremy remarked. He'd appeared at the door of the downstairs bedroom he used as an office, arms folded as he watched Taffy wriggling in his brother's arms. "Too bad—it might be an improvement."

"Bite me," Jake said amiably. At the same time, he experienced another of those pangs. He'd just taken for granted having his brother around to trade barbs with, to roam through Flagstaff's forest trails with when they'd both had enough of staring at computer monitors and needed to take a break to clear their heads. Soon, though, Jeremy would be almost a thousand miles away. There was always video chat, but that wasn't the same thing.

As if picking up something of his brother's mood, Jeremy asked, "You're still going through with this crazy plan?"

"Yes," Jake replied. He'd informed his brother about what he intended to do, and hadn't gotten much of a response except, *Mom and Dad are going to go ballistic.* Which probably was true, but no matter what they said, he wasn't going to change his mind.

Jeremy shook his head. "And the local tribe is really okay with a bunch of Wilcoxes invading their territory?"

"I wouldn't call Addie and me 'a bunch,'" Jake said. "But yes, we have permission from the guy who acts as the tribal elder, so we're set. I'm just here to get the dog and bring your truck back—and take care of some business."

For a few seconds, Jeremy didn't reply, only stood there and appeared to absorb that information. When he spoke again, his tone sounded almost plaintive…for him.

"And what about Trident?"

Jake had wrestled with that problem on the way to Flagstaff—a thirteen-hour drive gave you a lot of time for rumination. "Well, I'll expect you and Laurel to keep it going," he said. "And I can stay in touch long-distance. This is the twenty-first century, after all—it's not that hard to stay in the loop."

"No, but you were always supposed to be the point man when it came to working in the field," Jeremy returned. "That's not my area of expertise, and Laurel—well, she's enthusiastic and everything, but I don't know if I'd feel comfortable sending her into dangerous situations."

"Whereas you were just fine with sending me."

His brother ran a hand through his hair, mussing it even worse than it already had been. Sometimes Jeremy's hair looked like he styled it with a blender. "That's just the point. I wasn't *sending* you. Trident was your baby, and you were the one taking the risks. Besides, Laurel's talent as a healer is a valuable one, but you have to admit that your telekinesis is a lot more practical when it comes to physical confrontations."

That was only the truth, so Jake didn't bother to argue. At the same time, he thought Jeremy was overstating his worth just a little. He could direct things long-distance, and there were plenty of Wilcox cousins with unique gifts who could come to work at the Wheeler Park facility. They just had to determine who would be best suited for the job.

"We'll figure it out," he said. "Right now, though, I just want to go home and crash. I've been on the road since seven."

Jeremy only shrugged. "Okay. My truck?"

"Parked in front." Jake fished the key fob out of his pocket. "The Gladiator?"

"In the driveway."

They exchanged fobs, and Jeremy went to fetch Taffy's food and bowls from the kitchen. He was silent during all this, as if he'd realized that it didn't matter which arguments he tried to make in favor of having his brother stay in Flagstaff—Jake had already come up with ways to shoot them all down.

"Good luck tomorrow," Jeremy said, and Jake clapped him on the shoulder.

"Thanks. They'll be upset, but I think eventually they'll come around."

"I hope so."

There wasn't anything to say after that, so Jake guided Taffy over to his truck—pausing to let her pee on the lawn before they got in—and drove off. He wished he could call Addie to let her know he'd gotten to Flagstaff safely, but she was at work and wouldn't be reachable.

Still, when he got home, he sent her a quick text because he knew she'd check her phone when she was able to take a break. *At the house. I'm fine. Taffy sends her love. Call me in the morning. Love you.*

And that was that. He went upstairs and collapsed in bed, and slept the sleep of the just.

18

IT FELT STRANGE TO WAKE UP AND NOT HAVE Jake lying there next to me, even though we'd only spent a single night together. I reached out with one hand, feeling the empty space in the bed, reassuring myself that his absence was only temporary. Just a few more days, and he'd be back for good.

At least I had his text from the night before, letting me know he'd made it to Flagstaff without incident. There was no reason why he shouldn't have, of course, but the last few weeks had taught me not to take anything for granted.

Arizona was an hour behind Wyoming, and so even though it was almost nine in the morning where I was, I knew there wasn't much point to checking my phone so early in the day. Most likely, Jake had collapsed into bed once he'd gotten home and might very well still be passed out.

So I made myself get up and shower and get dressed, then ate the last of the frozen waffles as I drank my morning coffee. It was another almost blindingly bright sunny day, with not a cloud in the sky. I figured I'd take advantage of the good weather by heading to the grocery store, since the items Jake and I had bought for our picnic lunch and spaghetti dinner weren't exactly staples. I needed more waffles, and coffee and eggs and probably some frozen dinners as well, just to tide me over until he got back to Riverton. And laundry detergent; the house had a stacked washer/dryer combo in a little alcove off the kitchen, and I realized I was starting to run out of clothes. The stuff I'd bought when I went shopping with Laurel—on a shopping expedition that felt as if it had taken place in another lifetime—had only been enough to last me for five or six days at the most, and I was stretching my limits. Probably, once I felt truly settled, I'd buy some stuff online or maybe plan a shopping expedition with Jake to someplace like Casper, which I vaguely thought was a lot closer to Riverton than Cheyenne.

My trip to the grocery store kept me occupied enough for the first hour after I was done getting ready for the day. And before I could get too antsy, my phone rang just as I'd finished putting my first load of laundry in the teeny washing machine.

Jake's voice came through the speaker on my

phone, warm and so very welcome. "Hey, sweet-heart. How are you doing?"

My heart thrilled a little at the endearment. He'd uttered the word in a casual tone, but still, it was the first time he'd ever called me that. "I'm fine," I told him. "Just doing some laundry, kind of hanging out until it's time for me to go to work. How about you?"

"I just got back from taking Taffy on her walk. I'm about to head over to the Jeep dealership and see about trading in the Gladiator."

Ouch. Even though I knew intellectually that he needed to get something less conspicuous, another guilty pang went through me at the thought of him being forced to get rid of his beloved truck. "Maybe that's not necessary—"

"Yes, it is," he said, interrupting me, but gently, as if he didn't want me to let myself get too worked up over the subject. "And it's okay. Really. Anyway, I figured I might as well get that handled, along with some other logistics, since my parents are both at work and I won't have a chance to talk to them until late in the afternoon."

Right. I'd forgotten that both his parents had nice, normal jobs. All part of keeping up the façade that there wasn't anything particularly noteworthy about the Wilcox family. "Is it a good thing that you can't talk to them right away?"

A small chuckle sounded in my ear. "Well, I'm

not big on confrontations, so yeah, in a way it's good. On the other hand, I'd rather just get this over with so I can get back on the road. With any luck, though, I'll be on my way early tomorrow. A lot depends on whether I can get someone to watch my house on such short notice."

"Can't you have Jeremy keep an eye on it?"

"I could, but he's got his own place to take care of, in addition to his work at Trident. I'd rather he keep his focus there." A faint, breathy sound that might have been a sigh, and Jake went on, "I've got enough cousins that I'm sure there's someone who'd be glad to crash at the house until I decide for sure what to do with it. I just need to get the word out."

Don't feel guilty. Don't feel guilty. I knew it wasn't how Jake wanted me to feel, but once again, guilt tugged at me. My fault that he had to give up his truck and his beautiful house and...well, pretty much everything and everyone he knew. He'd made starting over in Riverton sound like a grand adventure, and maybe it would be, but he was still the one who had to make a huge sacrifice.

"That makes sense," I said, glad that my voice sounded steady and not as though I was standing there and giving myself a mental beating.

"It'll get taken care of," he reassured me. "Worst case, I might have to stay here an extra day to get everything handled, but I hope not."

No, I definitely didn't want him to stay in

Flagstaff any longer than he had to. There was no reason for me to believe I was in any kind of immediate danger, but I felt so much better when he was around. "Well, if you do, it's not that big a deal," I said, still doing my best to sound casual. "I'll be working most of the time anyway."

Well, that was a slight exaggeration. One thing about swing shift was that it did leave open a decent chunk of the day to get stuff done, like my grocery shopping expedition earlier or my current foray into laundry. I'd have plenty of time to miss Jake pretty damn hard. But one upside was that I'd probably be so tired when I got home from work each day, I'd basically collapse into bed and not lie there and brood about his absence.

And, as he'd said, he was going to do his best to get back to Wyoming as quickly as he could. With any luck, he'd find a cousin right away who was willing to take care of his place while he decided whether to rent it or sell it…and his talk with his parents would go more smoothly than he thought, eliminating yet another obstacle.

"True. And everything was okay at the casino last night?"

"Same old, same old," I replied. Maybe I shouldn't be referring to a job I'd held for a grand total of a week as "same old," but I could already tell there wasn't going to be a lot of variation in the work. Sure, the customers would shift from day to day—although I already recognized quite a few regulars—and yet the job itself didn't change all that much. "Oh, someone hit the big jackpot last night and won fifty grand, but that was about it for excitement."

"Good," Jake said. "I'm a big fan of 'boring' right now."

I had to smile. "You and me both."

A pause, and he said, "Well, I should let you go. I have a lot I need to get done, so I'd better get started."

"It's fine." My turn to hesitate, but I told myself that we'd already said the words to one another, so it really wasn't that big a deal. Besides, I needed to reconfirm our connection, to make it as real as possible, despite the miles that separated us. "I love you, Jake."

"Love you too, Addie. I'll be back before you know it."

"I know you will. Good luck with everything today."

"Have a good day at work."

I assured him I would, and we ended the call. For a moment, I held my phone cradled in my hand, staring down at it as if the device still resonated with the sound of Jake's voice. But of course, that was silly. He'd gone on to handle the day's business, and I needed to do the same.

If I kept busy enough, maybe I wouldn't notice how much I missed him.

The other bar servers had informed me that Wednesdays tended to be the slowest days at the casino, thanks to falling in the middle of the week and not even having the attraction of the tribal dance demonstrations held there throughout the summer on Tuesday evenings to give attendance a boost. Even so, I was busy enough fetching and carrying that at first I didn't notice how the place started to empty out a little past six. It was only when Blake the bartender waved me over, his expression strained and not looking anything like his usual cheerful self, that I realized something strange was going on.

"Fire," he said tersely when I approached, and I stared at him in alarm.

"Here at the casino?"

"Not yet," he replied, reassuring me a little. At least the third floor wasn't on fire or something. "I guess the fire started out near Midval and looked as though it was going to stay away, but the wind shifted directions and now it's coming at us from across the prairie. People are leaving so they can go check on their houses."

"It's that bad?" I asked as I did my best to push

back the panic that had started to percolate somewhere in my gut. But there was a good reason for my panic—I'd seen prairie fires before, had seen how they seemed to flare up out of nothing and then race across miles of grassland, consuming everything in their path.

"I don't know yet," he said with a frown. "You can't see a damn thing in here."

Which was true. Like pretty much every casino the world over, the Wind River facility was dark and cloistered, effectively shielding its patrons from anything that might be happening outside. "They'll evacuate us if it gets bad, won't they?" I asked, doing my best to keep the worry from my voice.

"I suppose so," Blake replied, although his tone was dubious and his frown deepened, as if he wasn't quite sure what the procedure would be for such an eventuality, since he'd never encountered this particular one before. "It's getting pretty dead in here, though—why don't you go take a look outside and see for yourself? I'll cover for you, and that way you can come back and give me a report."

"Sure," I said. His proposal sounded like a good idea—although if things looked bad enough, I didn't plan to stick around once I'd gone back to Blake and let him know what was going on. The spot where the casino was located was exposed and surrounded on three sides by bare land with dry scrub grass and not much else, whereas most of

Riverton was much greener and would, I supposed, be less likely to burn. I had a feeling I'd be much safer at my rented house, which was located almost half a mile past the natural barrier the Wind River provided.

Flashing Blake an encouraging smile, I hurried toward the nearest exit, which opened onto the southern section of the parking lot. As soon as I emerged from the building, a hot, dry wind caught at my hair, pulling a few strands loose from the barrette that secured it at the back of my neck. With that wind came the acrid scent of burning brush, and I realized then that the light itself looked odd, the westering sun tinted an angry dark orange as billows of smoke blew past me.

From where I stood, I couldn't see much except the parking lot, since the bulk of the hotel blocked the view of the highway and the open land beyond it. Trying not to breathe too deeply of the smoke-tainted air, I hurried down a little ways, dodging cars as they sped out of the lot.

Once I reached a spot where the hotel was no longer obscuring the view, my breath caught in my throat. No, the fire wasn't at the casino yet, but it also appeared frighteningly close, maybe no more than a mile away, if even that much, a wall of hungry flame consuming the dry brush as it went. Sirens screamed against the thick air, and I thought I heard the whir of a helicopter, although I couldn't see one, thanks to the thick smoke that swirled overhead and covered most of the sky.

This was bad. Really bad. Why they hadn't evacuated us, I didn't know, although maybe the fire had moved so quickly that management hadn't had enough time to react.

I wasn't about to take that risk, though. Maybe I'd get fired for leaving early, but right then, I didn't much care. At the same time, however, I told myself I should go find Leona or someone else in a position of authority and ask whether it was time to let any nonessential employees go before we all got trapped and couldn't get out even if we wanted to.

As I turned to go back to the casino, I stopped abruptly. Carson Archuleta stood there in the parking lot a few paces away, his lined face heavy with concern. Leona was with him as well, relief clear in her expression as she caught sight of me.

"Blake said you were out here," she said. The dry, hot wind played havoc with her sleek black hair as well, strands flying in front of her face as she spoke. "We've decided to evacuate—I just got off the phone with the fire department, and they don't have any estimates on containment. With this wind—"

She stopped there, reaching up to vainly push her hair out of the way. I looked from her to Carson.

"It's really that bad?" I asked, even though I'd

seen with my own eyes how dire the situation appeared to be.

"I'm afraid so," he replied. "The highway provides something of a barrier, but when the wind blows like this, it can easily carry sparks much farther than that. And the casino is concrete and steel, true, but if the fire is fierce enough, that hardly matters."

I looked away from him, staring up at the multi-storied building that towered above us. It certainly looked solid and sturdy enough, but that appearance of solidity wouldn't be enough to save it if the fire continued to race forward and gain in strength. And the weather had been warm and dry for weeks, apparently, with the last real rainstorm in the area occurring sometime at the beginning of May.

The last real rainstorm....

A heavy rain would put out the fire. Yes, the skies were clear—or at least, they would have been if they weren't obscured by smoke—but that didn't really matter when I was around, did it?

You can't, I told myself. *You're supposed to be lying low, remember?*

Oh, I remembered.

But....

I could try to convince myself that the casino wasn't such a big deal in the grand scheme of things, and maybe it wasn't, compared to climate change and wealth inequality and all the problems of everyday life in the twenty-first century. It was a big deal in Riverton, though. The casino employed hundreds of people and attracted tourists to the town, tourists who shopped and dined and stayed there. If the casino was lost, the local economy wouldn't recover for years.

Jake and I wanted to make a home in Riverton…but could I honestly face the people who might one day be our neighbors and friends, knowing I could have helped them but had been too afraid when the moment came?

Just one good rainstorm. That's all it will take.

For an agonizing second, I hesitated. Maybe I should try to pull Carson away from Leona so I could speak to him privately. Then again, I'd probably draw more attention to myself by doing such a thing rather than making the offer without going into any specifics.

I had to hope that Carson would know what I was talking about.

"I can help," I said, keeping my gaze focused on him. I tried my best to ignore the anxiety that roiled in my gut and made icy chills run down my spine, despite the hot, dry wind that blew all around us, but I couldn't say I was all that successful.

Leona stared at me as if I'd lost my mind. "I appreciate that, Addie," she said. "But you need to get out of here. There's really nothing you can do."

However, Carson only regarded me with sad, dark eyes, and gave a single knowing nod. When he spoke, the worry was clear in his voice. "You would be taking a very great risk, wouldn't you?"

"I—I don't know for sure," I replied. Was that the truth? I didn't know...or maybe I did, and just didn't want to admit it to myself. "Maybe. But I don't want you to lose your casino."

Leona looked from him to me and back again, as if she couldn't begin to figure out what the hell we were talking about. Before she could comment, however, Carson held up a hand.

"We would be very greatly in your debt."

I didn't reply, only nodded.

Jake is going to kill me.

But there were more important things in the world than my own safety. I knew if I stood by and allowed so many people's livelihoods to be destroyed, I wouldn't be able to look at myself in the mirror ever again.

A breath, and then I focused on the power the way Joanna had shown me, let my consciousness rouse my gift so it reached out to the very air itself, forcing the water molecules in the atmosphere to swell and grow, clouds appearing in a sky that had previously held none. They began to loom over the casino, pregnant and dark, a brooding light pulsing from within.

"What in the world…?" Leona breathed, shock clear in her face.

Thunder crackled, and lightning leapt from cloud to cloud, the glare illuminating the few cars left in the parking lot. Immediately afterward, the wind grew cold, with a drop in temperature so severe that goosebumps appeared on my bare forearms.

I could smell the moisture on the wind, even thicker than the scent of smoke. In the next second, rain began to fall, so heavy and sudden that we were drenched in just a few seconds.

"Hurry," Leona said, and the three of us ran for the shelter of the portico that protected the rear entrance to the casino. From there, we watched as the rain pounded down, flooding the parking lot, cascading down the sides of the building.

A moment passed, and then a few more as we stood and breathed in the cold, damp air. A phone rang, and Leona startled, then reached to pull it out of her jacket pocket and put it to her ear. Almost at once, her taut expression relaxed, and she smiled, looking serene and beautiful despite the wet hair plastered to her cheeks and brow. "You're sure?" she asked. A pause, and then she said, "We've sent most people home, but I'll let everyone know. Thank you."

Carson said, "The fire is out, isn't it?"

"Yes," she replied. "That was Chief Mackinnon

from the fire department. The rain drenched everything so thoroughly, they're not sure even any hot
spots are left. They'll check the fire lines to be sure,
but—"

"But it's over," he finished for her. His gaze
moved to me. "Thank you, Addie."

About all I could do was give him a weary
smile. I honestly didn't want to think about what
I'd just done, didn't want to consider the ramifications of such a powerful storm appearing here out
of nowhere, when the forecast had been for
continuing hot and dry conditions for the next
week.

Once again, Leona glanced from Carson to me
and then back again. Brows pulled together in
confusion, she said, "Why are we thanking Addie?"

"No reason," I told her. Suddenly, I was
exhausted, even though using my talent didn't
usually tire me out. "Just—just forget about it," I
added. "Forget he said anything."

Carson still studied me, eyes now full of
compassion. A brief brush of his fingers against my
arm, and he said, "Go home, Addie. You've earned
the rest of the evening off."

I wanted to protest that I'd rather stay at work,
but there didn't seem to be much point in doing
that. Not when most of the casino's patrons had
already left and probably wouldn't be coming back
until they were absolutely certain it would be safe.

So I shrugged and said, "Sure. I just need to get my purse out of my locker."

Not quite meeting Leona's eyes, I moved past the two of them and into the casino. As I went, my footsteps dragged, although I told myself that the best thing for me to do was go home and change out of my wet clothes.

I'd saved the Wind River Casino...but I had no idea at what cost.

19

JAKE HAD JUST DROPPED THE PAPERWORK FOR his new Jeep—a white Wrangler Rubicon that, while loaded with pretty much everything he could have wanted, still didn't make his heart sing quite the way the Gladiator had—on the kitchen counter when the doorbell rang. He frowned. While he guessed that Jeremy could have simply decided to drop by, that possibility seemed pretty unlikely. They'd already talked earlier in the day, and there wasn't much need to have an in-person discussion, although Jake supposed his brother might have wanted to come by and hash things out in person.

The doorbell rang again. While he was tempted to ignore it, he figured that probably wasn't a good idea. He'd put out the call for potential house-sitters on the Wilcox family bulletin board, and it was entirely possible that someone had gotten over-eager and had decided to show up in person to state their case for why they should be the one to live in the house while he mulled renting or selling it.

However, when Jake opened the door, about the last person he'd expected was standing outside, wearing a formidable frown.

His cousin Connor.

"What the hell is this about you moving to Wyoming?" he demanded, clearly upset enough that he'd decided to dispense with the pleasantries.

"Come in, Connor," Jake responded. No point in airing their grievances so the entire neighborhood could overhear them; he stepped aside and let his cousin enter the house, then shut the door. At the same time, he wondered how the clan's *primus* had gotten wind of his plans. His post on the clan bulletin board? Maybe; the main reason Jake had felt safe posting there was that Connor didn't use the boards all that often—and Angela likewise seemed to prefer to stay away from them, maybe to allow people their privacy—but it was entirely possible that someone had reached out to the *primus* to alert him to his cousin's plans. "Do you want something to drink?"

"No." Connor shoved his hands in his pants pockets and gave Jake a hard stare. "You can't move to Wyoming."

A flat ultimatum was not something Jake had

expected from his normally laid-back cousin. "Why not?"

"Because that's not how it works. We stay in our territories!"

"Yeah, and it's not safe for Addie to be here," Jake told him. "We've tried to cover everything up, but there's no guarantee Randall Lenz won't eventually put it all back together and come after her again if she's here. In Wyoming, we'll be anonymous."

"And hundreds of miles away from help if anything goes wrong."

Privately, Jake couldn't help but agree with Connor on that particular point, but he wasn't going to admit such a thing. No, he needed to stand his ground. "That's not entirely true. The elder with the local tribe already said he and his people would watch out for us. It's not as if we're going to be left completely on our own."

It didn't seem as if the *primus* had been expecting that particular piece of information. His head tilted slightly as his gray-green eyes—so like Addie's—narrowed. "That's probably better than nothing, but I'm not sure how much help they can give if Lenz really decides to come after you in force."

"How much help could we Wilcoxes give?" Jake countered. He was doing his best to keep his voice calm, since he had a feeling that Connor didn't want a knock-down, drag-out fight over this any more than he did. At the same time, he couldn't quite prevent an edge from entering his tone. "When you get right down to it, we can't afford open war with the U.S. government any more than the people on the Wind River Reservation can. At least in Wyoming, we'll be someplace that Lenz and the rest of his agency won't have any reason to look for us."

"That you know of."

"I'm pretty sure of it, actually. Jeremy has scrubbed all images of Addie from any surveillance cams that might have picked her up. There's no trail to follow."

Connor rubbed his chin. Jake got the feeling he would have liked to find a hole somewhere in that assertion, but he knew just as well as anyone else how good Jeremy was at that sort of thing. If he said the footage didn't exist, then it didn't.

At last, the *primus* said, "You really care enough about her to give up your whole family?"

"Yes," Jake replied. His feelings for Addie were the one thing he was absolutely certain of. "She'll be my family."

"She *is* your family…distantly," Connor pointed out, although Jake wasn't quite sure what his cousin had intended with that particular argument.

"So was Sarah." Strange how it didn't seem difficult at all to say her name now, where even a few months ago, he'd still had trouble allowing those two syllables past his lips. Being with Addie had smoothed the grief, had finally made him understand that it was all right to go on with his life, that he could mourn what might have been while still looking forward to the future.

"And Addie's *my* family, you know," Connor said next. "I was sort of looking forward to getting to know her better, to having my kids enjoy having an aunt."

Oh, hell. Jake knew he'd been so wrapped up in his and Addie's problems that he hadn't even stopped to think that by disappearing to Wyoming, he was preventing Ian and Emily and Miranda from getting to know the woman who was the children's closest blood relative. After all, Angela was an only child, and Connor's brother Damon had been dead for years…not that Damon Wilcox had ever been the sort of person you could imagine romping in a backyard with a bunch of little kids.

But Addie was that sort of person. She'd played with her nieces and nephew during their one visit to Jerome and looked like she was having a grand time. And although she hadn't said anything to Jake when he hatched this plan to have the two of them settle in Riverton rather than risk returning to Flagstaff, he had to wonder whether she'd been saddened to realize she wouldn't be there for her newly discovered relations. He thought it probable that she had been; losing her mother had changed her world forever, but at least she'd had the prospect of forging bonds with Connor and Angela, with the twins and Miranda. Now, she wouldn't have any of that.

She'd only have him.

"I know she's your family," Jake said quietly. "And maybe—maybe this doesn't have to be permanent. Maybe all it'll take is us lying low for a few months or so, and then we can come back here."

A long pause as Connor appeared to consider the possibility. Then he gave a small shake of his head. "Do you really believe that?"

Jake wouldn't lie—he'd spent enough years lying to himself that he wouldn't do it to another person. "No. Randall Lenz isn't the sort of person to give up, from what I can tell. But maybe...." He let the words trail off, and decided to leave the matter there. Connor could draw whatever conclusions he liked.

Somehow, Jake knew there wouldn't be any further argument. Seven years earlier, Connor had been forced to make some hard decisions of his own, decisions regarding his brother Damon that had forever changed the fortunes of the Wilcox clan —and, by extension, the fortunes of all the Arizona witch families. Now, as he watched his cousin come face to face with some difficult choices in his own life, Connor most likely had realized that this was no time to draw a line in the sand. All he could do was stay out of the way and hope for the best.

And, like Jake himself, prepare for the worst.

Alamosa turned out be a little more than the "wide spot" Lenz had characterized it to himself back at HQ. The small town was nestled at the base of the Sangre de Cristo mountain range and was quaintly picturesque, with its older buildings and an impossibly blue sky overhead.

However, he wasn't there to sightsee. He'd checked into the local Best Western hotel, along with his pilot and a man named Ives who'd worked several missions with him and could be counted on to be quick, efficient...and discreet.

Lenz had no idea how long they'd be waiting there. Instinct had sent him back to that part of the country—along with that glitch Dawson had found, the one that might or might not have been a scrubbed image of Adara Grant—and he had to hope that he hadn't jumped the gun, following a hunch that might not bear fruit for days or even weeks. The bean counters generally left him alone, but they might get a bit annoyed at having to spend taxpayer dollars to house personnel at even a modestly priced hotel for an indeterminate amount of time.

He'd told Ives and the pilot—a former Air Force captain named Tolliver—that they were officially off duty but to remain on call. Where they'd gone, Lenz didn't know, but this wasn't their first rodeo; they'd be sure not to wander more than ten or fifteen minutes away from home base at any time.

For himself, he'd put his duffle bag on the stand in the closet and briefly contemplated heading out for a bite to eat before deciding that could wait, since it wasn't even seven o'clock yet and daylight lingered for a long while at this time of year. Instead, he sent Dawson a quick text letting her know he and his team had landed safely, and then opened his laptop and began poring over maps of the region, hoping that maybe seeing a certain location might make his intuition kick into overdrive.

So far, though, he hadn't gotten a single twinge. The lack of feedback wasn't enough to dissuade him, however, and he kept scanning maps of Colorado and Wyoming, of New Mexico and Utah, figuring that a more-than-passing familiarity with the region could only be a benefit in the long run.

His phone rang, and he immediately pulled it out of his pocket and looked at the screen.

Dawson.

"Lenz here."

"Sir, I think we have something."

At once, he sat up straighter, anticipation beginning to hum in his veins. "What is it?"

"A thunderstorm in Wyoming, in the Wind River Reservation."

Even though he wanted to believe this storm was a sure sign of Adara Grant's weather talent manifesting itself, he knew better than to allow himself to get too excited. Tone unconcerned, he said, "It's summer, Dawson—thunderstorms happen all the time."

"Not like this, sir. The region has been dry for weeks, and there were no storms in the long-range forecast. Also, a large grassfire was burning in the immediate area and threatening homes and the local casino. But before the fire could do any damage, a storm came out of nowhere and put it out."

That particular circumstance did seem just a bit too convenient. "Any confirmed sightings of Ms. Grant in the area?"

"Not so far, sir, but it's likely our hacker friend has done his best to make sure she was erased from any surveillance footage that might have been captured over the past few days. However, because the storm was so anomalous—and because it seemed to appear precisely to put out a fire—I think it's worth investigating."

He thought the same thing. "Is there an airport in the vicinity?"

"Yes, about two miles outside the town center. You can be there in a little over an hour. I'll make sure there's a vehicle standing by."

So much for Alamosa, or the Mexican restaurant down the street that had looked interesting. Well, this trip wasn't about sampling the local fare, but something far more important.

"On my way."

He ended the call, then contacted Tolliver and Ives, telling them to meet him at the hotel. Since he hadn't unpacked yet, he was out of there quickly enough, explaining to the desk clerk that an important matter had come up and that he had to be on his way.

Then they were all in the SUV they'd rented from the kiosk at the airport, the other two men crowding the passenger and the back seat with their bulk as they headed back to return the vehicle and board the sleek little jet Lenz used for all of his "business" trips. Most likely, anyone who met him while on one of these missions probably thought he must be some sort of high-powered executive, rather than an agent of the United States government... and he did his best to maintain that façade. Fewer questions that way.

Wheels up, and they were in the air, streaking toward Riverton at a tidy five hundred miles an hour. Lenz got a protein bar out of his laptop case and consumed it in silence, figuring he needed the sustenance. He was just carefully folding the empty wrapper in order to stow it in the trash receptacle near his seat when his phone buzzed in his pocket.

"Got something for you, sir," came Dawson's voice.

"Go on."

"Well, I couldn't find any surveillance footage

that definitely showed Adara Grant, but I went on a hunch and started poking around at some of the local establishments to see if they had any new hires. After all, she would have needed to find some way of supporting herself."

"And you found something." Otherwise, what would be the point of this call?

"Yes, sir. A new hire at the Wind River Casino named Addie Wilcox."

The alias Adara Grant had been using. For some reason, the name "Wilcox" felt as though it held its own significance, but Lenz couldn't say why. His memory was still a blank when it came to those important hours between the time he confronted Adara at her mother's home in Kanab and when he awoke in a motel room in that same town days later.

So, Adara had been working at the casino outside Riverton. And as someone trying to make a safe home for herself in a new place, she would have had a vested interest in making sure the casino continued to operate, didn't burn down in a wild prairie fire. It would have been taking a terrible risk to bring the rain that saved the casino, but she probably had believed she had no choice.

Excitement surged through him again, the anticipation of a hunter closing in on his prey. "Does she have an address listed in her work record?" he asked.

"Yes. Fifteen East Jackson Avenue."

"Thank you, Dawson," Lenz said, then added, "Good work."

"Thank you, sir. Best of luck."

But he didn't need luck. He knew his quarry, knew that her talents were ones to be respected. This time, he would have to catch her unaware, so she wouldn't have the opportunity to strike back.

You're mine, he thought, and smiled.

20

Despite the near-miss from the fire—or maybe because of it—the casino was closed for the rest of the night, although the hotel would continue to operate.

"Enjoy your evening off," Leona told Blake and me and the rest of the staff on duty. "You'll all get paid for the shift, so no need to worry about that."

Her words appeared to hearten everyone, and we all went to collect our things and head home. I noticed Blake giving me a hopeful look, as if he was mulling the possibility of asking me out for a drink or something, despite my sodden clothes. However, I hurried out the employees' entrance before he could say anything, and let out a sigh of relief as I slid behind the wheel of my Fiat and turned on the engine. Thank God for leather seats; at least I didn't

370 | CHRISTINE POPE

have to worry about doing too much damage to the upholstery, despite my wet dress pants.

Not that my relief lasted for very long. All during the short drive home, I was at war with myself, wondering if I'd completely blown it by summoning such a large, conspicuous storm...even as I knew deep down that I could never have stood by and let the casino be destroyed.

Right then, I felt like the living embodiment of "damned if you do."

But I made it home without incident, even though I kept looking over my shoulder, wondering if a SWAT team was going to emerge from the hedge that separated my rented house from the property next door, swoop down, and scoop me up. The neighborhood looked calm and friendly in the late afternoon light, however, with a couple of boys who appeared to be around nine or ten riding their bikes down the street, and a group of much younger kids playing on a slip-and-slide in their front yard, laughing and shrieking with excitement.

Had I ever been that carefree?

In that particular moment, I sort of doubted it.

I put my purse down on the little round table in the dining area and pulled out my phone. No messages from Jake, but then, I hadn't really been expecting any. We'd talked before I went to work, and of course, he could have no idea what had happened in the intervening hours. In his mind, he probably thought I was calmly going about my duties, working my way through yet another uneventful shift.

Unfortunately, life—as it often did—had intervened.

I knew I should call him and let him know what had happened. Or...should I? He was a thousand miles away. It wasn't as if he could do anything to help me if the worst happened. All I'd do was succeed in making him crazy with worry. If I could even get hold of him. It was not quite seven o'clock, and Flagstaff was an hour behind Wyoming. Jake had said he was going to talk to his parents after they got off work, which meant he was probably having that discussion even as I brooded over my phone and tried to figure out what to do next. I had a feeling that exchange with his parents was going to be tense enough without a phone call from me to disrupt things, especially once Jake started asking questions about why I wasn't at the casino.

Well, that seemed to decide matters.

However, I wasn't quite ready to throw up my hands and let the universe handle things. I picked up my phone, extracted the business card Carson Archuleta had given me from the pocket where I'd stowed it in my purse, and made the call.

He picked up after the first ring, his voice calm and unruffled as ever. "I thought I might hear from you."

No point in beating around the bush, then. "Carson, I'm scared."

"Have you seen anyone?"

"No, but…it might take them a little time to find me."

"I'll have someone keep a watch on your house."

Even though that was ostensibly why I'd called him in the first place, now that Carson had offered his assistance, doubt assailed me. The last thing I wanted was to put anyone else in harm's way. "I'm not sure that's necessary—"

"Oh, I think it is," he broke in, but gently, as if he knew exactly why I'd made the protest. "After what you did for the tribe this afternoon, it's the least we can do. Go about your evening—you'll never even know they're there."

They. Which seemed to indicate Carson thought the situation was serious enough to warrant sending out more than one person to keep watch over me. Once again, I opened my mouth to tell him that wasn't necessary…and then closed it again without voicing my concerns. Somehow, I knew he would view such objections as an insult, an indication that I didn't think he and his people were capable of taking on such a responsibility. That wasn't it at all, but I could see that he believed it was his duty to ensure my safety.

"Thank you," I said quietly.

"No thanks are necessary. We honor our debts."

He ended the call then, and I slipped the phone and his business card back into my purse. Since there didn't seem to be much else for me to do, I went ahead and nuked one of the frozen dinners I'd bought at the store earlier—even as I kicked myself for not picking up a bottle of wine or a six-pack of beer when I was grocery shopping. Right then, I thought I could have used a drink to take the edge off.

However, as the evening wore on and full dark fell, I actually found myself relaxing despite the utter lack of alcohol in the house. I'd called down the thunder and the rain, and so far, nothing had happened, except the Wind River Casino still stood and I'd gotten an unexpected evening off.

Since I didn't much feel like watching TV, I got out my laptop and cruised around on some real estate sites, looking at property in Riverton for sale, setting up a free account on Trulia so I could save the houses I liked best. As far as I could tell, it looked as though our money would go a lot farther in this part of the country than it would have in Flagstaff. Not that buying a house would have even been an issue if we'd stayed there, since Jake already owned a place.

I ached for him then, wishing he was there to put his arms around me and tell me it was all going to be okay. Yes, it helped a little to know there were people hiding in the dark, keeping silent guard on the house, but that knowledge couldn't replace the comfort of actually having the man I loved at my side.

Well, he'd be back soon enough. Maybe late the following night, if all went well. I'd have to tell him the truth then, but by that point, I'd be ready to laugh about the situation and point out that obviously, it didn't matter if I exerted my powers here, since I'd already done my worst, so to speak, and nothing had happened. In a way, it was good that I'd been forced to reach out and summon a storm, if for no other reason than to prove Riverton truly was the sanctuary we hoped it would be, that we really could look forward to a safe future there.

With those thoughts humming in my mind, I took a quick shower, then went ahead and got ready for bed. Just as I was about to turn out the lights, my phone buzzed, and I went to pick it up.

Jake had sent me a text. *I know you're still at work,* it said, *but I just wanted to let you know that everything is great here in Flag. Connor & my parents are cool w/everything, & I got someone to watch the house. I'll be on the road early tomorrow morning.*

Silly as it was, I lifted the phone to my lips and gave it a quick kiss, leaving a faint smudge of Burt's Bees lip balm on the screen. I grinned as I wiped the smudge away and deposited the phone back in my purse.

See? I told myself as I went into the bedroom. *Everything is going to be fine, and Jake will be home tomorrow night.*

Still smiling faintly, I leaned over and turned out the light. Because the night was warm, the bedroom window was open, but all I could hear was the sound of the wind sighing in the trees, and the low singsong of crickets in the grass. That summer evening lullaby drew me to the borders of sleep, my body relaxing as it released the day's cares.

I slept…and then startled awake as a man's hand came down on my mouth, strong and cool as iron. Fear shrilled along all my nerve endings, and I struggled in vain against his heavy grip, knowing I had to free myself, had to get away before the worst happened. Thunder rumbled overhead, and lightning broke through the night…and yet I somehow knew it wouldn't be enough.

Not this time.

Randall Lenz's voice came to me in the darkness, low, almost regretful. "Sorry to be so uncivilized about this," he said. "But you leave me no choice."

A sharp sting against my neck, and I was gone.

Jake and Addie's story concludes in *Winds of Change*.

(Paranormal Romance)

Sympathy for the Devil

Charmed, I'm Sure

A Wing and a Prayer

THE WITCHES OF CANYON ROAD*

(Paranormal Romance)

Hidden Gifts

Darker Paths

Mysterious Ways

A Canyon Road Christmas

Demon Born

An Ill Wind

Higher Ground

Haunted Hearts

THE WITCHES OF CLEOPATRA HILL*

(Paranormal Romance)

Darkangel

Darknight

Darkmoon

Sympathetic Magic

Protector

Spellbound

A Cleopatra Hill Christmas

Impractical Magic

Strange Magic

The Arrangement

Defender

Bad Blood

Deep Magic

Darktide

THE DJINN WARS*

(Paranormal Romance)

Chosen

Taken

Fallen

Broken

Forsaken

Forbidden

Awoken

Illuminated

Stolen

Forgotten

Driven

Unspoken

THE WATCHERS TRILOGY*

(Paranormal Romance)

Falling Dark

Dead of Night

Rising Dawn

THE SEDONA FILES*

(Paranormal Romance)

Bad Vibrations

Desert Hearts

Angel Fire

Star Crossed

Falling Angels

Enemy Mine

~

STANDALONE TITLES

Hearts on Fire

Taking Dictation

Night Music

Golden Heart

* Indicates a completed series

ABOUT THE AUTHOR

USA Today bestselling author Christine Pope has been writing stories ever since she commandeered her family's Smith-Corona typewriter back in grade school. Her work includes paranormal romance, fantasy romance, and science fiction/space opera romance. She makes her home in Arizona's beautiful Verde Valley.

Don't miss out on any of Christine's new releases —sign up for her newsletter today!

Christine Pope on the Web:
www.christinepope.com